POINT OF CONTROL

ALSO BY L.J. SELLERS

THE DETECTIVE JACKSON SERIES

The Sex Club

Secrets to Die For

Thrilled to Death

Passions of the Dead

Dying for Justice

Liars, Cheaters, & Thieves

Rules of Crime

Crimes of Memory

Deadly Bonds

Wrongful Death

THE AGENT DALLAS SERIES

The Trigger

The Target

The Trap

STAND-ALONE NOVELS

The Lethal Effect

(previously published as *The Suicide Effect*)

The Baby Thief

The Gauntlet Assassin

L.J. SELLERS

POINT OF CONTROL

THOMAS & MERCER

Published by Thomas & Mercer, Seattle
www.apub.com

Amazon, the Amazon logo, and Thomas & Mercer are trademarks of Amazon.com, Inc., or its affiliates.

ISBN-13: 9781503951495
ISBN-10: 1503951499

Cover design by Marc Cohen

Printed in the United States of America

CHAPTER 1

Friday, March 13, 8:05 p.m., San Jose, California

Nick Bowman had never felt more alive. He'd just had the best sex of his life with a spectacular younger woman who expected nothing from him, and his research had hit a breakthrough that had just earned him an exciting job offer. Plus, he'd finally won the International Metallurgy Award. Nearly euphoric, he strode down the hall of the hotel, eager to climb into his new Jaguar XE, rev the engine, and fully enjoy the moment. Soon enough, he would be home, boxed in by a wife who didn't appreciate him and two surly kids who didn't seem to have his DNA.

As he stepped into the elevator, Nick shoved aside the negative thoughts and replayed his session with Carly, a long-legged model he'd met at the gym. She was incredible—sexy, smart, and independent. She'd waved him off after their second round of sex, telling him to move along so she could shower and have the room to herself for a while. Carly understood that he had to get home to his family before it seemed suspicious, even for a late night at work.

In the basement parking garage, warm, muggy air engulfed him, and he pulled off his sports jacket. Out in the night air, with the Jag purring under him, the air would be fantastic. He loved living in central California—so much more civilized than the dull Iowa landscape and cold winters he'd grown up with. Nick hurried toward his car, whistling softly. He only had twenty-four hours to consider the job offer, and he didn't know if he would take it, but the money was exciting to think about. He was already doing quite well. A lucky, lucky man.

A sudden movement startled him. He spun toward the big concrete post he'd just passed, and a man in dark clothes rushed toward him. No, two men, one behind the other, and both wearing ski masks. The lead guy's arms jerked up, holding something dark. Before Nick could cry out or swing his fists, a heavy cloth bag came down over his head, and the man spun him around. Powerful hands grabbed his wrists from behind and pulled them together. *What the hell?* Fear shot from his belly into his throat. "Hey! Stop! You've got the wrong guy!" His words sounded garbled inside the cloth.

A hand clamped the bag against his open mouth. "Quiet! We don't want to hurt you."

Nick didn't believe him. Heart racing, he prayed for the first time since he was a kid.

CHAPTER 2

Sunday, March 15, 7:20 p.m., Washington, DC

Zach Dimizaro stepped out of the bar and tried to shake off the jitters. Head down against the wind, he hurried toward the nearby park, wishing he hadn't downed two beers on an empty stomach. But this meeting made him nervous, and he needed the alcohol for courage. The buyer had insisted on a late-night transfer in a part of town he normally didn't go to, especially after dark. All of it made him uncomfortable. Except the money he was about to put in his pocket. The first step toward forming his own start-up company, making the lifestyle apps he was really interested in.

The crisp night air penetrated his coat, and he pulled it tighter. Zach picked up his pace, anxious to get the deal over with. He passed two dark storefronts and another bar. Across the street he could see the seedy park, where a cluster of dark figures hung out on the corner. *Gangbangers?* Heavy footsteps snapped his attention toward the alley beside him. A big man walked toward him with a gun aimed right at his chest. *Oh god, a mugger!* Zach couldn't take his eyes off the silver weapon gleaming in the moonlight.

"Get into the alley. Now!" The mugger's voice was low pitched and menacing, even through the scarf covering the bottom of his face.

Run! But he couldn't. His body was too heavy, too out of practice. Why had he let himself get like this?

The man stepped out of the alley, grabbed his elbow, and threw him up against a brick wall. "Give me everything in your pockets!"

Shit! His iPhone was practically new. He'd been lucky to get it before the production slowdown and shortage. Now cell phone resale value had shot so high, everyone was a target for thieves. That's what this guy wanted.

Why the hell was he worrying about his damn iPhone? It was the prototype phone and the microchip he needed to focus on. They both had the algorithm. How to distract the mugger from them?

"I've only got about forty dollars, but you can have it." Zach pulled his wallet from his back pocket and opened it. The microchip was inside, and as he fumbled with the bills he managed to slip it out and palm it.

"Hand me the whole thing!" The man with the gun reached for it, and the scarf slipped off his chin. Brown skin, wide nose, long black coat, wool cap. That's all the detail Zach could process in the dark—while scared shitless and a little drunk.

Zach clenched his jaw and handed him the wallet, keeping the chip wedged between two fingers.

"Phones too. And whatever else you've got on you."

Shit! Shit! Shit! Phones, plural. Why would the bastard assume he had more than one? The device prototype he was carrying was worth fifty thousand, and the man he was supposed to meet had a satchel of cash waiting for him. The damn mugger wouldn't even know what he'd taken. "I've got an iPhone," Zach said quickly. "That's it." He slipped the cell from his jacket and held it out.

The mugger snatched it and shoved it into his own coat.

In the brief second that the big man glanced down, Zach slipped the microchip into his mouth. A cab drove by, the only car on the street, but with the chip in his mouth, he couldn't call for help.

"Empty your pockets!"

He worked the chip under his tongue to hide it. "I've got nothing else!" Zach heard the fear and bullshit in his own voice and cringed.

The mugger shook his head, and a sharp pop echoed in Zach's ears. Heat and pain flared in his chest, and he realized he'd been shot. His mouth fell open, and a strange squeak came out. He tried to step back, but his knees buckled and he went down. His last thought was that he would die without ever having a real girlfriend.

CHAPTER 3

Monday, March 16, 12:05 p.m., Washington, DC

Special Agent Andra Bailey closed the report she was writing. Time for lunch. She heard the distinct footsteps of her boss' boot heels and realized she'd waited a minute too long. She turned in her chair and gave a practiced smile to the striking woman glaring down at her.

"I need to see you in my office." SA Lennard was six-one with short platinum hair and a grim expression that somehow didn't hurt her looks.

Bailey stood, feeling short at five-eight. "I'm right behind you." She had no idea what her boss wanted, but projecting confidence was a lifelong habit. She followed Lennard down the hall.

FBI headquarters in Washington, DC, was a blue-chip assignment inside the bureau, and Bailey felt lucky to be there. Not that luck really factored into it. At her original assignment in Denver, she'd simply worked harder than her peers to earn the promotion. She also knew how to manipulate people to get what she wanted—and to make them feel good about it. Her mindset usually felt like a gift. At other times, such as late at night, alone in her apartment, her sociopathic nature was painfully limiting. She was reasonably attractive with thick ginger-red hair that people liked to touch, so she didn't lack for male attention. She just wasn't capable of bonding the way empathetic people were. She'd had her share of affairs when she was younger, but her lovers had wanted more than she could give. In time, she'd simply stopped dating.

After several twists and turns in the maze-like building, they came to a corner office. Brent Haywood, the bureau's second in command, stood outside Lennard's door. *Good news.* If the assistant director was involved, this case was a big deal. Bailey nodded at the AD, and the three stepped into the office. Lennard closed the door and took a seat behind her shiny metal desk. Haywood, an ex–football player who shaved his head to hide the gray, continued to stand.

Lennard glanced at him, then looked at Bailey. "We have an issue developing that could turn out to be nothing, or it could be a global crime spree."

Intriguing! Bailey leaned forward.

"Ten days ago, Milton Thurgood, an Australian scientist, disappeared. His wife came home and he was gone. Some of his clothes and personal items were missing too, and his car was found at the airport."

She'd heard the name recently but couldn't place it. "Why does he sound familiar?"

Lennard squinted. "Unless you're a science buff, there's no reason it should. Thurgood lost the International Metallurgy Award recently to another scientist named Nick Bowman, of California."

"What else?" Bailey was a voracious reader who filed information for later use, but this Australian scientist's disappearance hadn't made major headlines.

"Three days ago, Nick Bowman also disappeared, after work in San Jose, and his wife reported him missing. This morning, hikers found his body in the Sunol Regional Wilderness, northeast of Silicon Valley."

"Murdered?"

"Most likely." Lennard ran a hand through her bristly hair. "His body was broken in just about every conceivable way, as if he'd taken a horrible beating. But with Thurgood missing—and having a history of irrational behavior—we think the events could be connected."

There had to be more to it. "Did Thurgood get on a plane?"

"He took a flight to Los Angeles. After that, we don't know."

"It's rather bizarre." Bailey wasn't usually assigned homicide cases—they were generally too easy—but this one was unusual and could involve a lot of travel.

Lennard continued. "The local sheriff's department called our San Jose field office for help. One of our monitors hit on the possible connection to the Australian scientist."

As a field agent in Lennard's Critical Incident Response Group, or CIRG for short, Bailey kept busy with high-impact events. The monitors watched global news feeds around the clock to connect and anticipate incidents. Bailey wanted to run the unit someday—and she would.

She'd been racking her brain for what she knew about Thurgood, and now it came to her. She'd read an article about that science award and some of the inventions that had earned nominations. "Thurgood and Bowman are both metallurgists," she recalled aloud, "and Thurgood is developing an extraction process for rare earth metals." She started to suggest a theory, but the AD cut in.

"We think Thurgood went off the rails and killed Bowman out of jealousy and to keep him from reaching a breakthrough before he did." Haywood finally sat down but perched on the edge of his chair.

"That's one possibility," Lennard added.

The assistant director gave her a silencing look. "It's the strongest possibility." To Bailey, he said, "Focus your investigation in that direction."

They obviously disagreed. Bailey weighed the advantage of making the AD happy by agreeing with him against the harm of pissing off her direct supervisor. A draw. So she wouldn't comment. She still didn't understand why she'd been chosen for this assignment, but she was happy to get out of DC. The snow was driving her crazy. "You need me to go to California. And Sydney too?"

Haywood nodded. "Start in San Jose. To the best of our knowledge, Thurgood hasn't returned to Australia."

"Why is this even a bureau concern?" As soon as the words were out of her mouth, Bailey realized it had been too blunt. Sometimes her carefully crafted filters didn't work.

Neither boss seemed ruffled by the question, though. Lennard handed her a thin file. "It's possible that Thurgood might target other scientists in the field. We need to find him and stop him."

A scientist serial killer. How unusual. She couldn't wait to get started. "Does the San Jose field office know I'm coming?"

"Yes. Don't worry about stepping on toes. Just dig deep and do what you do." Lennard gave a tight smile. "I chose you because you have that rare combination of a highly analytical mind and a charisma that opens doors."

Was Lennard giving her an unspoken message to think beyond the AD's directive?

Haywood was silent.

She probably wasn't his first choice. Too bad. She would prove him wrong. Bailey focused on her boss. "I need the field offices to report anything unusual they might pick up involving metallurgists."

Lennard nodded. "It's done."

Bailey was already making a mental list of things to do, starting with buying a plane ticket. "I'll catch the first flight I can."

"Report directly to both of us," Haywood said, standing. "And if the San Jose field office holds a task force meeting, conference us in."

Lennard added, "If this case gets too complex, we can assign other agents to the investigation."

Bailey preferred to work alone, but collaborating was part of the job. She stood. "I'll keep you posted."

Back at her desk, she scheduled a flight for that evening and made a hotel reservation near the San Jose FBI office. One of the perks of being an agent. Airlines and hotels always made room for her. She stuffed the file into her satchel and headed home to pack.

Another reason Lennard had picked her was flexibility. No spouse or kids to slow her down or pressure her to wrap up quickly and come home. She loved that about her life, but at times hated it too. Other successful sociopaths managed to make deep connections and establish families. At her age, she accepted that she wouldn't have children—and wouldn't want the responsibility of raising a sociopath, as her father had had to do. But she did want to fall in love someday, and so far, it hadn't happened.

CHAPTER 4

Monday, March 16, 1:55 p.m., Washington, DC

Detective Jocelyn Larson inhaled a quick dose of nicotine vapor before she walked into the department's forensics building. She loved that the vapor had almost no smell and didn't ruin her breath or her clothes. The joy of smoking, without the disgusting part or the guilt. At her age and with her body type, she was tired of taking crap for her bad habit.

At the security counter, she showed her badge. "I'm here for the John Doe autopsy."

The woman behind the safety glass barely glanced at the ID. "Lucky you." They'd had this exchange a few times. Jocelyn was a career detective, all of it spent in DC, and had attended more autopsies in this building than was healthy for the soul.

The desk clerk pressed the button, the door to the left buzzed, and Jocelyn headed past the crime lab to the morgue. In the small front room, she pulled on a gown, hairnet, and booties, grateful she didn't have to wear the gear at crime scenes, because technicians collected and processed the evidence. Inside the autopsy center, stainless steel and constant disinfecting didn't mask the slight stench of decay that hung in the air.

An assistant medical examiner looked up from her microscope. "If you're ready, we'll get started." The ME had a fresh young face, but the rest of her body was covered in puffy blue scrubs.

Jocelyn stepped toward the table. The John Doe who'd been shot and robbed in the Bellevue area lay on the shiny steel table, already uncovered. Why did she always get the bodies with no ID and no fingerprint match in the database? The ME pulled her tray of sharp instruments next to the table and turned on a bright overhead light. None of the autopsy would bother Jocelyn, except the Y cut into the chest with the saw. But that was later, and she would be a little numb by then.

The twenty-minute inch-by-inch search of his skin was uneventful, except for the ME's comment about his hands. "He appears to have some damage to the tips of his fingers, possibly from chemical burns. But it's not recent." She looked up at Jocelyn. "I'll know more after I send a tissue sample to the lab for analysis."

Jocelyn tuned out for a moment, wondering what else she could do to identify this guy—short of running a dead-face photo in the newspaper.

"This is interesting." The medical examiner's voice held surprise and excitement as she lifted something tiny with a pair of long-handled tweezers.

"What is it?"

"Some kind of microchip, and I found it under his tongue."

What the hell? Her investigation hadn't turned up any witnesses, but based on the location, she'd assumed some gangbanger had killed the man for his cell phone and wallet. The microchip made her rethink that. Clearly, the victim had hidden the chip from his assailant. What was on this bit of silicon that made someone kill him for it?

CHAPTER 5

Bailey sat in the Dulles Airport terminal reading the file on Milton Thurgood, a brilliant metallurgical engineer who'd discovered an acid-and-heat method for extracting rare earth metals from mining operations. He'd also been arrested several times for public meltdowns in which he shouted at and sometimes accosted strangers. Once he'd come after his wife with a shovel, but when police responded to the disturbance, she convinced them to let it go, claiming her husband had simply forgotten to take his medication. Thurgood obviously had violent tendencies, and if he'd quit taking his meds altogether, he might have been capable of plotting and carrying out a murder. Which could also make him unpredictable and hard to locate. The background data, which had likely come from the Australian Federal Police, didn't include Thurgood's actual diagnosis. Too bad. Mental disorders fascinated her.

Her own mental condition was often referred to as *antisocial personality disorder*, which sounded more palatable than *sociopath*, but they weren't the same diagnosis. The public, and even most mental health professionals, wrongly assumed all sociopaths were criminals or forces of destruction, just like people with ASPD. The truth was that sociopaths, an estimated 4 percent of the population, were specifically defined by their inability to empathize with other people or feel guilt about their own behavior. Those qualities alone didn't make them criminals. Instead, sociopaths fell along a continuum. Those on the moderate-to-low end, like herself, didn't take any pleasure in hurting anyone. They just didn't suffer guilt if it happened. Her emotional experiences were different from other people's too. If various emotions were like colors for empaths, hers were shades of gray. Low-end sociopaths included a lot of high achievers, such as rapid-rising CEOs and politicians. Not to mention some law enforcement personnel, who were attracted to the career because it offered both power and a firm structure to help keep themselves in line.

On the high end of the continuum were those commonly thought of as psychopaths, because they enjoyed tormenting and sometimes killing people. Many psychopaths were also brilliant and successful, but others lacked intellectual capacity or ambition and were often frustrated by their mediocre lives. Those types often ended up in prison. Sociopaths were as varied as any other group that shared a single characteristic or belief.

An elderly man approached and gestured at the empty seat next to her. "Excuse me. May I sit here?"

"I'd prefer that you didn't."

He looked taken aback.

Bailey smiled and shrugged to lessen the sting. She had to be true to herself when she could. He shook his head and walked away. She went back to reading. But there was little else about Thurgood that was helpful.

Her cell chirped and Bailey pulled it from her satchel. A 303 area code. Denver, her hometown, where her father still lived, but it wasn't his number. He didn't call often, so this would probably be bad news. "Andra Bailey here."

A robotic voice said, "You have a collect call from the Denver County Jail. Press One to accept the charges."

Her father had been arrested. *Damn.* She accepted the call.

After a short recorded message, her father came on the line. "Andra, thank you. Beth is in New York at a conference, and I didn't know who else to call." Beth was his third wife, and her absence explained why her father, also a sociopath, had stepped out of his behavior construct.

"What did you do?"

"I got into a fistfight, and the other man went to the hospital. I'm charged with assault."

Oh hell. At sixty-two, her father should have been long past that kind of impulse. This wasn't his first altercation, but the last one had been ten years ago, and he'd offered financial compensation to the victim to drop the charges. Bailey was grateful not to be a male sociopath; they had more violent tendencies. But the fact that her father, a university professor with a long history of stability, could fail to control his impulses meant that she was always at risk for the same thing. For the first time, the thought caused her real fear. She never wanted to be fired again and have to start over with a new career or in a new location. Or worse yet, end up in jail. Most negative consequences didn't faze her, but those definitely did.

"What can I do for you?"

"Wire ten thousand in bail money to Express Bail Bonds and have them post it for me."

"As soon as I can. I'm in the airport, waiting for a connecting flight to San Jose." Bailey kept her voice low, even though everyone around her was preoccupied and heading to the same city.

"You'll find a Western Union as soon as you land?"

"Of course." She owed him. He'd bailed her out of a few scrapes in high school and college, before she'd learned to control her dangerous impulses. Plus, she loved him and wanted to help. "Call your lawyer too."

"I already did."

"Can you get out of this?" An assault conviction could ruin his teaching career. She might have to help him out financially. He'd never been good with money and probably didn't have much saved. She spent hers freely too, but she had also made some great stock picks, so she had a nest egg.

"I don't know." Her father didn't sound upset. But he rarely did.

"I can't come to Denver now because of this assignment, but if I can help out later, let me know." She would do what she could—until his situation became too boring or uncomfortable to be around. He would understand when she walked away. Others didn't, especially after becoming attached to her. Another reason her friendships were few and seldom lasted.

"Thanks, Andra."

An overhead voice announced that her flight was boarding. "I have to go. We'll talk again later." They hung up without saying good-bye, a mutual understanding.

She'd known from an early age that her father wasn't like other people, especially other fathers. He hadn't hugged her when he dropped her at the babysitter's or school, and he hadn't reacted emotionally to her accidents on the playground or bicycle. Being impulsive and fearless, she'd had plenty. In her early years, she'd assumed his indifference was because her mother had died and he was sad. When she was eleven, he'd sat her down and talked about sociopathy, both his and hers. He'd apparently known, or assumed, since she was a preschooler that she had the disorder too. A particular incident when she was five had convinced him. During their sociopathy talk, he'd brought up the kindergarten incident, and she had remembered the day vividly. In recalling it at the time, she'd cemented the episode in her mind, because it had been a turning point for her.

* * *

The playground slide was hot from the sun, but she used it anyway—a beautiful afternoon in late May. Kindergarten was over for the day, and her teacher had let the kids out to play for the last few minutes before the adults arrived to take them home. Puffy clouds drifted across a blue sky, and she felt happy to be outside.

Jack's mother was the first to arrive. He picked up his backpack and waved at her. "Bye, Andra. My mom's here."

"Bye."

She saw her babysitter's car pull to the curb outside the playground fence. She would have time for one more ride down the slide.

The boy in front of her in line, Mark, turned to face her. "Why don't you have a mother?"

He'd asked her several times before, and she didn't want to talk about it. "You already know." She decided not to get on the slide.

As she walked away, he grabbed her arm. "My dad says your mom ran away."

What? Confused and angry, she shouted, "That's a lie!"

"Don't call me a liar! Just because your mother's a cheat."

A cheat? Not her mother! Her mother was dead. Bailey decided not to get mad or hurt, because she hated those feelings, and they didn't fix anything. But she had to put a stop to Mark's meanness about her mother. She pulled her fist back and punched him in the face as hard as she could.

He staggered back, holding his nose as blood gushed from it.

Intense feelings pulsed in her body. She didn't understand them, but she liked them. "Don't ever say that again!" She stepped forward to hit him in the stomach.

Their teacher was suddenly there and grabbed her arm. "Andra, no! We don't hit each other." The teacher bent over to look her in the eye. "Tell him you're sorry."

She rarely regretted anything—except not having a mother—and didn't understand the concept. "I'm not sorry."

"You should be. We don't solve our problems with violence."

That didn't make sense. She'd solved her problem with Mark with one punch to his mean face. She pulled free of the teacher's grip, ran through the opening in the fenced yard, and climbed into her babysitter's car.

Later at home, she asked her father, "Why did Mark say Mom left? He called her a cheat too."

Her father sat quietly for a long moment, and she couldn't tell what he was thinking. Finally, he said, "Your mother did leave us. But I didn't want you to know. I shouldn't have lied."

Her mother hadn't wanted to live with them? An ache she'd never felt before filled her stomach. "Why? I don't understand."

"It's complicated. But it was mostly about me. I'm hard to live with."

Mostly? "She left because of me too?"

For a moment, he looked hurt. "She just couldn't handle being a parent. She loved you." He hugged her, a rare moment. "I love you."

Her father went off to make dinner, and confusion set in. Her mother loved her, but had walked out of her life anyway. Her father loved her, but had lied to her. Adults could not be trusted. Love could not be trusted.

She'd been expelled, and her father had explained how, in the next school, she would have to obey rules even when she didn't understand them. And she would have to apologize even if she didn't mean it. It was her first realization that she was different from other kids. Eventually, she learned not to be violent. *If you hit, you sit*—in the principal's office, grounded in her room at home, or in jail. Confinement was the worse consequence of all. That early incident with Mark had also been her first exposure to the internal conflict she would face her whole life—should she do what came naturally to her, or what was socially acceptable? Her own perspective always seemed more logical than others', but when she acted on it, she usually ended up alienated or in trouble.

Later, in college, when Bailey had studied the literature on sociopaths, she wondered if her condition was based purely on the genetics passed down from her father or whether a lack of bonding with a mother had stunted her emotional growth. Or maybe her own lack of emotion had driven her mother away. Did genetics dictate how her mind worked, or had her experiences caused her brain to form pathways of antisocial thinking? Or some combination? Either way, she had to live with it. There was no treatment for sociopathy.

The hardest part had been to develop a sense of self. In high school, she'd been a chameleon, adapting her music and clothes and speech patterns to mimic whoever she was around. She'd done those things to fit in and make people like her, but also to manipulate people for her own benefit. Her father had eventually encouraged her to find or create her own identity, ideally through a career that would provide expectations and guidelines. Years later, he'd been surprised by her choice of the FBI, but being an agent was now her identity. It also gave her a code of ethics to live by, to compensate for her lack of intrinsic morals. She knew she would adapt and remake herself if she ever lost her job, but without a core sense of self, it would be challenging.

At thirty-nine, she'd already done all the self-analysis she could handle. A quick check of her phone indicated she still had twenty minutes until her flight took off, so she called the Australian scientist's wife again. Mrs. Thurgood hadn't answered earlier or returned her call. As the phone rang, Bailey calculated the time difference. It should be around one in the afternoon in Australia.

A soft voice with a lovely accent answered. "This is Leslie Thurgood. Who is calling, please?"

"Agent Bailey, US Federal Bureau of Investigation."

"Goodness. What could you possibly want with me?"

"I'm looking into your husband's disappearance, and I need to ask some questions."

"But why? The Australian authorities say he walked away." The woman made a muffled sound of grief. "Not that I believe it."

"What do you think happened?" It was always good to hear what people closest to the scene had to say.

"Milton is obsessed with his research. Wherever he is, he's working."

"He didn't tell you anything about where he was going?"

"No. And I'm mad as a cut snake. He's had some fuckups before, but this one's bonzer."

Was she a little drunk? "Did your husband ever talk about Nick Bowman?"

"Aye, he did. Especially after the award was announced, but not so much lately. Why do you ask?"

"Nick Bowman has been murdered."

Mrs. Thurgood sucked in a quick breath of air. "I'll be stuffed. But don't think my Milton offed him. I know he's a bit bonkers when he's off his pills, but he's been taking them."

Would she have known for sure if he'd stopped? "How was he behaving in the weeks and days before he left?"

"The same. Working hard. No peculiars."

"Your husband took a flight to Los Angeles. Who did he know there?"

"Don't know that."

This was getting nowhere. "Where do you think he is?"

Mrs. Thurgood muffled a cry. "I don't know. But it's not like he's gone walkabout. He'll be back."

"Did anything unusual happen recently? A problem at work? A job offer? A birthday?" Sometimes people reacted strongly to external events.

"He got a call he didn't want to talk about. He took the phone in the bedroom and it lasted a while. Milton said it was about his extraction process and not to worry."

A recruiter? But why the secrecy? "Was he having an affair?"

The woman laughed. "Oh, that's ace. Milton's not a pretty man and has no social skills. I love him, but I don't see anyone else getting in his pants."

If he had no social skills, Milton Thurgood could be a sociopath, one who'd given up playing by the rules and indulged in his darker nature. She gave the woman her name again and her cell number. "Call me if you think of anything important. I'm trying to find your husband."

"If you do, tell him to get his arse home. G'day."

Bailey hung up and joined the line boarding the plane. What else besides revenge and mental illness might have driven Thurgood to leave his job, his wife, and his country without a word?

Money came to mind.

CHAPTER 6

Tuesday, March 17, 6:15 a.m., San Jose, California

Bailey hurried out of her hotel room for a quick walk. Exercise for the sake of exercise bored her, but her desk job, combined with the sitting required for travel, took its toll on her body. So she made herself go for at least one short walk a day, and she preferred to go early because she hated to sweat. The only time she made an exception was during long overnight operations. Takedowns she loved, but stakeouts were the pits. Being trapped in a surveillance van with another agent for long stretches really tested her mental discipline and social skills, which were mostly contrived. But since joining the CIRG team, her work rarely involved stakeouts anymore.

She surprised herself and walked all the way to the bay and back, enjoying the scenery and the warm air. In the hotel, she checked her watch, surprised she'd been gone forty minutes. Forty. Her next birthday loomed over her, and she dreaded it. Forty was hard to wrap her head around. How could she keep thinking of herself as young after that? She could look the part, though. Enzymes and laser facials had helped her look and feel better for years.

Bailey showered, dressed in dark forest green—to look serious without actually wearing black—and climbed into her rental car. Her first stop would be the morgue to see the dead man for herself. It would have been better to examine the crime scene, but the bureau was typically called in after the fact, unless they were working a multistate serial killer. She'd been on two such cases, so she had some experience searching for globe-trotting murderers, but she usually ended up with oddball investigations that didn't fit standard categories. This one could turn out to be both.

With the help of GPS, the medical examiner's office was fairly easy to find, a few blocks off the 880 highway. But the parking was limited, and she had to find a space a block or so away. Inside, she showed her ID, waited while the receptionist made a call, then followed her back to the autopsy room. A dark-skinned man with a glistening bald head greeted her with a slight Indian accent. "Ms. Bailey. Thank you for coming. I'm Dr. Sharish." She nodded, relieved he didn't offer his gloved hand.

"Where's the body?" Too abrupt, she realized.

"This way." He spun toward a wall of large stainless-steel drawers, pulled one open, and removed the white covering.

Bailey stared at the dead man. His skin was purple and his limbs contorted.

"You can see from the bruising that he took quite a beating, then died immediately afterward." Dr. Sharish scowled, the wrinkles on his forehead rippling up toward his scalp. "But there are no edges to any of the contusions and they overlap, so I can't determine the weapon."

Nick Bowman had been pushed out of a plane or helicopter. A rather elaborate way for a mentally ill man to commit a revenge murder. But Thurgood was a scientist, and he may have had a reason. She looked up at the medical examiner. "This man was dropped from the sky, and I need to know exactly when."

The ME's eyes widened. "That would certainly explain the condition of the body." He stepped back and checked a clipboard on a nearby counter. "I estimated his time of death at between five and ten a.m. Saturday morning. It's fortunate that his body was discovered so quickly. He could have just as easily lain there for weeks."

Someone had flown over the state park and dumped him in the dark or early morning. Had the killer planned to push him out or had Bowman caused a problem during the flight? Who had been piloting the craft while all that went on?

She was starting to think Thurgood might be another victim rather than the killer. On her flight the night before, she'd researched rare earth metals. China produced 95 percent of the world's supply, and in the five months since it had stopped exporting, the shortage of gallium, indium, and dysprosium had become critical for computer and cell phone manufacturers. Other industries—such as electric cars, wind turbines, solar cells, and batteries—had been hit hard too. The US government was pushing to ramp up mining in American facilities, but the biggest problem was extraction, which was complex and expensive. Meanwhile, cell phone production everywhere except China had nearly come to a halt. The price of electronics had shot up, and in some cases, they were disappearing from retail shelves. The whole industry was in turmoil, and manufacturing companies were in a state of panic. The biggest problem was the lack of dysprosium, which had magnetic qualities and was used to make speakers, microphones, and hard drives. Because it was scarce and hard to extract, Bailey assumed companies and researchers had to be desperately trying to produce a replacement material, which was Bowman's specialty. What if someone had coerced or kidnapped the scientists because they needed both of their vital skillsets or knowledge?

But where was Thurgood? And why had they killed Bowman? If the kidnappers had known they were going to kill him, they probably hadn't filed a flight plan. Still, the plane or helicopter had taken off from and landed somewhere, and she would investigate that.

Bailey looked over Bowman's body, noting his once-excellent muscle tone and appendix scar. "May I have gloves?"

The ME hurried to grab some. Bailey pulled them on and lifted Nick Bowman's right hand. "Anything under his fingernails?" She didn't expect the scientist to have struggled.

"No, but he was bound by his wrists, at least for a short while."

She'd noticed the red mark against the white skin on the inside of his wrist, one of the few places he wasn't bruised. But she was interested in the skin condition of his palms. In the grooves was a brown discoloration, like a stain or burn. "Please test his hands for chemicals and tell me what you find. I want his toxicology as soon as possible." She smiled and made a don't-hurt-the-messenger gesture with her hands. "I know the blood work could take weeks, but you need to pressure the lab to prioritize this one." She leaned toward Dr. Sharish and whispered, "This case is related to national security, and the bureau needs your full cooperation."

"Of course." The ME blinked. "What chemicals? Was he making bombs?"

"I can't say, but you'll be in the loop when I know more."

Bailey studied the corpse, searching every inch of his bruised and broken skin. "Let's turn him over."

The ME started to protest, then clamped his jaw shut and stepped to the other side. They rolled the body so she could see his back. Not nearly as much bruising, but he still looked contorted by the broken bones. Bailey spotted a round reddish mark and leaned in.

"That's a burn," the ME said. "Most likely from a stun gun."

Tasers had two prongs. "Where's the second mark?"

"His right leg, to the inside."

When had they stunned him? When they originally grabbed him? Or later, in the plane, to control him? The kidnappers' MO was critical, especially if more scientists were at risk. She pulled a business card from her pocket and handed it to Dr. Sharish. "Here's my email address.

Please send me the full autopsy report immediately. And I'd like the toxicology details in a few days."

He swallowed hard. "I'll do what I can."

She hurried out, eager to talk to witnesses and dig into the investigation. Agents in the San Jose field office had filed a report, but she would go back over the same territory. The local agents hadn't known what they were dealing with when Nick Bowman's wife reported him missing, so they hadn't asked the right questions, or enough questions. Investigators often assumed missing adults had walked away on their own—for good reason, since it was nearly always true. Although two disappearing metallurgists created a whole new investigation. Her next stop was New Age Fabricators, the company Bowman worked for. His coworkers had been the last people to see him.

Outside in the bright sun, she focused on the food cart she'd noted on the way in and turned left. As she reached the corner, she realized her error. Wrong direction. Her topographical disorientation had tripped her up again. The short walk to her car had seemed easy, especially after registering the food cart as a direction signal. Had the owner moved the damn cart?

Bailey backtracked and found the rental car without further mishap. Before GPS had become commonplace in cars and phones, her life had been more challenging, including getting through the fieldwork segment of the bureau's training. But her IQ and analytical skills had made up for it. The agency's psychological exam had worried her the most. Though lying was easy for her, knowing when to lie on the test and what they wanted to hear had taken a lot of preparation—but she'd gotten through. As long as she was good at her job, what difference did it make?

New Age Fabricators took up half a block in an industrial area south of San Jose, a concrete-bunker-style building with a row of glass-framed offices on the top floor. She could never be one of the workers on the ground floor with no windows, but that was their choice. She parked next to the entrance in the open visitors' space. Who would drop in at a company that produced unusual metals? Not spotting any security, she pushed through the double doors into a small lobby. Beyond its back wall, the hum and thump of machinery vibrated the walls. She ignored the guest chair and stepped through an open door to the left. A claustrophobic office space with an old guy behind a cluttered desk. The tag on his wrinkled white shirt said *Security*. She suppressed a smile and introduced herself.

"You're here about Dr. Bowman?"

Doctor? Oh right. Bowman had a PhD in materials science and engineering, and obviously exploited the title. She added arrogance to his profile. "Yes, and I need to speak with Clare Jones and David Seabert. Ms. Jones first." The last two people to see Nick Bowman alive. She'd gleaned the names from the field office report.

"Clare's on the second floor, left side of the building." The old guy coughed up some phlegm. "Mr. Seabert has the corner office on the top floor."

No surprise. Seabert ran the company his father had founded. But little information was offered on their website, and she wanted to know more about the company's research, particularly what Bowman had been working on. Bailey remembered to say thanks as she walked out. She didn't see stairs so she took the elevator, then encountered a chubby middle-aged woman as she got off on the top floor. Based on the field office report, Bailey took a guess. "Ms. Jones?"

"Yes?" Her eyes registered fear.

"Agent Bailey, FBI. Let's go to your office and talk about Nick Bowman."

"I don't know anything. I already told the other agent that." Her voice was thin and childish and didn't match her appearance.

Bailey decided to dive right in. "Tell me about the last time you saw Bowman."

The woman let out an exasperated breath. "We walked to the parking lot together, then got into our cars and left. That's it."

"What did you talk about?"

"I don't know." She shrugged. "I mentioned a restaurant I wanted to try."

"Did Bowman say what his plans were?"

"Just that he was stopping for a drink." Jones rolled her eyes, then blurted out, "But he was having an affair. It was so obvious."

That hadn't been in the report. "With who?" Now she had to consider a jealous husband as the suspect. Maybe the scientists' shared career was a coincidence.

"I have no idea. Can I go now?" Jones seemed flustered and probably regretting sharing the gossip about Bowman's love life.

She would need special handling now. "You seem like the kind of person your coworkers would confide in. I'm surprised he didn't tell you about the affair."

A pleased expression swept over the woman's face, even as she shook her head. "No, Nick probably knew I wouldn't approve. He has a lovely family."

"Did his wife know about the affair?"

"I doubt it."

"Does she strike you as a volatile personality? The type to get angry enough to take revenge?"

Jones' eyes and mouth popped open. "You mean would she kill him for cheating on her?"

"It happens."

A blank stare now. "I don't know his wife at all."

Bailey dreaded talking to the widow. Distressed people's emotions got in the way, and it took forever.

"Thanks for your time." She had to move on. The likelihood of find-ing a witness to the abduction was slim—unless she found Bowman's mistress or could trace his steps on the evening of his disappearance. Bowman's car hadn't turned up, and no one had seen him after he left work. The local agents had requested the dead man's phone and finan-cial records, and she would soon have access too. But first, she needed to know what the scientist had been working on. Matching his research to another company's needs could be the key to finding the suspects. She headed for the corner office to question the CEO.

David Seabert was forty-something, wore a dark-blue pullover, and sported a well-groomed beard. Not a scrap of paper cluttered his high-gloss desk. Just a palm-sized recorder and, near the front, a business award he'd won. A nonconformist and a control freak. She would have to work him carefully. Bailey introduced herself, and he offered a quick handshake but no smile.

"Thanks for seeing me," she said. "I know you're a busy man."

"Have a seat." He gestured and sank into his own chair. "How can I help you?"

"Tell me everything you know about Nick Bowman's research."

He drew back, eyes tightening. "You think his death is connected to his work?"

"Yes."

"I just heard he was having an affair. Maybe it was a domestic issue."

"Unlikely. What was he working on?"

Seabert folded his arms across his chest. "Our research is proprietary."

"I understand, but this could be a matter of national security." She would appeal to his ego. Bailey leaned forward and touched his hand. "I'll tell you something confidential in exchange. Another metallurgist from Australia disappeared two weeks ago. I don't believe Nick Bowman's death was a domestic issue or a random act of violence. Something big is happening here, and I need your help."

For a long moment he stared past her, vacillating. Finally, he said, "I can only give you a broad idea of Nick's research, but it involved the development of a new material, something that could replace dysprosium in manufacturing." He met her eyes. "Do you know what that is?"

"A rare earth metal in very short supply."

"It has been all along, even before China's embargo. So Nick had been working on it for years." The CEO finally relaxed his arms and confided in her. "China's control of the supply has always worried the technology industry, but no one expected them to completely shut down exports. It's chaos here in the Valley. Employees are either being laid off or recruited at crazy salaries."

"Already?"

"Five months is a lifetime in the tech industry. But our company is somewhat immune, because we produce a variety of specialty metals."

"What about your competitors? What company would have the most to gain by appropriating or stopping Nick Bowman's research?"

Seabert's eyes narrowed. "Everyone in the digital device business could benefit. As well as companies that make hard drives and lasers." He stroked his short beard. "But dysprosium is essential to cell phones, and startups with only one product line, such as Celltronics and ZoGo, will be the hardest hit. I heard Celltronics is facing bankruptcy."

Bailey had dossiers on both. She'd only had time to glance through them, but she'd noted the name of ZoGo's CEO: Shawn Crusher. A search of the databases had revealed his birth name as Shawn Ming Crutcher, but he'd changed it to Shawn Crusher at the age of twenty-two, when he'd left college to start his technology career. A smart move, even if it had been driven by a fragile ego. He'd gone to work for qPie, the search-engine giant, and had quickly been promoted up the ranks, his new moniker giving the news media easy wordplay shots at his propensity for *crushing* the competition. Then, just five years into his reign, he'd been fired. Speculators claimed it was over a cell phone he developed that didn't make it through focus groups—after qPie had spent millions on it. Now he manufactured his own burner-style phones. Recent business reports called him "brilliant" and "prescient" for investing in low-end phones before the crisis began to render high-end electronics unaffordable for many consumers. The analysts also admired his marketing skills, claiming he possessed "a rare combination of technical and promotional savvy." ZoGo was one of the few companies holding its own in the new shortage-driven market.

Mark Ziegler, Celltronics' CEO, was nowhere near as flashy or high-profile. He was older and had started his company after a long career in software design. Celltronics made middle-of-the-road phones and marketed them to large employers who bought cell phones by the thousands.

While Bailey couldn't rule out the big three—Apple, Samsung, and Nokia—it seemed highly unlikely that someone inside one of those reputable companies had suddenly gone rogue. Not that it couldn't happen. People like her, with little or no conscience, could easily step outside social boundaries in their quest for power or money. But it made sense to start with the newcomers, who were vulnerable and fighting hard for their share of the pie.

CHAPTER 7

Tuesday, March 17, 9:15 a.m., Mountain View, California

Shawn Crusher's phone rang, interrupting his morning scan for market-share data. Annoyed, he glanced at the caller ID. No name appeared, but he recognized the number. This wouldn't be good. He popped in a tiny earpiece and pushed the Answer button on his Tones, a new neck-wraparound wireless device. "Hello, Max." It was the only name he had for his financier, and Shawn suspected it was phony.

"We have a couple of problems."

Even though he'd known blowback was coming, the man's cold, flat tone made his neck muscles tighten. The voice was enough to intimidate him, and he hated that. "Yeah? Like what?"

"What the hell happened with Nick Bowman?" Max had quickly switched to shouting.

How did he know? Had Bowman's body surfaced already? "What do you mean?"

"Don't bullshit me. Someone found the body. What the hell is going on?"

Shawn swallowed hard. Nick Bowman's death was unfortunate. He'd never planned to harm the scientist. But Shawn had already tucked away his guilt and moved on. That's how he survived. Besides, what he was trying to accomplish was far too important to let other people derail him.

"Bowman was totally uncooperative from the beginning," Shawn explained. "When he caused a problem on the transfer flight, my crew had no choice but to deal with him." He'd been a lot less complacent when Harlan and Rocky had reported the incident.

"There's more." Max resonated with controlled anger now. "My source in the bureau tells me someone made a connection between Thurgood and Bowman, and now they've sent an agent to investigate."

Fuck! Shawn had a dozen questions, but he knew his contact wouldn't stay on the phone much longer. "Who is the agent and what do you know about him?"

"Andra Bailey. And I hear *she's* brilliant."

He already hated her. But she wasn't smart enough to stop him. He'd been planning his takeover of the cell phone market for years. During an obligatory trip to China to visit his mother's family, he'd set up a meeting with a rare earth metal analyst, hoping to cut out the middleman and save money on raw materials. After too many baijius, the man had slipped and hinted at the government's plan to cut back on exports. A promise of cash had lubricated the analyst further, and he'd confirmed that it might even be a total shutdown. That moment had changed everything. Wild, ambitious thoughts had starting bouncing around in his brain, and within weeks, he'd starting looking at mining operations.

"Don't worry," Shawn said. "I'll handle the agent."

"No more bodies turning up! And get a replacement for Bowman ASAP. I recommend Dana Thorpe. Her synthetic is probably as advanced as Bowman's, and she's in Seattle, not far from the lab." Max shifted gears. "My partners have changed their minds about encryption.

They think it's the key to getting consumers to shift to a new brand. So now they want the best of the best. They've heard there's an unhackable version out there, but only a few coders know the key. Figure out who they are and bring one on board."

"That wasn't in our agreement." He didn't have time to develop a whole new software standard, and that wasn't the kind of phone he was manufacturing. Feeling a familiar tightening at his temples, he grabbed his bottle of dextro and swallowed one. He'd been taking too much of it lately, but the ADHD medicine kept him focused.

Shawn cut off whatever Max was saying. "I have it handled. You know I have an encryption expert in-house, and she's within days of finalizing an algorithm that'll deliver exactly what you're after." *Maybe.* It was true that Jia, his wife, had been working on the problem for months, but so far her hacker-testers kept breaking through everything she tried. But telling people what they wanted to hear was often more advantageous than the truth. At least in the moment. He'd learned that at an early age from parents who expected perfection.

"Having your wife working on it isn't good enough. We want the hacker-proof software that's already out there, developed by the best in the business. Make it happen. We've invested too much in this project to fail at a key marketing objective." Max was gone.

Shawn clenched his teeth, caught himself doing it, and sat back in his $2,000 office chair. He didn't care about encryption, and neither had Max in their first conversation. What had changed? The big competitors, Apple and Samsung, were already embedding software that kept federal law enforcement from easily accessing phone data in their devices. Apparently, his financiers had decided that ZoGo cell phones needed to offer that level of security too, so consumers would buy them as replacements now that the name brands had become insanely expensive and nearly impossible to find. He disagreed. Once they dominated the market, consumers would buy whatever was available. That day was rapidly approaching.

Because he'd known the shortage was coming, Shawn had studied rare earth mining and researched every facility—operating or abandoned—that had the right potential. A West Coast location and the presence of bastnäsite were the two primary indicators. He'd found the perfect mine in central Washington. Because the facility had been shut down for years, he'd bought it relatively cheap, hoping to soon have the money to invest in state-of-the-art extraction technology. Still, the payments had been hefty and stressful while he waited to see if the analyst had been right. After six months, China had cut off rare earth exports and all hell had broken loose. Two weeks later, Max had approached him, wanting to invest in ZoGo and to help it gain control of the market.

When his private cell phone had rung, he hadn't recognized the number and had almost rejected the call. But the southern area code intrigued him, and he finally picked up. "Shawn Crusher speaking."

"This is Max. I'm an investor with an interest in your cell phone company. Can you meet me in an hour?"

Flustered and curious, Shawn asked the obvious. "Max who? What equity group are you with?"

"We're private venture capitalists. We've been watching the metal shortage and the production slowdown, and we think it's going to get ugly very quickly. A lot of companies won't survive. Our pockets are exceptionally deep, and we'd like to invest in the winner."

A shimmer of excitement rolled up Shawn's back. He'd been planning for this paradigm shift for years. He'd laid the groundwork, leveraged himself to his eyeballs to find and gain control of a mine, only to end up staring at a brick wall. He didn't have the capital to hire an extraction specialist and provide him with the necessary equipment. And now, a call out of the blue, offering the cash he needed? If it sounded too good to be true, it probably was. But he'd be a fool not to find out. "Sure. I'll meet with you. It sounds like we have interests in common."

"Eleven o'clock. In the middle of the food court in the SunView Mall."

"What do you look like?"

"I prefer to remain anonymous, so I'll find you." The man hung up.

Shawn paced the office, trying to figure out who the investors were, then decided he didn't care. They could be demons from hell as long as they provided the money to buy extraction equipment and recruit a top-notch specialist. He had an Australian in mind. He picked up his keys and left his office. Should he call Jia about the development? No, he'd wait and see how things went at the meeting.

A little later, at the food court, two teenagers vacated a table just as he arrived, and Shawn sat down, too keyed up to care about the mess they'd left. He was seven minutes early and waiting made him jumpy. He should have bought something to drink so he didn't look out of place sitting there. He checked his watch ten times, counting each nervous glance. At two minutes after the hour, a voice behind him said, "I'm here, but don't turn around."

The clandestine nature of the meeting sent Shawn's pulse up a notch. "I've never had a conversation like this before."

"Don't worry. I'll do most of the talking."

From behind, Max set a small duffle bag on the chair next to Shawn. "There's a hundred thousand in cash in the bag for seed money. We're prepared to invest considerably more through bank transfers. But you have to work within our timeline and agree to the software standards we impose."

The big money made his throat dry, and he itched to open the bag. "What standards?"

"Mostly quality and security, but we'll talk about that later."

Shawn didn't care much about security. He manufactured inexpensive, untraceable phones that people bought with cash and easily disposed of. But he wanted to be cooperative. "My wife is a coder with a specialty in encryption. I'll get her working on it."

"That's not the big issue. Our main concern is timing. We want to capture the market while it's in turmoil and before the government steps in."

He'd been thinking the same thing. But he had to ask. "Why me?"

"We're impressed with your foresight and ability to adapt. We think you've got a solid business model for the shortage-driven future." Max made a soft chuckling sound. "And you bought the mine we had our eye on. Whoever controls the resources controls the market."

Shawn was pleased with himself too, but how did Max know he'd purchased Palisades? He'd been careful to shield his ownership in case monopoly issues were ever raised. "How do you know I bought the mine?"

"We had our eye on it too, but you beat us to it. Now we need you to acquire the extraction equipment and get up to full production immediately. Plus bring in a rare earth extraction expert." Max's voice tightened. "Even that won't be enough. Dysprosium is so rare and so hard to process that we need to find a replacement. Without it, our competitors won't be able to produce microphones or speakers, and they'll go out of business. Meanwhile, we'll introduce a new generation of devices made with our own metals or synthetics."

Max's plan was similar to what he'd envisioned. Only more complex. Shawn hadn't thought about replacement materials. But he did notice the use of "our" when Max mentioned the synthetic. "How much stake do you want in my company?"

"Fifty-one percent."

Controlling interest. Could he live with that?

"You'll make millions and millions in the first year," Max assured him. "We have some promotional ideas that will exploit the shortage and increase our market share very quickly, and you're the right person to employ them. It's a once-in-a-lifetime opportunity." Max paused. "We think you know that already."

Shawn knew he would take the deal, but elements of it seemed daunting. "What about the dysprosium replacement material? I don't know the industry or who to recruit."

"This will be the most challenging aspect. I can give you the names of two metallurgists who are doing cutting-edge research, and you need to get one of them on board quickly, before another company recruits them. But we don't need them long term, we won't give them credit for their breakthroughs, and they'll need to sign a secrecy agreement with tough enforcement clauses. All we can offer is a lucrative bonus. That will make recruitment very difficult."

Why were those hurdles necessary? Max represented some peculiar investors. "What if I can't recruit anyone?"

"Be creative. Be ruthless. We don't care how you do it as long as we're kept anonymous."

What was Max suggesting? "Do you mean bribe them with a duffle bag of cash?" Another idea came to him. "Or do you mean blackmail?"

"That's too messy and not foolproof. If you can't recruit one of the best, you may just have to grab one and use forced labor." Max paused. "With a cash payment when they produce, of course."

Holy shit! This guy was talking about kidnapping scientists. "That sounds extreme and dangerous."

"No one has to get hurt. Just inconvenienced a little, then extremely well paid after a month or so when you release them."

No wonder Max wanted to keep his identity secret.

"Keep in mind," Max said, "you'll make more money than you can ever spend. And you'll be Silicon Valley's go-to guy, the one CEO who not only survived the meltdown, but profited."

Shawn wanted that more than anything. Could he do this? More important, what if he said no? The investors would take their money to a competitor, and someone else would make the millions and rise to the top. By the time he could afford the extraction technology for the mine, another company would be making phones with synthetic metals. Freaked out and excited at the same time, he could barely sit still.

"Can you handle it?" Max asked.

This was the litmus test. If he wanted the payoff, he had to go all in. But he would do everything he could to recruit experts first. Shawn swallowed hard. "I may need help with the logistics."

"I'll send a guy to help with the dirty work. He's also a pilot with his own plane, which will come in handy. And you can trust him."

He had so many questions! "Where will the scientists work? I don't have a lab for materials research."

"Find a facility and we'll fund the equipment. We can have the money in an account for you within twenty-four hours."

It was happening so fast, it was surreal. He needed to test Max's resources—and generosity. "I'll need five hundred thousand for myself up front, just as a bonus."

A pause. "I'll give you half in cash in a few days, delivered to you. And the other half will go into your account after you've brought in an extraction specialist and geared up the mine. We expect timely results."

Shawn heard a threat in his tone. What would they do if he failed? He wouldn't fail. Even more than the millions, he wanted control of the market. He wanted to be the King of Silicon Valley and show the bastard who fired him years ago what a colossal mistake it had been. "I'm ready to sign."

"There won't be a contract. You keep your end of the deal, and we'll keep the money flowing. But I want to reiterate that timing is critical."

"Why?" He thought he knew, but he wanted to hear the investor's reason.

"The electronics industry is collapsing, and consumers are getting unhappy very quickly. We've heard rumors that the White House is talking about nationalizing mines that have rare earth capabilities. We need to make our money before that happens."

The urgency made even more sense now. This was a unique window of opportunity, and he wouldn't let it pass by—or screw it up. If it came to taking the scientists by force, he would need help. Harlan, his best friend and special-ops employee, would do almost anything for him. And Max had mentioned sending a pilot capable of providing muscle, if need be. The two of them could handle that part. But Shawn could never tell his wife. Jia was ambitious and ruthless, and he loved her for it, but kidnapping would freak her out.

"Do we have a deal?"

He snapped back to attention. "Yes. I'll get started today."

He felt movement behind him and realized Max was leaving. Shawn turned and caught sight of his back, a medium-build man in a dark overcoat and baseball cap. Who the hell was he? Then it hit him. One of the major players, probably Samsung, wanted to capture the low-end phone market, but only as a silent investor so they didn't ruin their brand. He almost laughed. If the material shortage continued, his burner phones would become the high-end market. The iPhones that did everything would cease to be made—at least for the masses—because the cost would be too prohibitive. Consumers were already switching, and his market share had increased nearly 20 percent since China had choked off the supply.

Curious to see if he could recognize him, he hurried after Max, but the secretive man had disappeared in the crowd.

CHAPTER 8

He'd had other conversations with Max, but that had been their only in-person meeting. Now he had to focus on the present and his new problem. Shawn sat down at his Brazilian-hardwood desk, pressed the flashing button on his headset, and said, "Call Jia." FaceTime would open automatically, so they could see each other.

While he waited, he stared out the window of his second-floor corner office. Thousands of people were out there in the Valley, working hard in their labs and offices, pushing for the next technology break-through, hoping to be the guy with the startup that gets an IPO and is suddenly worth millions. He was about to be that guy, only without the IPO. His company would stay private, and he wouldn't answer to anyone. Except his financial backers. But eventually he'd buy them out. Analysts had been skeptical when he started manufacturing economy cell phones—entering a market dominated by giants. But he'd quickly proved them wrong and grown his company into one that tech experts wanted to join. He'd anticipated the earth-metal shortage too, and now he was going to cash in. He'd come a long way for a college dropout, and his parents would finally be proud of him.

His wife finally answered his call, breathing hard. Even while exercising she was pretty—delicate features with an upturned nose and downturned eyes. The perfect blend of Caucasian and Chinese, just like himself. "Make it fast, please," she said, not smiling. "I'm working out."

He'd known that, of course, even though only her face showed on his phone screen. She was using the stair climber in her office at the other end of the building. "Any update on the EC software?" he asked.

"No." She paused her workout to give him an exasperated sigh. "I'll let you know the minute I do."

He wanted to warn her not to talk to the FBI agent when she came around, but Jia didn't know about the kidnapped scientists and he needed it to stay that way. The only thing he could do was get her out of town before the agent questioned her. "I need a favor from you, sweetheart."

She hesitated, her dark eyes wary. Finally, she nodded. Her Chinese upbringing required her to be polite and hear him out. "What is it?"

"Will you go stay at the Washington mine to keep an eye on things? I think the manager is slacking, and you're the only person, besides me, who can keep people in line."

Her first tiny smile. "I've known you a long time, Shawn. You're flattering me to get what you want. Tell me what's really going on."

He gave her his most charming smile. "We really do have a problem. The production manager is behind schedule, and one of us needs to be there to push him hard. I can't go right now, but we'll take turns." He would miss her, but it was a sacrifice he had to make. She was one of the few people he knew who was smart and edgy enough for him to enjoy talking to. But they could do that through Skype. Their relationship had never been about sex, or even love, in the beginning. Their families had introduced them, and they shared a passion for technology. People married for worse reasons. But they'd come to love each other, in their own way.

"It's too cold up there. And I thought you wanted me to focus on the encryption algorithm. Send Harlan."

"I need him here." Shawn smiled again, a practiced skill. "You never go outside, so what do you care about the cold? And you only need to stop in at the mine for a few minutes each day, just so they know we're watching." He shifted his voice to assertive mode. "Just pack and go today. I'll call ahead and have someone make sure the place is warm and ready." He'd bought a piece of property with a small house a few miles from the mine just for the convenience.

Jia glared at him. "I'll stay a week. That's it."

"Thank you."

They clicked off, and Shawn felt himself relax a little. But not much. He could never stop thinking, moving, and planning. His parents, his mother especially, had pushed him as a child—to study, to play an instrument, to join the chess club, to get an after-school job. Sitting still hadn't been an option, and he'd never learned how. But the only activity he'd really loved had been music. His mother had wanted him to play the piano or cello, a "dignified" instrument. But in high school, he'd taken up the guitar and played in an alternative rock band. Like other young musicians, he'd dreamed of record labels and sold-out concerts. And he'd had the talent. In college, while taking IT classes as a backup plan, he entered the *American Idol* contest and made it to the semifinals. His parents had been frustrated with his pursuit, calling it a waste of time, but he'd hoped they were secretly proud too.

The shame of that night burned his cheeks even now as he remembered. He had failed spectacularly! A cold had clogged his ears and given him a headache. The music had sounded distant, and his voice went scratchy a few lines into the song. His mortification had only made things worse. He'd run from the stage as soon as it was over and hadn't picked up a guitar or sung since. His backup plan became his focus, and he moved to Silicon Valley to pursue another kind of success. After that one early setback, he was about to achieve it.

Unless his crew fucked things up. But he couldn't do everything himself. Now he had to deal with the ramifications of Bowman's body being discovered. He pressed the button on his wireless again and said, "Call Harlan."

Absentmindedly, Shawn counted the rings. He tracked almost every piece of information he might need later, a compulsion since fifth grade, when he'd first realized he was smarter and more driven than his classmates. The only thing he'd lacked was the ability to focus for long periods of time, but the right medication had finally given him that.

"Hey, Shawn. What's up?" Harlan, his go-to man, always sounded upbeat—the by-product of a simpler mind. Harlan had defended him from bullies in school and stuck by him through his adult failures. His loyalty made him a true friend, even if they didn't have much in common.

"We need to talk. Get Rocky and come to my office." He clicked off before Harlan could ask any questions.

While he waited, he researched Dana Thorpe and discovered she was giving a public lecture the next evening. Maybe that was their opportunity. A half hour later, the two men entered his office, Harlan Romero in front, looking worried. His pudgy body never seemed comfortable in the tight black jeans and pullovers he wore, but Harlan liked to emulate Shawn, including how he dressed. Only Harlan didn't have his super-toned physique.

"What's going on?" Harlan crossed the big office and stood in front of his desk.

"Nick Bowman's body turned up. How the hell is that possible?"

Harlan blinked and his chubby face blushed. "We pushed him out over a wilderness area. I can't believe someone found him already."

Shawn's right temple pulsed, and he pushed to his feet.

Rocky, his new pilot and strong-arm man, stepped forward. "It was my idea. I thought the coyotes would eat him long before anyone found him."

"You *thought?*" Shawn shouted. He turned back to Harlan, who should have been in charge. "Why would you leave something like that to chance?"

Harlan grimaced, then looked down. "The odds were against it." Harlan had been his best friend in high school—his only friend—and now the dropout was his right-hand man. More accurately, his left-hand man, who needed coaching on everything.

Shawn exhaled, trying to calm himself. Blood pressure medicine wasn't magic. His high level was a side effect of the dextro. "You should have landed and buried him."

"I'm sorry." Harlan looked up, distressed. "I never expected to have to kill him. We were only supposed to transport him to the mine."

"You got lazy and stupid, and now the FBI is looking into his death."

"Oh shit." Harlan shuffled his feet.

Rocky cut in. "I filed a flight plan under Celltronics' name, like you said to do. So that should help."

Shawn nodded but didn't praise him for following directions. Casting suspicion on his competitor probably wouldn't be enough. He might even need to plant evidence to keep the feds off his back for a few months.

"What do you want us to do?"

"An agent named Andra Bailey is investigating. If she contacts you, tell her as little as possible, then walk away. Then make yourself unavailable."

Harlan blinked, obviously alarmed. "Do you think she knows what's going on?"

"No. But once we take Dana Thorpe, the connection might be obvious." Shawn mapped out their directions, just to be clear. "Just grab her after her speech tomorrow night and take her directly to the mine." He'd tried to recruit Thorpe right after partnering with Max, but she'd turned him down. Her mistake. He hoped she would be more cooperative and easier to handle than Bowman. But Bowman's kidnapping had initially gone well, so Shawn wasn't afraid to try again. "You can find the details of her location online."

Harlan nodded. "Got it."

Shawn's mind went back to the federal agent. Just because she was investigating didn't mean she would focus on him. He processed the possibilities out loud. "We're only one of dozens of US companies with an obvious interest in rare earth materials. And there are hundreds more around the world. So this agent has a big job, and we'll stay one step ahead of her."

"But you think she'll come here and question us?" The crease in Harlan's brow deepened.

"Yes." Shawn made up his mind. "We're all going to relocate to the Washington facility. So pack a few bags before you fly up today. You'll be there for a while." Getting away from their well-known headquarters seemed like a good move.

Both men were silent for a moment.

"For how long?" Harlan asked, obviously unhappy. He had family in town.

"Until we have what we need and this investigation goes away."

His special-ops man shook his head. "What if it doesn't? What if the FBI gets too close to the truth?"

"We'll take care of the agent. Only this time, you'll be more thorough." The thought was repulsive, but he was in too deep to take chances. Fortunately, the mining facility in central Washington seemed like an ideal place to mulch a body and make it disappear forever.

CHAPTER 9

Wednesday, March 18, 9:05 a.m., San Jose, California

Bailey drove to the dead man's address again, hoping to catch his widow at home, and got lucky this time. She'd made the trip to the upscale neighborhood yesterday afternoon and also checked in with the local bureau, but neither had been productive. Today she needed to make some progress. Mrs. Bowman opened the door, and Bailey did her usual quick assessment: excessive makeup and jewelry this early in the morning indicated she was insecure, but her eyes were inquisitive, indicating at least some curiosity, if not intelligence. The widow might be capable of killing her cheating husband, but pushing him out of a plane wouldn't have been her style. Bailey held out her hand, gave a charming smile, and included her first name to soften her first impression. "Agent Andra Bailey. I need to ask a few questions."

"Again? I've talked to a cop and someone from the FBI. I'd really like to be left alone."

"I'll be brief. I promise. And I'll ask different questions."

Amy Bowman let out a long sigh as she stepped aside to let Bailey into the oversized house. They took seats on barstools at the edge of a massive kitchen.

"How are your kids?" Bailey asked, keeping her voice low and warm.

"They're struggling." Mrs. Bowman blinked back tears. "I sent them to school because they wanted to go. But they're also seeing a counselor."

"That's good." Bailey had never lost one of the few people she loved, so she didn't know how grief would feel. But she was about to find out. A longtime friend was terminally ill. Bailey hoped her brain would reject grief the way it did pain, fear, and stress. "Let's get the hard question out of the way. Did you kill your husband because he was cheating on you?"

Anger flashed in the widow's eyes. "No! That's a heinous accusation."

Technically, it hadn't been an accusation. But Mrs. Bowman's body language indicated she was telling the truth. Her hands stayed in her lap, she made reasonable eye contact, and she didn't overexplain.

"Had your husband received a job offer recently?"

"Yes, why?"

"Tell me everything he said about it."

Mrs. Bowman shook her head. "Nick said he couldn't talk about it, but that it would mean a lot of money. He acted like it was a big secret and he only had a short time to decide."

That seemed unusual. But the tech industry was weird and paranoid—with good reason. They liked to poach one another's employees. But Bowman had been a metallurgist who worked outside the tech hub in Silicon Valley. "Tell me exactly what he said about the company."

The widow sat up straight. "What are you saying? You think a competitor killed him because he didn't take the job?"

"So he turned it down?"

"I don't know. Nick had pulled away from me. I think that's why he didn't tell me much about the job offer."

"Tell me the words he used to describe it."

Flustered now, Mrs. Bowman twisted the ring on her finger. "I think he called it a startup. And he said the money would make him filthy rich." Her mouth tightened in anguish. "That's when I knew he planned to leave me, because he said it would make *him* rich, not us." She burst into tears.

Bailey jumped up from her barstool and stepped back, irritated by the crying sounds. She had to get the widow talking again or get out. "Did your husband say anything else about the company or the job offer?"

After a moment of sobbing, the widow finally choked out, "He mumbled something about *sacrifice*, but I don't know what he meant."

"Thanks. You've been helpful." Bailey headed for the door. What kind of sacrifice? A move to work somewhere else? Or more likely a cash payoff in exchange for giving up all rights and credit for any potential discovery.

In her car, she realized she'd forgotten to offer condolences to the widow. Oh well. Words didn't change anything.

She wanted to question the mistress, but they hadn't found her yet. Bailey keyed *ZoGo* into her GPS and started the rental car.

The phone rang in her hand. A California number she didn't recognize. "Agent Bailey."

"Mike Shatner with the FAA returning your call."

"Thank you. What did you find out?" She'd asked him to track down all the small-craft flights that had been registered to fly when and where Bowman's body had been found—on the off chance the kidnappers had signed in.

"Three flights Saturday morning in that area: MidValley Agriculture; Ross and DeVinter, a law firm; and Celltronics."

Score. The startup device manufacturer was near the top of her suspect list. "Do you have the name of the pilot?"

"No, there was some last-minute change."

"Thanks." Bailey hung up. She loved having leverage going into an interrogation. She deleted *ZoGo* from the GPS search field and typed in *Celltronics*. She would investigate the other company as well, but she had to follow the obvious lead. What strategy would she use with the CEO? Careful at first, probing without accusing. Asking for his help, rather than putting him on the defensive. She could be intimidating and usually enjoyed it, but she saved the tough-guy act for when it was most effective.

Celltronics sat between two other businesses in a little manufacturing mall on Phelan Avenue. A newer building with a bright exterior and no landscaping to water. Another car waited to pull into the hub from the other direction. Bailey gunned her rental and turned in front of it, a small thrill just to keep her juices running. She parked in the only open space, pleased that she'd been aggressive. Whatever saved her time. This case had too much going on to waste even ten minutes.

She strode to the entrance, unimpressed by the facility. Did they actually manufacture phones here? More likely, they were produced in a foreign country, like most other tech products. China made a good portion of them, which explained why it had quit exporting rare earth metals. Their supply was running low, and they had to keep their own factories operating. South Korea and Vietnam were likely hurting from the shutdown too, but the United States, which imported materials from all three countries, was in the most serious trouble.

Inside, a young receptionist chatted on the phone. It sounded like a personal call. The woman held up a finger, indicating Bailey should wait a moment. *The twit.* Bailey pulled out her badge and commanded, "Hang up, now!"

The receptionist went silent and her mouth dropped open. She started to say something, but Bailey cut her off. "This is a federal investigation. Where can I find Mark Ziegler?"

The receptionist blinked, as if confused, then said, "He's in the first office on the left."

Bailey walked away without comment. There was nothing to gain by being charming to a rude receptionist. At the first door, she knocked loudly, waited a full second, then grabbed the knob. Catching people off guard could be effective, but she changed her mind and waited. A moment later, the door opened and a tall silver-haired man stared at her.

"Do you have an appointment?"

"No, I'm with the FBI." She smiled, meeting his eyes for a long moment. "Agent Bailey."

The CEO's face tightened and he stepped back. "Come in and have a seat."

Bailey waited for him to settle into his worn office chair, then sat across from him. "You're Mark Ziegler?"

"Yes. What is this about?"

He wasn't an aggressor. She could tell by his casual posture, soft eyes, and concerned tone. But maybe someone else in his company was. "Rare earth metals. Where are your products made?"

"Some parts are made in Vietnam, but we assemble the phones here. Why?"

"Is your factory having trouble getting the materials it needs to keep up with production?"

"Everyone is."

"Who's your supplier?"

"We were buying them from Zing Metals in China, but we're looking for a new producer now."

"Is your manufacturing shut down?"

"Almost."

So they were getting desperate. "Do you know Nick Bowman?"

The CEO hesitated. "I'm familiar with his work. What's this about?"

"Someone killed him. What do you know about that?"

"What?" A startled expression. "Why ask me?"

"Why did you take a flight over the Sunol Regional Wilderness Saturday morning?"

He recoiled, as if physically afraid. "I didn't. I was right here at my desk."

"Can you prove that?"

"Yes. My manager was working too. What is this about?"

She would check his alibi, but it didn't mean anything. He could have hired a contract killer. "Nick Bowman was pushed out of a plane Saturday as it flew over the forest." Bailey kept constant eye contact and scooted toward him. "Celltronics was one of the only companies that filed a flight plan in that area at that time. Who was on that plane if you weren't?"

"I don't know." But Zeigler was thinking about it. His eyes shifted as he processed the possibilities, and his lips twitched with worry.

"Who in your company would kidnap and kill a metallurgist trying to produce a replacement for dysprosium?" It occurred to her that they might have stolen Bowman's research, then dumped him because they no longer needed him.

The CEO seemed stunned into silence. Bailey tapped her hand on the desk. "I need answers, or you're the one coming into the bureau with me. You won't like our interrogation room." She hadn't seen the one in the field office, but they were all the same.

He grimaced as if in pain. "Only my partner owns stock in the company and would benefit directly from such a thing." A disbelieving headshake. "But Miguel isn't capable of murder."

He might be surprised. Even empaths could commit murder out of passion, anger, or greed. If his partner was a sociopath, he wouldn't even feel guilty about it. "I want to speak with him right now. What's his name and where can I find him?"

"Miguel Carina. He's out of town on business."

"Where?"

"Seattle. He'll be back in two days."

Bailey stood. "We believe more scientists' lives could be at stake, so don't warn him about our conversation." She handed him a business card. "Text me his contact information. And call me if you find out anything."

The drive across the Valley to ZoGo was slow and frustrating, but mostly uneventful. The GPS guided her smoothly with no wrong turns, and nobody in traffic pissed her off. That almost never happened. Was she mellowing with age? Relief and disappointment surfaced at the same time, and Bailey laughed at herself. She was feeling good about this assignment—the challenge and the potential payoff when she resolved it. The sunny California weather was helping too.

ZoGo's headquarters occupied a significantly more valuable piece of real estate than their competitor's. A prime location north of Willow Glen and a new building with metal sculptures and a small courtyard off to the side. ZoGo—a stupid name, but in keeping with other internet darlings—had less operating capital than Celltronics, so it had to have considerably more debt. Or an off-the-books source of revenue.

The interior was trendy too, and the lobby had stone-and-laminate walls, a high ceiling, and a travertine floor. The receptionist's counter was a long piece of black-and-rose granite. Gorgeous. A middle-aged woman with a nice smile greeted her pleasantly. "How can I help you?"

"Agent Bailey, FBI. I need to speak with Shawn Crusher."

The receptionist pressed her lips together. "He's not here."

Liar! Bailey leaned toward her. "It's a crime to lie to a federal agent, punishable by up to six months in prison. Let's try again."

The receptionist blinked rapidly. "He's in a meeting, but I'll let him know you're here."

Bailey turned and headed for the elevator.

The woman came around the counter and trotted after her on noisy high heels. "Please wait here. Mr. Crusher hates to be interrupted. I could get fired."

Bailey ignored her and got on the elevator. The woman tried to keep the door from shutting. Bailey shook her head. "Get out of my way. He's not worth it. Neither is your job."

She let go and the door slid shut. What kind of prick was Crusher? He was already a more-likely suspect than the mild-mannered CEO of Celltronics. Except for the flight plan. Bailey got off the elevator at the top floor and glanced in both directions. An office at the end with a wide glass door caught her attention. That was the prime spot in the building. Before she reached the entrance, an attractive man stepped out of the office. Five-eleven with thick dark hair, cut short on the sides but full on top—a style that was currently fashionable with male models. A nice face, but he wouldn't catch her attention on the street. Dark slacks and an off-white button-up shirt. No tie and no jacket. What did that mean? In DC, it meant you didn't care about image or power, but here in Silicon Valley, Crusher was probably dressed for success.

He spotted her coming and smiled stiffly. The receptionist had warned him.

"Agent Bailey?" He held out a hand, still smiling.

"Yes." She shook it, intending to match his phony charm. "Can we sit and talk for a minute?"

"I'm sorry, but I'm late for an important meeting." Crusher carried a bulging satchel.

"I'll walk with you. I just have a few questions."

"Fine." He walked toward the elevator.

Bailey matched his stride. "Do you know Nick Bowman?"

"The metallurgist?" He turned and widened his eyes in surprise.

Was the reaction real? She suspected not. "Yes. When did you see him last?"

"We've never met, but his research is fascinating."

How did he know about it? Bowman's boss had labeled his work proprietary.

Crusher glanced at her, but didn't hold eye contact. "Why are you asking about him?"

"He was kidnapped and murdered."

They stopped in front of the elevator, and Crusher turned to her with a look of shock.

Only, it wasn't quite right. She knew from her own personal experience. Bailey's gut told her Crusher was an accomplished liar. But was he also a killer?

He reached for the Down button. "Perhaps you should talk to Mark Ziegler, the CEO of Celltronics. He tried to hire Nick Bowman a few months ago."

The door opened and Crusher stepped in. Bailey followed. "How do you know?"

"Competitive intelligence. It's my job to know."

"Did you try to hire him?" The elevator started down, and Bailey shifted closer to Crusher, hoping to make him uncomfortable.

"No. Bowman is too expensive, and we have a reliable source of materials."

His confidence was interesting. "Who's your supplier? Everyone else is experiencing a shortage."

A dark displeasure flashed on his face, then he quickly masked it. "That's confidential information."

"I can easily get a subpoena. Who's your supplier?"

"We're done talking." The elevator opened again, and he strode off without another look.

The phony smile and the flash of anger, followed by the mask, were red flags. Was he a sociopath or just a narcissist? Bailey followed him out of the building. "Where are you headed?"

He ignored her and hurried toward a silver car in the front of the parking lot. As he climbed in, he put in an earpiece and made a call.

Bailey would have given anything to have a tap on his phone. She jogged to her own rental car and climbed in. She would follow him just for kicks. She put the key in and waited for him to pull out. Instead, the receptionist came out, trotting awkwardly in her high heels. The rattled woman got into a car behind Bailey and started it.

What the hell? As soon as she realized what was happening, Bailey threw her car into reverse and backed up. But the receptionist continued pulling into the area behind her, and their cars collided with a crunch. *The bitch!* Rage engulfed her, and she wanted to use the car like a battering ram. But she wouldn't be able to lie her way out of it, and the consequences would be too significant. She shut off the engine and counted to thirty while Shawn Crusher drove away.

It didn't matter. She knew where he lived and worked. She also possessed a variety of skills that would allow her to access his personal information. But first she had to determine if the other company, Celltronics, had really tried to hire Nick Bowman, or whether Crusher had lied to throw her off.

CHAPTER 10

Wednesday, March 18, 6:55 p.m., Seattle, Washington

Dana Thorpe hurried down the backstage hallway, rehearsing her speech. She rounded the corner and passed two men in coveralls. They stood near an electrical panel with their backs to her, but the shorter man glanced over his shoulder, then turned away. Why were they working so late? *Because stuff happens.* She turned her focus back to her opening statement. This was her last lecture on rare earth metals. She loved sharing her research, but public speaking always terrified her, and her work was too important to take time away from. Now that the global supply had dried up and technology manufacturers were desperate, she, or some metallurgist, needed an immediate breakthrough, or the device and hard-drive markets would collapse. Lasers, metal halide lights, and liquid-fuel injectors would become scarce too.

Thinking about her colleagues made her glance back over her shoulder at the men in coveralls. They were still there, talking in hushed voices. Milton Thurgood, an extraction specialist she'd met at a conference in Sydney, had disappeared weeks ago. The incident hadn't made national news, but people in the industry knew and were worried. Then

Nick Bowman, who was working on a material similar to hers, had been abducted and murdered. Her heart skipped a beat. Would they come after her next? Dana shook off her paranoid thoughts and walked out onto the stage. She had to convince this group of scientists and analysts that they needed to step up the effort to find replacements for, and new sources of, earth metals before the shortage became a national crisis.

The lecture went smoothly, with only one rough spot when she projected that without new materials or an increase in rare earth metal production in other countries, cell phone and tablet manufacturing would come to a halt soon. One audience member coughed. Some people still didn't want to believe how few precious metals were left on the market.

With the audience still clapping, she scurried off the stage, relieved to be done. She'd done her part. Now she had to get back to her lab and continue working on her latest development—a synthetic dysprosium. She'd mentioned the compound briefly in her lecture but didn't want to raise false hopes. Her work on the substance was very close to completion, but its shifting properties made it unusable for manufacturing—so far. She was still looking for a way to stabilize it.

Dana stepped into the backstage hall again, and a cool shiver ran up her spine. The evening's host congratulated her as she walked by. She nodded and picked up her pace, eager to see her son, who was waiting for her in the lounge. As she passed the electrical panel, she noticed the men in coveralls were gone, and another wave of relief washed over her. There was the door to the waiting room. She stopped and grabbed the knob. Sensing someone behind her, she started to turn, but a man's body pressed against her from behind. Dana opened her mouth to scream, but a hand clamped over it. A sharp medicinal smell filled her nostrils and her thoughts drifted away on a dark cloud.

CHAPTER 11

Garrett Thorpe heard the doorknob turn and closed his Kindle. *Good.*
The lecture was over and they could finally grab some Thai food. He was
starving. He shoved his reading into his backpack and looked up. The
door had swung open a little, but his mother hadn't stepped through
it. Loud footsteps moving away from the room brought him to his
feet. Several people were jogging down the hall. What was going on?
Some kind of emergency that made security escort his mother from
the building?

He ran to the door, still awkward on his prosthesis, and peered out.
The dark hall was empty. To his right, he could hear the muffled sounds
of hundreds of people leaving the lecture hall. Garrett glanced left and
caught sight of his mother's red dress rounding a corner, flanked by
men on either side.

Please let them be security! Leaving his coat and backpack on the
couch, he ran down the hall. The damn fake foot slowed him considerably, and he cursed his lack of coordination. He turned at the intersection where he'd seen the three people and spotted an *Exit* sign, glowing
red above a metal door. The short space between him and the exterior

wall was empty. He charged forward, yanked open the door, and called out, "Mom!"

The backstage exit opened into an area filled with huge recycling bins. Beyond the cracked and stained cement, an SUV sat in a narrow alley. His mother was in the backseat, sagging lifelessly against the door. One of the men stretched his arm around her shoulders and rocked her head away from the window. The taller man climbed in the front seat and slammed the door.

No! They were kidnapping her! Garrett ran toward the vehicle, stumbling and shouting. He didn't even know what he was saying. But he had to stop them. The engine roared, and the vehicle lurched forward. The man in back turned and stared.

For a moment, they memorized each other's faces. Then the vehicle was gone, racing down the alley. Garrett fumbled for his cell phone in his pants pocket and called for help.

"What is your emergency?"

"My mother's been kidnapped! Two men in a dark SUV. From the alley behind the stage at Kane Hall." He shuffled down the dark alley as he shouted. The taillights of the SUV were still ahead of him.

"Calm down and tell me what happened." The dispatcher was female and sedate.

"I just did! Don't waste time asking questions. Get the police out here now."

She didn't balk at his tone. "At the UW campus?"

"Yes, but the vehicle just left the alley and is headed west." Garrett kept jogging, hoping to reach the street in time to see where the SUV turned next. His heart pounded so violently, he thought it would explode. What the hell did they want with his mother?

"Are you still on the line?" The dispatcher was so calm he wanted to slap her.

"Yes." Garrett reached the end of the alley and stopped. Cars drove by in both directions, and he couldn't spot the SUV anywhere. *Damn!* "I don't see the car anymore. Put out an alert for it!"

"I already have. What's your name? And your mother's?"

"Garrett Thorpe. My mother is Dana Thorpe."

"Can you provide more details about the car?"

Garrett struggled to come up with anything specific. "It was big, like an Expedition. Maybe jacked up a little. And dark, probably black or blue." He remembered a brief thought that it looked expensive. "I think it has custom rims too."

"Great. That helps." The dispatcher cleared her throat. "Any idea who would take your mother or why?"

"No. She's a scientist, so she's not rich." Far from it, thanks to him. His mother never talked about money, but eight years earlier, she'd spent everything she had on a lawyer to get him out of trouble when he'd been wrongfully accused of a crime as a teenager. For that alone, he would've owed her everything. But she'd done so much more! Like paying for his ridiculously expensive prosthetic after his accident when the insurance company hadn't been willing. She was his saint, and he had to save her!

"Do you need me to stay on the line until the police arrive?" the dispatcher asked.

"No."

"I'm going to disconnect now. Just wait there for an officer." The voice disappeared, and he was alone on the sidewalk, staring into the dark. *Alone.* Oh god, what if his mother never came back? He couldn't imagine his life without her. She was his best friend. His source of emotional support. His backup when things went wrong.

Man up and form a plan! Her voice echoed in his head.

Garrett squared his shoulders. His mother had been taken for a reason, and it probably had to do with her research. Nothing else made sense. Glancing at the cell phone still in his hand, Garrett knew what he had to do. He called his father.

As it rang, he counted back. Five years since they'd spoken. Ten since his father had been in their lives. His parents' marriage had already been on the edge when Garrett, at age sixteen, had gotten involved with an older woman who turned out to be a criminal. His mother had wanted to do everything possible to help him. But his father, an FBI agent, had argued that he needed to suffer the consequences of his marginal involvement by accepting a plea that included a year in juvenile lockup. His mother won the argument, but lost her husband in the process. Garrett still felt guilty about it. Because of his stupidity, she'd gotten divorced and spent her savings on lawyer fees. But his mother had always insisted it was her choice and she'd wanted out of the marriage anyway.

"Garrett?" His father's abrasive voice was suddenly there, sounding surprised. "It's good to hear from you."

"It's about Mom. She's been kidnapped."

"What?" Total skepticism.

So typical. "I watched it happen. They took her from backstage at Kane Hall, where she gave a lecture tonight. I need the bureau to help me get her back."

"Who took her?"

As if he knew. "Kidnappers. Two guys in a dark SUV."

"What is this really about? Did you get involved with criminals again?"

"Fuck you." Garrett hung up and fought the urge to cry. He still needed help, but he couldn't deal with his father. Hopefully, the jackass would take him seriously and get the bureau involved. Garrett didn't have much faith in the Seattle police. He didn't even want to talk to them, and they would be here any moment.

Limping now because his leg hurt, he backtracked to the lot where his car was parked. He'd driven his mother here tonight because she claimed she was nervous about her speech and wanted time to go over her notes on the way. He knew that was just an excuse to get him behind the wheel, part of her campaign to help him get over his fear of traffic. The accident had been almost two years ago, but it had been a long, slow recovery. He'd lost the bottom part of his left leg, but he had no regrets. The little boy might have been killed if he hadn't stepped into the street to save him.

Garrett sat behind the wheel for a long moment. He couldn't just go home. He had to do something—and right now. Once the police arrived, they would ask him a million questions and not let him leave. They'd probably treat him like a criminal. That's what his father had thought. He pulled out of the lot.

For a while, he drove around, cautious as always, looking for the kidnappers' vehicle, but eventually he accepted that it was pointless. Frustrated and scared, he headed home to his mother's house, where he'd been staying since the accident. First he would call to see if the police had found her, then he would try to retrace her steps over the last few days. Maybe he'd find a clue in something she'd done or someone she'd met.

CHAPTER 12

Thursday, March 19, 5:55 a.m., San Jose, California

A ringing woke Bailey and she sat up in the dark. What time was it? She grabbed her cell phone off the nightstand. When the screen illuminated the room a little, she remembered she was in a hotel in California. She recognized the number. Her boss. "Bailey here. What have we got?"

Agent Lennard was wide-awake in a different time zone. "Another scientist has been taken. Dana Thorpe in Seattle."

"A metallurgist?"

"Yes. Thorpe teaches at the University of Washington and conducts research into synthetic metals, much like Nick Bowman."

Was she meant to replace the murdered scientist, who hadn't worked out for the kidnappers? Another piece in a complex puzzle. "When did it happen and what do we know?" Bailey put the phone on speaker and pulled on yesterday's clothes as Lennard spoke.

"Thorpe was taken by two men last night behind a lecture hall where she had just given a speech about the rare earth metal crisis."

"Any witnesses?"

"Her son saw her in the vehicle. But no one has questioned him yet."

"Are the police watching the airport and train station?"

"Of course."

"I'll catch a flight to Seattle this morning." Bailey worked through the possibilities. A scientist from Australia, one from California (now dead), and one from Seattle. Where were they keeping them? It had to be a research facility somewhere. The scientists would need tools and equipment. The abductors had used a plane or helicopter to dump Bowman, but now they were in a vehicle. Was Seattle their home base? Or somewhere nearby in Washington State? Assuming Thurgood was still alive. But he might not be, and Dana Thorpe might be dead soon too. Bailey didn't think so. If all they wanted was data, they could have stolen it or hacked into computers. She would have to look at a list of every manufacturing company in the Seattle area and see if anything popped up. But she would start with recent transactions and see what facilities had been bought and sold since the metal shutdown, then expand the search from there.

She would buy a plane ticket, then take a brisk walk, shower, and change. If she handled this assignment well, she'd be next in line to run the Critical Incident Response Group—with the power to give important assignments. She'd been paying her dues for a long time.

After securing a flight for late that morning, she went for a walk. The bright California sun coming up over the horizon was a welcome treat compared to East Coast snow, and she enjoyed the warm, quiet morning. Until her phone rang. Brad, her best friend's husband. *Oh no.* She'd better deal with it now rather than later, when she would be focused on work. "Hey, Brad."

"Cass died this morning, and I thought you should know." His tone was businesslike.

The news hit her hard and she stopped walking. Her funny and sarcastic friend, whom she'd known since college, had ceased to exist. The ache in her chest was overwhelming, and it was hard to breathe. "Thanks for letting me know," she managed to say. "When is the funeral?"

"Monday." Brad was still giving her the cold shoulder.

He'd been mad at her since she'd stopped visiting Cassidy two months ago. But watching her die had been painful and stressful, and Bailey just couldn't subject herself to it. Without guilt to motivate her, walking away had been the only choice. It didn't make her a bad person. No one would spend time with a dying cancer patient if they didn't have guilt pushing them. "I'll try to be there for the service, but I'm working an important case, and I can't promise."

"Whatever." Brad hung up.

His rudeness bothered her. She couldn't help who she was. She'd been born this way, but at least she'd finally learned the rules and did her best to obey them and fit in. Other sociopaths churned through their lives without regard for anyone but themselves. She'd also found a job that gave her structure and benefitted society. What else did he expect from her? He expected her to be normal. Everyone did. Because they didn't know her mind was different from theirs, and she would never tell them. Hiding the truth was imperative. People assumed that all sociopaths were monsters who needed to be locked up. She let out a distressed laugh. If society locked up everyone who didn't feel remorse, some of the most successful people in the world would disappear. Few people made it to the top without guiltlessly crushing the competition.

The chatter in her brain ran itself out, and Cassidy's death hit her again. Tears welled in her eyes, then spilled over. Bailey let out a sob, then started walking again, the sun no longer a thing of joy. She rounded the corner, hurrying now, eager to get to work and push the pain of Cassidy's death out of her mind. Cass was the only person who'd come close to knowing the truth about her, though they'd never discussed the *sociopath* label. It was too harsh, and Cass was too kind. She'd also been Bailey's conscience in college, chiding her when her behavior was out of line or hurtful.

In her sophomore year, Bailey had been questioned by an FBI agent about a man she'd dated who'd been involved in a minor fraud scheme. The agent's work had fascinated her, and she'd ended up interviewing him about the various types of assignments available. During their conversation, she'd decided to focus on criminal justice, then apply at the FBI. It seemed like an ideal way to be herself and stay out of trouble. A career that would give her structure and power at the same time. Once she'd made it into the bureau, she'd been ruthless on occasion in pursuing better assignments, but she'd never hurt another agent to further her own career. Except that one time. And the misogynistic jackass had deserved it.

Another early morning walker passed her going the other way, a woman in yoga pants and a baggy sweatshirt. Bailey nodded but didn't smile. Grief seemed to have frozen her face. Back in her hotel room, she showered and packed her suitcase. Her flight was in three hours. She had just enough time to grab some breakfast, then catch a cab to the airport. It felt wrong to leave San Jose without concluding her investigation, but if the kidnappers were in Seattle, that's where she needed to be.

On her way, she'd call the local FAA office to see what noncommercial flights had left the area yesterday. She suspected the kidnappers hadn't filed their trip, though, and she admired their audacity. It took balls to make unregistered interstate flights, at least on the East Coast, where the military might shoot you down. That wasn't a risk out here, but still, whoever was masterminding the criminal enterprise was taking huge risks. That meant he or she believed there would be a huge payoff.

CHAPTER 13

Thursday, March 19, 12:02 p.m., Washington, DC

Jocelyn heard footsteps approaching her table and looked up from the menu. Ross was coming her way. Overweight and balding, her estranged husband wasn't aging well, yet she'd recently discovered she still loved him anyway.

"Hi, Ross. How's your day going?"

"Boring so far." He kissed her forehead and sat down. "But after last month at the bureau, boring is fine. What are you working on?"

She loved that they were back to discussing cases. They'd been separated for months and she'd almost filed for divorce, then a homicide case involving political activists had brought them together. They'd been dating since then, but he hadn't moved back in. She was afraid of the old patterns.

"I've got another homicide victim with no ID." She made her frustrated face. "But we ran his photo in the paper this morning. Maybe I'll get a call soon."

"A homeless guy?" Ross glanced at the menu, but he would order what he always did.

"No, a younger man, decently dressed. Shot to death at close range." Jocelyn leaned forward and whispered, "Get this. At the autopsy, the ME found a computer chip in his mouth." She had his full FBI attention now.

"What kind of chip?"

"I don't know one microchip from another, but I took it to our cyber team at the new consolidated lab. I'm waiting to hear from them."

"You should take it to the bureau's cyber forensics lab. We have better techs and better equipment."

She shrugged. She knew he was right, but she had to give the DC police department the first crack at it. If they failed, she'd let Ross call in a favor with the FBI lab. It helped to be connected to the bureau and its deep pockets. Her husband's job had better hours than hers, but he spent a lot of time at his desk and it had taken its toll. She liked the mobility of murder investigations, which took her to every corner of the capital to track down witnesses and leads. This one was a dead end, so far. She decided to run it by Ross—an old habit. "No one saw the murder, and even though I found the nearby bar where the victim drank two beers before his death, no one at the bar had ever seen him before."

"What neighborhood?"

"Bellevue. The Dog's Head. It seems too working-class for the way he was dressed. Plus the chip."

"What was he doing there?"

Jocelyn laughed. "If I knew, I would have solved it already."

A food server took their order, and Jocelyn asked for a Mountain Dew.

"We don't have that." A flat tone from a waitress older than her.

"Just water then." Jocelyn would buy a soda at the little store nearby. She'd finally cut back to two a day and hadn't had a Mountain Dew since breakfast. No other caffeine tasted good to her, and she couldn't do this job without it.

"I'll bet he was there to sell the chip and got mugged," Ross blurted out.

"That's my thinking. But until I know who he is and what's on the chip, I can't even make a list of suspects."

"If you bring it to us, I'll call the director at the forensics lab and ask her to bump it to the top of the list." Ross winked. "Maybe it's a matter of national security."

"That's my real concern." In Washington, DC, where so many federal agencies were located, it was certainly possible. "The victim could be a spy or a traitor. The person who shot him may have stolen other secrets he was carrying, even though the vic was able to hide the chip before being shot."

"Was he assaulted? Tortured?"

Jocelyn recalled the scene, just a nameless body in the alley with a fatal gunshot wound. "Hit with a handgun from a few feet away. That's it. If not for the microchip, I would write this one off as a mugging."

"Did you run facial recognition software?"

"Only against our databases, with no hits. I'll send you the image to check against the international lists, if you're willing."

"I'm glad to. As I mentioned, it's been a dull week so far."

Ross brought up their son, who was away at college, and they talked about him until the food came.

"When are you going to let me move back in?" Ross asked abruptly halfway through his patty melt.

"I don't know. I like things the way they are." They had several meals together each week, and he slept over on Saturday nights, then spent Sundays with her, which usually meant brunch and a movie.

"Paying double housing expenses is just stupid," Ross argued. "And it's making Kyle worried. I think it's affecting his grades."

"He's twenty; he can deal with it." She worried about their son too, but she wasn't going back to living with someone who didn't talk to her. "When you're around me all the time, you forget I exist. I can't stand the silence."

He leaned back, frustrated. "I won't let that happen again. I promise."

"I'm not ready." She pushed her plate away. Time to get back to work. Jocelyn's phone rang, and she grabbed it in relief. Her partner, Detective Snyder. "Larson here." She stood and dug a twenty out of her purse.

"Our victim's coworker just called. He says the dead man is Zach Dimizaro, and they worked together at DigSec."

Jocelyn put the money on the table, kissed Ross good-bye, and hurried toward the exit. "What do we know about the company?" she asked Snyder, who was still on the phone.

"Only that it's a tech firm that develops encryption software and security apps for mobile devices. They're located off M Street, not far from the department."

"I'm in the area. I'll head over and see what I can find out."

"I'll see if I can find next of kin."

"See you back at the office." She hung up as she stepped outside. *Shit!* The rain was really coming down and she didn't have an umbrella. Jocelyn jogged toward her car, two blocks away, hating every moment of the rain and the run. Parking in DC was a pain, even for law enforcement.

The tech firm's lobby was small, beige, and shabby, making her feel sorry for the receptionist. After briefly questioning the young woman—who seemed indifferent to her coworker's disappearance—Jocelyn asked to see the boss. They walked through an open room with a dozen desks. Every employee was male, and most looked under thirty-five. The silence and the intense focus on computer screens were a little freaky. Only two guys even glanced up at her, then quickly went back to their work. A room full of jeans and either black or white T-shirts. Where was the life and color? She subconsciously touched her burgundy blazer.

At the back wall, the receptionist knocked on a wooden door and waited. Someone yelled, "Give me a minute" from inside. The receptionist nodded at Jocelyn and walked away. What a cold work environment. Was it cutthroat too? Was this a room full of suspects? She knocked again and walked in. "Detective Larson. Sorry to interrupt, but I have a homicide to solve."

The clutter in the tiny office was worse than the bland beige in the lobby. The whole building was an aesthetic nightmare.

"What homicide?" The manager popped up from behind his desk, eyes wide. Forty, with curly black hair and a narrow face.

Little white boxes covered the extra chair, and Jocelyn gestured at it. She needed to sit. Running through the rain had hurt her feet. "Tell me your name."

"Larry Osterhaudt." He spelled the name for her. "Who was killed?" He charged around the desk and scooped up the boxes from her chair.

"Zach Dimizaro. I understand he worked here."

"Zach's dead? Oh my god." His surprise seemed genuine.

"When did you see him last?"

"Friday. He quit at the end of the day."

"Did he say why?"

Anger flashed on the manager's face. "No, but now I think he took a prototype with him."

"What prototype?"

"A cell phone embedded with our newest encryption software. We're beta testing it."

"He stole it?"

"I can't prove it, but he and the device both went away at the same time." The manager rubbed his face. "But murdered?" He sat back down. "Shit. Zach was probably trying to sell it."

"To who?"

"I don't know. But after Snowden, everyone wants unbreakable encryption software right now."

She needed names, details, people to question. "Who's everyone?"

He let out a derisive laugh. "Every cell phone and tablet manufacturer that wants to protect its customers."

There were no such companies in DC. But someone could have traveled here to buy the prototype. "Was Zach an encryption expert?"

"One of the best. I was lucky to hire him." His mouth tightened into a grim line. "Or so I thought."

"So, how effective is the software?"

A look of pride on Osterhaudt's face now. "It's unhackable as far as we know."

Even by law enforcement agencies? She would ask Ross, not trusting the tech guy to be honest about his product.

The manager abruptly slammed his fist into his messy desk. "I can't believe Zach stole the damn prototype. I mean, he wrote most of the code, and I'm sure he felt proprietary about it, but the software belonged to the company."

A struggle that many creative people had to deal with. "Do you have any idea who might have contacted him about the software?"

He shook his head.

"I'd like to take the computer Zach was using." She would search his emails, then turn it over to the cyber lab.

"Not a chance."

"Don't make me get a subpoena. It just wastes my time."

A shrug. "We've already searched the hard drive, purged personal files, and put it back into commission. We didn't know he'd been killed."

Jocelyn held back a sigh. "I still need to see Zach's emails."

"We deleted those too."

She bit back a curse. *What were they hiding?* "Where were you Sunday night between six and eight p.m.?"

"Whoa!" The manager held up his hands. "Don't even go there. I did not kill Zach. We didn't even realize the prototype was gone until late Monday afternoon."

"So tell me where you were."

"Right here working, until about six thirty. Then I had dinner with my wife at BJ's Steakhouse."

"Give me your wife's name and phone number." Jocelyn slipped her notepad out of her pocket. Nothing she'd heard until now had required it. When he'd provided his wife's contact information, she asked, "When did Zach leave on Friday?"

"Around four, right after he told me he quit."

She remembered the discoloration on the victim's fingertips, but didn't have the tox report, which could take weeks. "What happened to Zach's hands? How did he get burned?"

Osterhaudt's tension eased. "Those were old scars. Zach had some accident years ago in high school chemistry. We're all nerds from way back."

"I still want his emails. You can recover them, correct? I mean, you're tech guys."

"Maybe."

"I'll be back with a warrant." Jocelyn walked out, having wasted enough time. Now that she knew the victim's name, she could get his phone and financial records. If someone had killed him for the encryption software, they had to have contacted him first. The technology aspects intimidated her, and her partner was even more of a Luddite. They would need to involve the FBI. On the way out, she called the department's tech team to see if they'd had any luck, but no one picked up. *Damn.* She needed to know what was on the computer chip found in Zach Dimizaro's mouth. Was it the unbreakable encryption software or something even more valuable?

CHAPTER 14

Thursday, March 19, 6:15 p.m., Seattle, Washington

Driving in Seattle confused and frustrated Bailey even with the GPS. Her flight had been delayed, and now it was dark, making her topographical dysfunction even more challenging. At the moment, Bailey was ready to pull over and scream. City driving had almost ruined cars for her. And she loved cars! The speed and power thrilled her. As a teenager, she'd done a lot of crazy stunts in cars and was lucky to be alive. As an adult, she had few opportunities to experience the real joy vehicles once offered.

She spotted a Chinese restaurant and stopped for a quick stir-fry, then studied the map again while she ate. Dana Thorpe's home was less than a mile away, which meant the hotel she'd reserved a room at was even closer. But it would have to wait. The investigation came first.

It took nearly half an hour, but she finally found the two-story home in the Queen Anne neighborhood. The three dark sedans on the street were conspicuous as hell. She supposed it didn't matter—this wasn't a stakeout—but still, it rankled. The agents in the house were expecting her, so she walked right up to the entrance and knocked. The door opened a crack, and a sliver of a face appeared.

"Agent Bailey. The AD sent me."

"Right." The agent stepped back and opened the door just enough to let her in. "Nelson is in the living room."

Two more feds sat on the couch, each with a laptop. The woman stood and offered a hand. "Special Agent Nelson. I'm handling this kidnapping. This is Special Agent Thorpe. He's in charge of the Seattle field office."

Thorpe? He stood, and she shook his hand too. "Any relation to Dana Thorpe, the victim?"

"She's my ex-wife."

That explained why the supervisor was out in the field. "Do you have any personal insight into this incident?"

Thorpe was built like a pro wrestler and had thick gray hair that didn't match his still-unlined face. He shook his head. "We've been divorced for more than a decade. But Nelson and I are handling this kidnapping, so I'm not sure why you're here."

They had the room set up as a command center, as though they expected a ransom call. Bailey didn't have to explain anything, but she wanted their cooperation. "You're not going to hear from the kidnappers, because this isn't about money."

"We realize that," Thorpe snapped. "But we can't make any assumptions."

"You should. I suspect they'll force her to share her research, then kill her." Before she could continue, a young man burst into the room.

"Kill her? No!" He turned his back on the other agents. "You can't let them do that," he said to Bailey. "You have to get out there and *find* her. Not just sit here like these guys!" He gestured over his shoulder at the other agents.

Even contorted with passion, his face was compelling. Bright blue eyes, with delineated cheekbones and jawline. He wasn't gorgeous, but still, she couldn't take her eyes off him. "I intend to find her. Who are you?"

"Garrett Thorpe, Dana's son." He glanced at Agent Thorpe and quickly looked away.

How old was he? Twenty-five? "You were with her when she was abducted?"

"Yes. I tried to follow and get a license plate, but I was on foot." He had a deep, pleasant voice and full lips.

Agent Thorpe stepped over, and she could see the facial resemblance. "We have his statement." He turned to his son. "Please stay out of this and let us do our job."

Pompous ass. Bailey moved toward Garrett and touched his elbow. "Let's go in the kitchen and talk." She needed as much intel as she could get from him, and Garrett was clearly intimidated by his father.

The son turned and led the way, his shoulders visibly relaxing as he went. She watched his body with enjoyment. He wasn't as bulky as his father, but he was taller than her and athletic, with a sexy flat stomach. Her attraction surprised her. Her sexuality tended to be responsive, rather than overt, so since she'd quit dating, she hadn't given much thought to hooking up. Bailey pushed the distracting thoughts out of her head. He was a witness, only someone to collect information from . . . unless he'd conspired with the kidnappers.

In the kitchen, he asked, "Would you like some coffee? Or something?"

"Sure." It would give her another minute to observe him.

His movements were an odd mix—his upper body and arms fluid and confident, while his left leg hesitated. He had an injury. But not just a physical one. His eyes held emotional pain. Everyone had insecurities, and she could usually pick up on them right away. His were likely connected to his parents. Angry with his father and some kind of guilt connected to his mother.

"Do you live here with your mom?"

"Yes. But only for now." A little defensive.

"Why now?"

He turned to face her. "I was in an accident and couldn't work while I was recovering. It was convenient to move back here." A little shrug. "My mother insisted. She likes having me here, because I help her out too." Anguish flooded his face. "Listen, I love my mother more than life itself. And I owe her everything. You have to find her."

Such passion. She'd never felt that intensely about anyone. Even her father, whom she loved despite his coldness. What would it be like to experience that? Joyful at times, but painful too. Was it worth it? She would never know. "Tell me about that night. Every detail could be important."

Garrett poured two cups of coffee and sat down. "I was backstage, waiting for her. Public speaking makes Mom nervous and she likes me to be there before and after."

So his mother was dependent on him, not the other way around. That gave Bailey a surprising sense of relief.

Garrett continued. "I heard the door start to open, but she didn't come in. Then I heard a bunch of footsteps walking quickly away, and I knew something was wrong."

The abductors had waited somewhere in the back of the theater. "Did you get a look at either of them?"

Garrett nodded. "After I followed them outside and they got in the car, I saw the man in the backseat. He was older, maybe fifty or so, with a wide, squarish face and flat nose. Like he might be part Alaskan Indian."

Clearly not either of the tech CEOs she'd questioned. But the megalomaniac who'd plotted the kidnappings obviously hadn't acted alone. "Would you recognize him if you saw him again?"

"I think so." Garrett reached over and grabbed her hand. "I'll look at all the mug shots you want. Whatever I can do."

His touch startled her, and she stared at the physical connection, liking it. "Go into your dad's field office. They'll set you up to do that." She handed him her card. "Report to me if you find him."

"I will."

Bailey studied his face, looking for signs of deceptiveness, and found none. Weakness, yes. He was emotional and eager to please. "Did anything unusual happen in your mother's life in the last week?"

He hesitated. "I've been thinking about that since the other agent asked me. She was in a strange mood last Thursday and asked me, hypothetically, if I would be okay here on my own if she took a job somewhere else for a while." Garrett gave a shy smile. "I said I'd be fine, of course. She tells herself I'm dependent on her, but I think she needs me more."

She could understand why. This young man was likable. "Did you ask her about the job? Do you think she was considering a position somewhere?" That would fit with her theory that Milton Thurgood, the Australian scientist, had been recruited and sworn to silence.

"All she said was that sometimes she wondered if she should work for a corporation instead of the university and finally make some real money."

"No mention of a business name or location?"

"Just Silicon Valley."

It didn't fit her theory that they were keeping the scientists here in Washington State. But she'd learned that Celltronics had tried to recruit Nick Bowman. Maybe its CEO had offered Dana Thorpe a job too. But their research was in demand, so maybe they'd both received multiple job offers. Then the megalomaniac had simply taken a shortcut and kidnapped them. Bailey stood, pulling her eyes away from Garrett's. "I'd like to look around, then glance through your mother's email."

Garrett's jaw tightened. "My father has her computer. He's been snooping in everything."

Was Dana Thorpe's connection to an FBI agent relevant? Bailey didn't think so, but she had to consider everything. "Show me Dana's office."

"Sure." Garrett led her upstairs.

Bailey didn't intend to spend much time here. The agents on the scene had scoured everything and filed their report with her boss, as ordered. They were waiting for a ransom or demand call because they didn't know what else to do. The unsub wouldn't make any demands of the family, because he already had what he wanted. It was up to her to find the research lab where he was keeping the scientists and hoping for a breakthrough. She had a long night ahead, searching online for businesses in the area. This case kept expanding and jumping around geographically, so she hadn't kept up with the background work needed. She hated to ask for help, but it was time to get a data person involved. She'd make the call before she left this house.

She and Garrett entered a cluttered room with a high sloped ceiling. How did anyone work in this mess? Photos on the wall caught her eye. Bailey stepped toward them. Dana Thorpe was featured in most, often receiving some kind of award. She was small, dark haired, and pretty, looking younger than her forty-five years.

A search of the papers on the desk produced nothing but personal bills and news articles. There was nothing of interest in the drawers either. Garrett stood in the doorway behind her, watching. Normally, that would have bothered her and she would have asked the resident to leave her alone to work, but she didn't mind his attention. After twenty minutes, she gave up the search. She would get Dana's laptop from Agent Thorpe and take it with her. She needed to get away from the other FBI people, and Garrett, to focus on her tasks.

"I'm done here." Bailey turned toward the door, but he didn't move out of her way.

"You're smarter than they are," he said. "I can tell. And I want to know what's going on. Who has my mother and why did they take her?"

"It's only a theory and I can't share it yet."

He still didn't move.

Bailey stepped closer, wanting to inhale his scent. "Step out of my way and let me do my job."

He locked eyes with her. "Keep me informed, please. And let me help if I can."

"I will." She pulled in a long breath. He smelled like a cyclist, with hints of sweat, rain, and nylon fabric. Oddly intoxicating.

Garrett finally moved and she brushed by, her arm making contact with his chest. A jolt of pleasure. Bailey suppressed a smile. It had been a long time.

Downstairs, she approached Agent Thorpe, who was still on the couch. "I need Dana's laptop."

"I'm not finished with it." The man glanced up briefly, then went back to staring at the computer in his lap.

"I have seniority in this investigation. I thought you understood that."

Agent Nelson came in from the kitchen. A thin older woman with deep lines around her eyes. She turned to Bailey. "What's your working theory?"

"The unsub needs Dana Thorpe to accelerate her research. If she cooperates, she might live long enough for me to find her."

"You don't think he'll contact the family?"

"No." Bailey grabbed the laptop from Thorpe and slipped it into the shoulder bag she always wore strapped across her chest. She disliked the special agent because he intimidated his son, so she kept her eyes on Nelson. "Please keep me informed of any developments. You have my number." Bailey headed out.

On the street, she turned left and walked half a block, not seeing her rental car, then realized her mistake. *Oh hell.* Wrong direction. She turned and heard footsteps. Someone was running at her from a dark vehicle parked on the street. Bailey reached for her weapon, but strong hands grabbed her arms from behind.

CHAPTER 15

Garrett watched Agent Bailey walk out the front door, disappointed that she didn't glance back. So intense, so sexy. He'd never been so attracted to a woman so quickly. He'd always liked women who were older—the gorgeous grifter he'd fallen for in high school had been twenty-three to his sixteen—but Bailey was a new extreme. She had to be in her midthirties. Impulsively, he followed her out of the house. He'd overheard her say that his mother might live if she cooperated with her abductors. The agent knew who'd taken Dana.

Outside, the air was cold and damp, but he barely noticed. He glanced left into the darkness, expecting to see her walking toward the corner, where there might be an extra parking space, but no one was on the sidewalk. Footsteps thudded in the other direction. A heavy, fast-moving person. Garrett pivoted toward the sound. A half block away, a dark shape charged toward a woman on the sidewalk. She seemed to sense the attacker and spun around. In the faint glow of a nearby streetlight, he recognized Bailey. Before Garrett could think or call out, another man had come from behind a shrub and lunged at Bailey, pinning her arms behind her.

Garrett charged across the lawn toward the struggling bodies, not knowing what he would do. He remembered the gun-carrying agents in the house. He shouted for help as loud as he could. Both assailants looked up. The closer one brought up a gun.

Oh shit! Garrett jumped behind a parked car. In midair he heard a shot ring out and felt a searing flare of pain in his arm. As he hit the ground, a second bullet slammed into the car with a crunch. He'd been hit! And they were still shooting! *Dear god.* He'd survived being struck by a speeding car, only to die here in the gutter in front of the house he'd grown up in.

* * *

Someone shouted, and the attacker loosened his grip. Bailey jerked both arms up, breaking his hold, then lunged for the grass to her right and rolled, finding her weapon as she came up on her knees. The sound of gunfire exploded. On the sidewalk, the man who'd charged at her from the street was firing at a shape diving behind a car a half block away. *Garrett?* She heard him cry out as he hit the street. She brought up her weapon and aimed at the shooter's head, but as she pulled the trigger, a boot smashed into her ear. The blow knocked her sideways, and she knew she'd missed her target. Pain seared in her temple, enraging her.

Bailey pushed to her feet and spun toward her assailant, her weapon aimed at his torso six feet away. She pressed the trigger but nothing happened. *Shit!* Her Glock was jammed.

The man, who appeared to be unarmed, sprinted for the SUV. The sidewalk shooter had already reached the vehicle and was climbing into the driver's seat. Bailey slid open the Glock's chamber and reloaded the cartridge. The car's engine roared as it took off. She brought up her weapon and fired at the back of the rig. The glass shattered, but the vehicle raced away. Where the hell was her car?

* * *

A door slammed shut. Dizzy and freaked out, Garrett stayed on the ground. An engine roared, and a big vehicle rushed toward him on the street. Garrett belly-crawled partway under the car he'd taken refuge behind. Bullets coming from several directions thunked into the back of the SUV as it raced down the street.

Holy hell! This was crazy. He eased out from under the car and glanced at the back of his upper arm. Blood seeped from under the sleeve of his T-shirt. Seeing it made the pain real again. But it didn't matter. All he could think about was Agent Bailey. Was she still alive?

Except for the voices on the porch, the night was suddenly quiet. No more guns. He clambered to his feet and hurried around the car. Bailey was running toward him on the sidewalk, blood oozing down the side of her face. Had she been shot in the head? "Do you need an ambulance?" he called out.

"No. I'm fine." She sounded so calm. As she reached him, she stopped. "What about you? You're bleeding."

He rotated his arm at the shoulder. "I think it's just a scrape."

"Good. I'm going after them." She took off running.

His father was suddenly there, a gun in his hand. "Everyone okay?"

Without bothering to answer, Garrett bolted down the sidewalk after Bailey, ignoring the pain and his distrust of the prosthesis. If she was going after the people who'd taken his mother, so was he. Her car had to be near the corner, as he'd expected.

Garrett caught up as she reached it. As she hopped into the driver's seat, he charged toward the passenger door and climbed in just as she started the engine.

"No!" she yelled, without looking at him. "Get out."

Garrett didn't budge. "Let's go! They're getting away."

"Oh hell." She slammed the car into gear and gunned it into the street. "Did you see where they went?"

"No, but the only way out of this neighborhood headed this way is Queen Anne to Highland or Mercer."

"Left or right?" she shouted.

"Right at the corner, then right again in two blocks." He barely recognized his own voice, so he pulled air into his lungs, trying to calm his pounding heart. "We have to get them alive. If they die, we'll never find my mother."

"I know that, but the Seattle police don't. I'm sure someone in the neighborhood reported the gunfire."

Bailey still sounded calm, as if unaffected by her near-death experience, but Garrett's mind was spinning, and his heart felt like it would burst through his chest. The thought of the cops chasing down these guys freaked him out. Cops operated in shoot-to-kill mode. God knew he wanted those bastards dead, but they might be the only link to his mother's location.

Garrett glanced over his shoulder, expecting to see his father's car behind them. But no headlights appeared. They were already racing through the neighborhood at a speed that terrified him, but he clenched his jaw and held on to the oh-shit bar. They had to get to the kidnappers before the police did.

* * *

Bailey loved the thrill of the physical chase! Lacking normal fear, she craved high-intensity situations, but rarely experienced them anymore. Adrenaline shot through her veins, making her body hum with pleasure. The young man in the car also excited her. She hated to admit it, but by following her and shouting for help, he might have saved her life. Knowing that only drew her to him more strongly. She would have expected the opposite effect. Intellectually, she understood the concept of gratitude—just as she understood empathy and regret—but she didn't usually experience those emotions unless she focused and made herself feel them. Most of the time, there was no payoff, and her mind quickly turned to something else. But she was feeling something intense toward Garrett now.

She careened the car around the corner, tires squealing. Taillights appeared at an intersection in the distance. *Yes!* She had the shooters in sight.

"There they are!" Garrett shouted.

The SUV continued through the intersection and stayed in sight. Bailey floored it and raced after them, shooting past quiet homes on the dark street. The two men were obviously amateurs. If her gun had worked properly, the tall shooter would be dead, and the one who attacked her would be in custody, telling her where to find Dana Thorpe. Logic told her they were both hired hands. The mastermind behind the kidnapping-for-research scheme was some tech CEO who was unlikely to get his hands dirty unless he was pushed into a corner. But she was about to push him there. Even sooner than she'd expected. *Don't let your ego get in your way.* Her father's voice echoed in her head. He'd coached her from an early age about how to handle herself and not let her peculiar mind land her in jail or the morgue.

The SUV hit the next intersection and turned left without stopping. Still riding the accelerator and pushing the car to its limit in a short stretch of residential road, Bailey let off the gas to make the corner but didn't brake.

Midway through the turn, the car skidded toward the curb.

"Oh shit!" Her passenger sounded terrified.

Bailey braked and held on to the steering wheel. She pulled out of the slide and gassed the engine again. "Don't worry. I've practiced this." She didn't dare glance over at Garrett while driving this fast.

A sports car suddenly darted into her path from a side street. She either had to brake or go around it. Bailey did both. But the driver took her move as a sign of aggression or horseplay and sped up, keeping parallel with her.

Stupid idiot! She honked and eased toward him.

"Hey! What are you doing?" Garrett shouted.

She didn't have time to explain herself. She honked again, but the driver—probably young and drunk—didn't let her pass. They were headed in a general downhill direction and gaining speed.

Her passenger grabbed her arm. "Slow down!"

Irritated, Bailey let off the gas and pulled back into the lane behind the sports car. At the next intersection, the driver stuck a hand out the window, flipped her off, and turned right. She slowed, realizing she'd lost sight of the SUV. "Did you see where they went?"

"No. I'm sorry. I was distracted for a minute."

Instinct told her the unsubs had probably gone north, rather than toward the downtown area, so she turned left on the main artery along the lake front. Light traffic in both directions forced her to drive more carefully. Still, she passed the car in front as soon as she had an opportunity. The access to the water made her nervous. What if the assailants abandoned their vehicle and escaped by boat?

A police car with flashing lights drove toward them.

She glanced in her rearview mirror. More flashing lights behind her. An officer was trying to pull her over. *Oh hell.*

"Look!" Garrett pointed at a short turnout along the lake, leading to an old boat ramp.

Without seeing what he was gesturing at, Bailey slowed and made the sudden turn. In the glow of a halide streetlight, she saw bubbles in the water at the end of the ramp. Something big had gone under.

"What if they pushed their car in the water?" Garrett asked.

"To change up the pursuit and get rid of any DNA." Bailey finished his thought. Garrett was smart as well as sexy.

She stopped the car and turned off the engine. The police cruiser parked behind her, lights still flashing. Badge in hand, she climbed out, hoping she didn't have to call her boss. She didn't have time for this bullshit.

CHAPTER 16

Thursday, March 19, 10:55 p.m., Mountain View, California

Shawn's phone rang just as he was getting into bed. Harlan, finally! He hurried out to the hall to talk so Jia wouldn't wake up. "Give me the update," he demanded.

"It didn't go well." Harlan's voice was shaky. "A guy came out of the house at the wrong moment, so we had to abandon the plan."

Shawn hated obfuscation. "The agent's still alive?"

"Yeah. I'm sorry."

Damn! "What about the guy who came out?"

"I may have hit him."

Disappointment morphed into anger. "So you failed the mission and left an injured witness."

"I'm sure it was too dark for him to get a good look at us. He just came out of nowhere and started shouting. It was unnerving, and I've never done anything like this before." Harlan, who'd always been a scammer, had taken to the criminal enterprise with surprising gusto. The kidnappings had gone well, but Shawn assumed that was attributable to Rocky, who was obviously an old pro or Max wouldn't have sent him.

Had Harlan fucked things up? As long as the criminal part never came back to him. He would just have to keep covering his own tracks as well as he could. "What about the stolen vehicle? Where did you leave it?"

"We pushed it into the water, then ran along the lake's edge. FBI agents were after us, and cops were coming too, so we had no choice." Harlan sounded a bit breathless just recounting the event.

"Was that Rocky's idea?" He wondered if Rocky had a record. If so, he'd probably wanted to destroy his fingerprints and DNA.

"Yeah. We hopped on a bus, then stole an Explorer from a dealership. We're in a hotel now, but we'll drive Rocky's Expedition back in the morning when we can blend into traffic." Harlan chuckled. "We totally smoked 'em."

"Except for getting rid of the agent," Shawn reminded him. "Get back to the mine early and check on our guests." Uncle Tai was keeping the researchers fed and supplied, but Tai was a simple man and needed some oversight. Rocky and Harlan needed their share of it too. But he trusted all three to never betray him, and that was most important. "I'll fly up there in the morning. We have another job to plan." Shawn had meant to leave the day before, but he'd had too many business issues to wrap up before taking an extended leave.

He went back into the bedroom and spotted his wife's slender leg sticking out of the covers. The sight aroused him. He climbed into bed, snuggled up behind her, and grabbed her breasts. Jia never denied him sex, just as she rarely argued with him. That was why their relationship worked. She was brilliant, but pliable—a rare combination. Her mixed race worked well for him too. Full-blooded Chinese women reminded him of his mother, but white women didn't sexually excite him, so Jia was the perfect blend. He hoped she never betrayed him or stood in his way. He loved her, but not enough to give up his dreams. He not only wanted to be rich beyond counting, but he wanted control too. He wanted powerful people—government officials, Hollywood executives, and especially the current tech kingpins—to come to him with their hands out.

The next morning, Shawn swam his usual laps, slipped on a thick terry-cloth robe, and pulled the cover over his pool. This would be his last swim for at least a few months. He hated the thought of leaving his sunny, luxurious Mountain View home for the small rural house in central Washington—in March—but it seemed critical. He had to monitor the scientists' progress and push the manager at Palisades to ramp up production. Plus, the mine seemed like a safe, remote place to hide out until things wrapped up. It worried him that the FBI agent was in Seattle. Since Harlan and Rocky had failed to kill her, he might have to take care of the job himself. Another reason to head north.

Shawn looked around his half-acre property and reminded himself that he would be back. If it didn't work out to come back here, he would sell this place and buy something better. Once he'd captured the cell phone market, he'd become a billionaire. But if he wanted to stay on top, he either had to develop or produce new manufacturing materials. The key to both was in the mining operation. He was already extracting gallium, indium, and yttrium. As soon as Thorpe finalized the dysprosium replacement, he would rush the formula to his manufacturing team in India, gear up production, and start shipping the new phones. ZoGo would be ramping up production and sales just as his competitors were giving up and closing down their facilities.

After securing the pool cover, he hurried inside and locked the back French doors. Their personal belongings were packed and loaded into their Escalade, and they'd leave soon. Jia would drop him off at the small airport where he'd arranged for a private flight, then she would drive their vehicle with their things. She hated to fly and refused to leave the car behind, and he couldn't afford to spend a day and a half on the road.

Jia saw that he was still wearing only a towel and called from the kitchen, "Let's get going before the traffic is bad."

"I'll be ready in five."

Shawn dressed quickly and made one last latte, then they climbed into the car. "We could still hire a driver," he said again as Jia settled in behind the wheel.

"I'm looking forward to a day or so away from my computer." Jia turned to him. "Don't worry. I'll think about encryption while I'm on the road. It might be just the thing I need to inspire me."

Shawn smiled and nodded, but he was no longer counting on her to produce a code that was secure enough to satisfy Max. A North Korean named Lee Nam had supposedly developed the best security algorithm out there—despite being shuttered away in that godforsaken country—and Kim Jong-un was sending him on a PR victory lap to trumpet how technologically advanced his country was. Lee Nam would be in Washington, DC, for a digital-security conference in the next few days, where he would, no doubt, pick up every security innovation he could before being sucked back into the black box. Shawn would send Harlan and Rocky to the conference to grab him. This abduction would be far riskier than the others, but Max wanted the encryption, so it had to be done to keep the money flowing. So far, they'd proven successful at kidnappings. It was the transporting and cleanup tasks that were obviously more challenging.

They pulled into the parking lot of the small airport, and the pink morning sky looked great for flying. Shawn's phone rang, and he glanced at the ID: *Uncle Tai*. Why was he calling? More bad news. He could feel it coming. When they'd been young, Shawn had teased his older, not-very-bright uncle. But Tai was the one person who'd never judged him or expressed disappointment in him. Shawn had come to love the strange, slow-talking man and had given him work as a janitor since the day he'd founded his own company. When Shawn had asked Uncle Tai to do a special job for him in Washington, he had agreed out of gratitude.

Jia had stopped the car, so Shawn jumped out and walked a few feet away. "Uncle Tai. What's going on with our guest?"

His uncle, a man who had to find and choose words carefully, spoke slowly. "Dana has a medical problem."

CHAPTER 17

Friday, March 20, 6:15 a.m., Palisades Mine, Washington

Dana Thorpe woke early, as always, even though no sunlight entered the small, sparse room. She sat up on the narrow bed, and her lower back cramped in pain. The lumpy mattress was too thin to cushion her body against the plywood underneath. A shiver ran up her spine, and she reached for her sweater. Might as well get moving to get warm.

She figured she was underground somewhere, god knew where. The chloroform they'd used had knocked her out, and she'd regained consciousness in the backseat of an SUV, hands and wrists bound. She had no idea how long she'd been out, and the blindfold had kept her from seeing where they drove, but she'd still tried to keep track of the time and listen for familiar sounds. Other than tires on a highway, she'd heard almost nothing along the way. The two men in the front had been mostly quiet too, with occasional whispered exchanges.

Dana stood and stretched, moving slowly to ward off muscle spasms. The cold and the lack of exercise made her vulnerable to cramping. How long would she be here? A month? A year? When it was over—and she'd either accomplished the breakthrough they wanted or completely failed and given up—they would probably kill her. Despair washed over her, and she collapsed back on the hard bed. How was she supposed to do her best work under these conditions?

The thought of her research gave her strength. If she could stabilize the new material and make it work the way she envisioned, syndyspso, as she called it, would revolutionize digital-product manufacturing, as well as provide an alternative to dysprosium in the manufacture of dozens of other types of high-tech equipment. She wanted the synthetic metal—the product of years of research—to be successful, even if someone else got the credit. When it came onto the market, would her university peers know it was her discovery? Either way, she would leave a legacy. If she was going to die in this bleak research lab, she should at least accomplish something first. And she had an idea she was eager to try.

Dana dressed and used the small bathroom to brush her teeth. She was grateful to not have a mirror. She didn't need or wear makeup or care that much about her looks, but she was afraid to see the expression in her eyes. Fear and despair were not normal for her. Poor Garrett had to be feeling the same. The thought of her son almost derailed her. She missed him dearly. The thought of his grief when she didn't come home nearly crushed her. But she'd raised him to be strong, and he would be fine eventually.

How would they even begin to search for her? Her ex was an FBI agent, so he was probably involved in her case, but what could they do? She had no idea who'd taken her or where she was, so why would they? Her only hope was to somehow escape, but that seemed unlikely.

When she was ready, she knocked loudly on the door, as instructed. It took the keeper nearly ten minutes to respond, but finally, a key turned in the lock. For a moment, Dana had a fantasy of assaulting him and running for her life. She'd had the same idea a few times, but always rejected it. At five-three and a slight hundred and ten pounds, she was no match for anyone. Especially without a weapon. No, she would have to be crafty and watch for an opportunity when she was in the lab.

The man opened the door and shuffled back, keeping his distance. A black bandanna obscured much of his face, and a hoodie covered his hair, but she had memorized what she could—dull brown eyes and tiny pockmarks on his forehead. Five-ten and two hundred pounds, with most of the weight in his chest. His legs were skinny, he had a stiff walk, and he was at least her age. She told herself these details mattered. One day, he would be on trial for keeping her prisoner. It was all she had to keep herself going.

Dana stepped into the concrete hallway and moved to her left, eager to be in the lab. The keeper, as she thought of him, couldn't be the person responsible for her abduction. His eyes were too dull to understand the complexity of her research. A hired hand, she suspected, and one without morals. The fact that he hid his identity gave her some hope she might eventually be released. But that was probably the point, to keep her spirits up so she would keep working.

At the end of the short hallway, the keeper opened another locked door. Dana walked into the lab and clicked on the lights. Constructed of concrete and covered in blond wood paneling, the room was ugly and windowless. But it held all the equipment she needed. More than she had at the university, actually—a small, cheerful fact that gave her an emotional boost. Someone had spent a fortune on this lab, so they expected to make an even bigger fortune.

"I'll bring food in a bit." Her keeper, still in the hall, locked the metal door behind her.

Dana moved to her workbench, ready to test her idea. The key was in the electrons. She just hadn't found the exact combination that produced a stable, magnetic-resistant material that didn't overheat. But she was close.

A tapping sound on the other side of the wall caught her attention. Her neighbor was up and working early. He usually came in a few hours after her and didn't seem to stay long. She'd never seen him but assumed he was a man, because most metallurgists were. When she'd asked about him, her keeper had told her to be quiet and mind her own business.

What was he working on over there? A material compound similar to hers, or something else entirely? Was that why they were keeping them separate? Collaboration might produce what they wanted faster. She'd tried communicating with him once by tapping on the wall, but he'd ignored her. Maybe he'd been instructed to ignore her. Too bad. Together, they might be able to force their way out.

Dana focused on her work, hoping the keeper would bring coffee soon.

Two minutes into her experiment, a blue aura of light appeared in her peripheral vision. *Oh no.* She was having a seizure. She'd known it could happen. Her medication was sitting at home in her bathroom. Would it be a minor one, or would it knock her on her ass? Her eyes blinked uncontrollably and the room started to spin. Dana dropped to the floor just before she blacked out.

Someone was calling her name and slapping her face. Dana opened her eyes and saw her keeper kneeling on the floor next to her. How long had she been out? Her temples ached, but that was typical after a seizure. Or it had been. This was her first in years.

"What happened? Are you all right?" His eyes looked worried.

"I had a seizure." Dana sat up. "It could happen again if I don't get my prescription."

"What is it?"

"Aptiom." She'd been taking it for only a few months. Before that had been Topamax. She'd been switching meds every six to nine months since the epilepsy had developed a few years earlier. None of her peers knew about her condition. In fact, no one but Garrett knew, and she'd sworn him to secrecy. She hadn't even told the professor she'd been dating for a few months. Nor had she told her son about the new man in her life.

"I need the medication right away. If I had one seizure, I could have many more." Dana crawled to her knees, thinking the worst. "If I fall and hit my head on this concrete floor, I could become useless to you."

"Do you need anything right now?" He spoke slowly, as if challenged. "A cold compress or something?"

Did she hear real empathy in his voice or just job-security concern? "For now, I need coffee. And eggs, please." As long as she had caffeine and protein, she could work and be healthy. But the seizures were unpredictable.

When she'd first been diagnosed, she'd been angry and bitter. She thought she'd never get any significant work done again. But the medication was mostly effective, and she'd kept right on working. At least it wasn't dementia. As long as her brain could think clearly, she wouldn't give up her research. She'd always visualized herself at ninety, skinny, wrinkled, and a little hunched over, but still in her lab, curious to see what she could develop or experiment on next. Retirement was for people who hated their jobs, and she loved hers. Even here, in this dungeon prison, her work still excited her. At least for brief moments.

The keeper struggled to his feet and left the room. Dana hauled herself off the floor, rotated her neck to work out a kink, and went back to her experiment.

CHAPTER 18

Friday, March 20, 9:00 a.m., Seattle, Washington

Bailey called the state's business licensing office and asked to speak to the highest-ranking person available. After a few false starts with midlevel managers, Nolan Fredrick came on the line and asked how he could help.

She repeated her identification one more time, pacing the hotel room as she talked. "I'm working a case that involves kidnappings and a homicide. We believe the abducted scientist is being held somewhere here in Washington and being forced to do very specialized work at a new business. What I need is a list of business-related real estate that's been sold in the last year."

"Can you narrow that down?" He gave a soft laugh. "You don't want car washes or fast-food restaurants, do you?"

"I do not." She'd meant to offer more specifics, but he'd cut in too soon. "I'm looking for unoccupied buildings, rural acreages, and anything related to technology or mining."

"That's a more manageable list, but it may still take a day or two."

"I don't have that kind of time. Not only is a woman's life at stake, but national security could be as well." An exaggeration. Or not, depending on what the megalomaniac kidnapper had in mind. "This request comes from the director of the FBI."

"I'll do what I can."

"I also need the name of the person or business who bought each property."

"Of course."

She made certain he had her contact information and started to hang up, then remembered it was important to say thank you. People were more likely to help if they were treated well, and she needed the information quickly. A lifelong question popped into her brain. What was the difference between pretending to be polite and actually being polite? She'd been faking and imitating her way through social situations for so long that she'd mostly become the person she pretended to be. The difference was, as a non-empath, she had another side that allowed her to use every tool at her disposal—as long as the benefit outweighed the risk.

Her next call went to Gunter Havi, a coworker at the bureau's DC headquarters. Havi was her go-to tech-and-data guy, one of best analysts in the CIRG. She liked Havi because he didn't care that much about rules either. Getting the job done was more important, and he was skilled at covering their tracks. His name and looks—a broad, square German face with dark coloring and soft brown eyes—suggested he was the product of a mixed marriage. But she'd never asked about his personal life, and most of their contact was by phone or email. "Havi, it's Bailey. I need your help."

"What's the case? I knew you were gone, but no one is talking about your assignment."

She summarized the crimes and her working theory. "I need to know about mining operations along the West Coast. Specifically, facilities with rare earth potential."

"I see your thinking." His computer keys clicked in the background. "The earth-metals market is crazy right now," Havi said. "China's export embargo has even Ayn Rand disciples talking about nationalizing our resources."

Bailey hadn't had time to pay attention to politics since she'd taken the assignment, so this was news to her. "I have to go into the local field office and check on a witness. Call me if you find any mines in Washington, Oregon, or California that have a new owner within the last year or so."

"I'm already on it."

"Great. If you need me to do a little hacking to get the intel, I'm game." She wasn't an expert, but with the right code and a little guidance, she could access non-secure data. Most of the information companies kept was non-secure. Only financial institutions and tech companies understood how grave the threat was.

"Let's see what I can find out first."

"Thanks, Havi."

The mining idea was a long shot, and some operations were on federal lands. But Thurgood was an extraction expert, so she had to explore that avenue. Another possibility was that the two scientists were being held in different locations. And for all she knew, Thurgood's participation could be voluntary. That was why she'd also asked the state business office to look at real-estate deals for abandoned buildings and rural properties. The megalomaniac may have purchased a variety of businesses to pull off his scheme. Whatever it was. Dominate the device market? Or did he or she simply want to make a fortune selling the metals other manufacturers needed? She needed to look at property transactions in other states too. The only rare earth mine she knew of was in California, not far from where the second scientist had been abducted. And Oregon was filled with remote areas where fringe groups could hide out.

Bailey pulled on a dark sweater—she refused to dress in a jacket like a man—and grabbed her satchel. Before she made it out of the motel room door, her phone rang again. Her boss. She stepped back inside and closed the door. "Bailey here."

"It's Lennard. Give me a quick update."

She'd filed a report that morning, but her boss apparently hadn't had time to read it. "The two men who kidnapped Dana Thorpe tried to kidnap or kill me last night in front of her house. They escaped by abandoning their vehicle in the lake and taking off on foot. We have a decent description of one unsub, and a local sketch artist is working on an image of him. I was just heading to the field office now."

"Good. We need a teleconference with the special agent in charge out there. I have directives from the White House, and you both need to hear them."

Oh hell. When politicians got involved in law enforcement, it was always trouble. They worried too much about public image and political correctness. "I'll be in the field office in twenty minutes or so. Text me with the meeting time when it's set." Bailey hung up, not worrying about etiquette. Her boss hated unnecessary chitchat too. She headed out again, wondering what the hell was going on that involved the president.

She found the Seattle field office with little trouble and put up with the screening process without complaint. On the other side of the metal detector, she asked, "Is Garrett Thorpe here? He's supposed to be looking at mug shots."

"In the second-floor conference room." The desk agent gave a we're-done-here nod.

Bailey hurried upstairs, eager to see Garrett again. She'd wanted to hook up with him the night before—after the exhilarating chase—but there had been too many cops and agents at the house. She not only accepted but embraced her attraction to him. Even though she wasn't a highly sexual person, she never felt any guilt or shame about her encounters.

At the door, she knocked once and stepped in. Garrett jumped up from his chair at the end of the long table and smiled. "Agent Bailey. I was just going to call you."

"You found the guy?" She walked toward him, feeling suddenly warm, and had to pull off her sweater.

"Maybe." Garrett gestured at the laptop on the desk. "He's younger and thinner in this photo, but I think it might be him."

"Excellent news." The new lead, combined with her unexpected sexual desire, filled her with an impulsive pleasure. Bailey touched the sides of Garrett's face and pressed her mouth against his, a deep, probing kiss that asked for much more. After a split second of shock, he responded, and their passion made her knees shake. Bailey drew back, suddenly aware the room might have video recording. She didn't want to be reprimanded for something so trivial. He wasn't the target of her investigation, so intimacy with him wasn't specifically against the rules. She only followed explicit rules, and only fought for self-control when it served her best interest. What was best for her in this situation was Garrett.

She smiled seductively. "Show me the photo."

Blinking with happy eyes, he sat down. Garrett scrolled back through three pages of images—all men between twenty-five and forty—then stopped and pointed in the upper left corner. "Him."

Jerry Rockwell. An ugly man with a broad face, a wide nose, and brownish skin coloring. She guessed Hawaiian or Alaskan Indian. In the mug shot, he looked twenty-five, but his birth date indicated he was fifty-two. The timing was about right, though. He'd been convicted of trespassing and vandalism of a federal building in Fairbanks in 1988. He'd done six months in prison, but hadn't been in trouble since. Unusual that he would be involved in kidnapping and murder now—unless he'd been a criminal all along and learned to be smart and careful.

"Are you sure?" she asked.

Garrett bit his lip. "Not a hundred percent. I mean, this photo is twenty-seven years old." He looked at the photo again. "But see this dark spot on his cheek? That's what caught my attention. I think I saw it on the kidnapper. But I was freaking out at the time, so I didn't really process it then."

"You did fine. It's a possible lead. I'll get my analyst to see if he can locate this guy."

Garrett stood and met her eyes. "That kiss. What does it mean?"

Bailey's cell phone beeped in her pocket. Relieved not to have to explain herself, she slid it out. A text from her boss: *Conference in ten minutes.*

She looked up at Garrett. "I have a meeting here in a few minutes. Did you get all the way through the mug shots?"

"I did."

"Then it's best if you leave now."

"Will I see you again?" Such longing in his expression.

His attraction intensified hers. "If I can. But this investigation could go anywhere."

"Give me your phone and I'll key my number in." He reached for it. "At least keep me updated about my mother. If we don't find her soon, she could—" He stopped and pressed his lips together.

"Could what? I need to know everything."

"My mother has epilepsy and without her medication she could have seizures."

A critical piece of information. "Why am I just hearing about this now?"

"She's very secretive about it. I'm the only one who knows, and she made me promise to keep it quiet. So I couldn't tell my father. That would've pissed Mom off." Garrett grabbed her hand. "Please don't put that in your report. If word gets out, the epilepsy could ruin her career."

Bailey loved that he was so loyal—and optimistic that his mother would survive this. "I'll do my best to protect her secret."

"Please call me." He stepped backward toward the door, not breaking eye contact until he had to.

When he was gone, Bailey felt relief. And a strange loneliness. But the emotion was distracting, so she tried to turn away from it. Compartmentalizing was usually easy for her, but not this time. *Well, hell.* Would hooking up with him cost her more than she would gain?

She moved to the other end of the room, where a large monitor hung on the wall, slid into a chair, and pulled out a notepad to prepare for the meeting. She had a few minutes, so she checked her email. The medical examiner in San Jose had finally sent lab reports. He'd attached the full printout, but he'd also summarized the findings in his email:

Nick Bowman had alcohol in his blood (.12) but nothing else worth noting. The brown stains on his palms were caused by handling gallium, which melts when it touches the skin.

Gallium was a rare earth metal used in devices, but she'd never seen it in person and didn't know much about its properties.

The doorknob clicked and she looked up, hoping Garrett had come back. Special Agent Thorpe stepped in. He was technically her superior, and she stood, more out of habit than respect.

He strode toward her. "Do you know what this is about?"

"No, but we'll soon find out."

Thorpe sat opposite her and clicked on the monitor, which stayed dark.

Bailey remembered she had a question for the field office. "Hey, what did the technicians find on the SUV that was pulled out of the water?"

"No trace evidence from the shooters." Like most law enforcement, Thorpe had a flat delivery. "The vehicle had been stolen earlier from Bremerton. We canvassed the area but didn't find any witnesses or abandoned cars."

The thugs were craftier than she'd expected.

A phone in the middle of the table rang, and Thorpe clicked the remote. Agent Lennard's face appeared on the screen. "Good. You're ready. Have you seen the news this morning?"

"Not since six o'clock. Why?" Bailey sensed something big had happened, but she hadn't been at headquarters with her unit to hear about it.

"A gang broke into a Walmart warehouse in Compton, California, looking for cell phones and tablets, and a group of bystanders joined them. When the news hit Twitter, a crowd started looting electronics from Best Buy in Florida City. The shortage has hit a choke point, and the White House wants to get it under control."

"What steps is the president taking?" Thorpe asked.

"For one, the National Guard is preparing its troops to protect warehouses and retail stores in the big cities." Her boss paused, as if in disbelief. "Plus Congress is drafting legislation that would nationalize rare earth mines. Possibly even the device industry."

As Havi had predicted. "How does this affect my investigation?" Bailey asked.

Lennard's mouth tightened. "We're calling you off. The Critical Incident group needs you back here."

No! How stupid. Was this Lennard's decision? Bailey studied her boss' face and noticed the pinched lines around her mouth. The decision had likely come from higher up, and Lennard had to support it.

Bailey still had to argue. "But we've identified one of the kidnappers. I just need a few more days."

"Who's the suspect?"

"Jerry Rockwell. He has an old conviction, but nothing since."

"Do you know where to find him?"

"Not yet."

"Then nothing's changed. The bureau has bigger issues to deal with—such as the wholesale theft of cell phone shipments. A truck was hijacked yesterday, and the driver was killed."

Criminals stole truckloads of things every day, including maple syrup. Cell phones were more personal and universal, but still, her boss was keeping something back, and it infuriated Bailey. "What is this about? Tell me the truth."

"Once the government nationalizes the industry, or its components, our unsub loses his profit and motivation. The problem goes away."

Damn. She was about to lose her chance for a big win. And never see Garrett again. "A woman has been kidnapped, and her family would like her back."

"Yes, what about Dana?" Thorpe added, with a dose of disbelief.

"We're not giving up. Agents in the field offices will pursue the individual cases. Bailey, we need your analytical prediction skills here in the CI room to help circumvent more looting—or rioting, whichever comes next."

Bailey had no intention of dropping the broader investigation. She would find a way to solve the disappearances and still keep her job. She motioned at Thorpe to shut off the monitor.

After the screen went black, he turned to her. "Of course, we'll continue to search for my ex-wife."

"Good to hear." Bailey walked out before she said something regrettable.

CHAPTER 19

Friday, March 20, 2:20 p.m., Seattle, Washington

The agents were still in his house when Garrett arrived home. *Damn.* They'd come back early that morning, after failing to catch the shooters the night before. The two women were drinking coffee and talking at the kitchen table, and his father was sitting in the living room, as if he'd just come in. Their presence was invasive and Garrett wanted them gone.

He sat down on the coffee table to look his father in the eye. "You guys need to get out of here. There isn't going to be a ransom. They don't want money. They want her research."

"I think you're probably right, but it's not only my decision." His father stood.

So did Garrett. "But it is mine." He strode into the kitchen with his father following him. Garrett looked at the older woman in charge. "Agent Nelson, I need all of you to leave. My mother is out there, and you need to go help find her. The kidnappers aren't going to call or bring her back." The thought crushed him, and he swallowed a lump in his throat.

"We have other people assigned to the task force, and they're looking too." Nelson gestured for him to sit. Garrett refused, so she continued. "This is protocol for kidnappings. It's only been a day and a half."

Anger flooded him. "Only a day and a half? She could be anywhere! She could be dead. Get the hell out of here. Sitting at our kitchen table isn't helping!"

The agent recoiled, then stood up. "Call me if you hear from the kidnappers." She handed him a business card and walked out. The other agent, whose name he couldn't remember, followed her.

His father stood in the hall and watched them go. "I should stay. I don't want you to be alone."

Garrett couldn't hold back a harsh laugh. "That's a first." His father looked hurt, and he regretted the remark. "I'm fine here. I'll call you if anything happens."

"What if the shooters come back?"

"They're not after me."

"You don't know that." His father crossed his arms and shifted into taking-a-stand mode.

They were eye-to-eye in height, but his dad's massive chest and arms intimidated him. Plus twenty-five years as a federal agent, and he was hard to argue with. Garrett took a quick breath. "I don't want you in the house, because I need my privacy." Bailey's kiss came to mind, sending a rush of pleasure through his body. He wanted her here, in his bed, but that wouldn't happen with his father around.

"Fine. I'll arrange for patrol officers to come by the house."

"Thanks." Garrett's phone rang in his jacket pocket. He hadn't even put down his car keys yet. What if it was Agent Bailey? "I have to get this." He paused, hoping the old man would take a hint.

"I'll grab my briefcase and let myself out."

Garrett headed for the privacy of his bedroom, slipping the phone out as he walked. *Bailey!* She either wanted to see him or had a new lead for finding his mother. "Hello. It's Garrett." *Dumb thing to say.* She'd called him.

"It's Bailey. I need your help, so we need to talk in private. Are the other agents still there?"

She wanted his help! Thank god he would have something constructive to do. "I just made them leave."

"Then I'll pick up some takeout food and come by in a couple of hours."

He sensed something was wrong. "Anything new about my mother?"

She hesitated. "No, but I have some ideas. I'll see you later." Bailey hung up before he could probe for more information.

At least she was still looking. That meant his mother wasn't dead. Garrett pulled off his jacket and collapsed into a desk chair. The thought that he might never see his mom again made his chest ache, but he fought the emotions. His father had never approved of tears, big on that old bullshit "I'll give you something to cry about." And he had sometimes. So his mother had compensated by making things too easy sometimes. The mixed messages had been confusing until they finally divorced.

His mother had never remarried, giving him her full attention when she wasn't working. She'd been good company, making Garrett think and laugh and appreciate everything around him. The world would be a bleak place if anything happened to her. How could he ever pay her back if she wasn't here? They had to find her before something horrible happened. If the kidnappers would attempt to murder Bailey, a federal agent, just because she was investigating their crimes, they wouldn't hesitate to kill a scientist after they'd extracted her research secrets. He prayed to the universe to keep her safe. *Please don't let them torture her.*

Garrett forced the image out of his mind. Constantly thinking about his mom was exhausting and unproductive. He either had to study and get caught up on his college classes or drop out for the term.

But that would set him back on earning his physical therapy degree. He picked up a textbook for his physiology class and tried to read, but couldn't concentrate. There had to be something productive he could do to help find his mother.

He sat down at his computer and googled her name. He'd done it before, but had never really read her research papers. Metallurgy didn't interest him and chemistry confused him, but now that his mother's life was on the line, it seemed important to understand her work.

Much of what she did involved doping one element from the periodic table with small quantities of another element to create either a shortage or excess of electrons. She'd started with inorganic materials, then moved on to small-molecule organics such as oligomers. Whatever the hell they were.

After a while, he couldn't process any more chemical terms, so he took a break and checked his email. A friend from the university had sent a brief note, asking if he'd received an earlier email with the homework assignment Garrett had asked about. Something about the email triggered a memory. His mother had sent him an email about two months earlier, a rare midday communication from her. But she'd been excited about a job offer and wanted to share it with him. Now it seemed important. He typed *job offer* into the search field, hoping the file hadn't been automatically deleted already.

Three emails came up, and the third one, from his mother, dated back to January. He clicked it open and eagerly read it again.

> Hey, kid. I was just offered a lucrative job by a tech company in Mountain View. But they wanted me to relocate immediately and sign a waiver agreeing to not talk about the position or the research. Of course I'll turn it down. I love my role at the university and don't want to work in the corporate world.

I'm not even sure why I'm telling you. Except
that it's exciting to be recruited. And the
money he offered was crazy! I could have
paid off my debts. Love you. M.

What if the recruiter had come back months later with a strong-arm man and kidnapped her? It seemed bizarre, but clearly *something* crazy had happened. Garrett wished she had named the company. He forwarded the email to Bailey, but except for the location, he didn't see how it could help them. There were dozens of tech companies in Mountain View.

Had she told one of her colleagues about the job offer? Two professors came to mind. He found their contact information on the university's website and called Eva Carmichael first. She didn't answer, so he left a detailed message and asked for a return call. Had the FBI already contacted his mother's coworkers? It didn't matter. The agents wouldn't have known about the job offer. The second call was to another metallurgist. The professor answered, sounding solemn. "Hello. This is Rob Davison."

"Garrett Thorpe. I'm Dana's son. We met once a few years ago."

"I remember. Any word on your mother? Her kidnapping has the whole department upset."

"Not yet, but I'm hoping you can help. Did she mention a job offer to you in January?"

"Yes, but she had turned it down. Why do you ask?" Student voices buzzed in the background, then a door closed, shutting them out.

"Do you remember the name of the company?"

"Oh boy." A short silence. "No, I'm sorry. And I sense this is important."

"It could be. Who else would my mother have mentioned it to?"

"Probably no one. It's best to keep that kind of information out of your current workplace."

Then why had she told Professor Davison? It seemed odd, but Garrett didn't want to get distracted. "The company that tried to recruit her may have kidnapped her, so I need you to remember the name."

"That's a wild idea. Does the FBI share your theory?"

"Yes. Can you give it some thought?"

"I'll try. But I'm not even sure Dana mentioned the name. She did say Silicon Valley, though."

Not helpful! "What other companies would be interested in her research? I know she was developing a synthetic metal."

"There must be a hundred manufacturers lined up, waiting for new sources of rare earth metals or replacement synthetics. But device makers would be my first guess."

Disappointed at the lack of specifics, Garrett decided to let that angle go. "Did you talk to my mother in the days before she disappeared? Did she say anything about being worried? Or mention being followed?"

The professor hesitated. "I had dinner with her the night before, but she didn't mention any concerns."

Dinner? That surprised him. "You're good friends with her?"

"Yes, we're very close."

What was he saying? "How close? Are you dating?"

"Yes. She didn't tell you?"

"No." Why wouldn't his mother want him to know? "I'm happy for both of you. Call me if you remember the company's name." Garrett hung up, feeling a little rattled. When had Mom planned to tell him?

The doorbell rang and he jumped up. Relieved by the distraction, he hurried toward the front door. What if it was Bailey? He stopped in the hall bathroom and swished mouthwash over his teeth. He hadn't eaten since breakfast, but he'd had coffee. He wanted to be ready—in case she kissed him.

The doorbell rang again, and he sensed her impatience. She wasn't a gentle soul, but that was a big part of the attraction—an older woman who wouldn't coddle him. He'd dated younger women, but they never held his interest for long. Their concern about clothes and shoes and what other people thought drove him crazy. He needed to be with someone confident and serious. He'd been to enough therapy sessions to accept that he wanted to date someone like his mom, but who wouldn't actually mother him. Bailey probably wasn't looking for anything long-term, but maybe she would help him get the older-woman thing out of his head. He laughed as he ran to the foyer. As if she was even interested in him. The kiss had been a fluke.

He pulled open the door and she was there. Stunning, in a snug green pullover that matched her intense green eyes. Her pulled-back hair only highlighted her strong cheekbones. She held plastic bags in one hand and a gun pointed at the floor in the other. The sight of the weapon in her hand stole his breath, in a way that had nothing to do with being frightened or concerned. Bailey was badass and it turned him on. Maybe he was weirder than he thought. "Come in." He closed the door behind her.

She'd caught him staring at the gun and slipped it into her satchel. "I was almost killed here last night, so I was being cautious." She turned toward the kitchen.

His father's comments came back to him. "I'm starting to think I should be armed."

She spun around. "Have they been back?"

"No, but my father seemed worried they might."

She moved toward the table. "It would be pretty stupid and risky, considering the agents they ran into here last time."

Garrett followed. "Why did they take my mom? I mean, I know it's about her research, but what do you think their plan is? To sell it?"

"Maybe." She put down the food. "A glass of water, please."

"Sure. We have wine too."

"I don't drink when I'm on a case like this." Bailey sat down, pulled out cartons of Thai food, and dug in. "If Jerry Rockwell's involved, he's probably a hired hand. I can't find anything new on him, so he's managed to stay out of trouble and the media." She ate with gusto and talked between bites, with some overlap.

He watched her, fascinated by how comfortable she was in her own skin.

"There's nothing in Rockwell's old file to indicate he has any real brains or ambition. Yet it's possible he's using an alias now." She noticed he wasn't eating. "You're not hungry?"

"I am." He helped himself to a beef dish. "Did you get the email I forwarded you from my mother?"

"Yes." Bailey scowled. "I'm still trying to figure out what it means and whether it's connected to one of two Mountain View companies I'm looking into."

"I made some calls to her university colleagues, but no luck in figuring out which company it was." Garrett remembered Bailey's earlier comment on the phone. "You said you wanted my help. What can I do?"

She hesitated for a long moment. "Garrett, I'm going to trust you with confidential information. But you can't share it with anyone. Especially not your father."

She was keeping something from the task force? "I don't understand."

A flash of disappointment on her face.

"But you have my word," he added quickly. "Please tell me."

"I've been pulled off the case." She put down her chopsticks and met his eyes. "But what's important is that there's a broader investigation that involves more than just your mother."

As he'd suspected. Why else would FBI headquarters send her to Seattle when they had local agents handling the kidnapping? "What's going on? And why did they pull you?"

She came around the table, bringing her chair, and sat next to him. "Your mother is the third metallurgist to disappear." Something dark passed across her face, only inches from his.

"What? You think she's dead?" He fought to suppress his fear.

"No, but the second kidnapped scientist was killed, so I'm worried for her." Bailey stroked his shoulder. "I can't tell you why they took me off the case, but I don't intend to give up, which is why I need your help." She gave a funny grin. "Without agency support, I need someone to do the grunt work."

A rush of excitement filled his belly. This would be so much better than reading his mother's research papers. "I'm in, whatever it is."

"I need you to call pharmacies all over the state of Washington. If they're keeping Dana alive, they'll need to get her some medication. It's the only lead we have."

A little deflated, he asked, "What do I say? Why would they tell me anything?"

"Tell them you're Agent Bailey, that a life is on the line, then give my badge number."

He wasn't a good liar, and it surprised him that she thought this was okay. "Why can't the other agents—" His voice trailed off when he realized she was helping him protect his mother's secret and hiding her own continued involvement.

"Will you help me?" She leaned toward him, kissed his cheek, then sat back.

Was she seducing him or just using sex appeal to enlist his help? He didn't care. "Of course I will." He forced himself to think about the task and how to get it done. "I can start calling after dinner. A lot of pharmacies are open until nine."

"I was hoping you'd say that." She stroked his leg. "I have a project of my own to take care of, and it could take a while."

No! He'd been sure they would have sex. "You're leaving?"

"Not just yet." Her voice was low and husky. "It's a computer project, so I can do it from here. But you can't ask me about it."

"I won't." He leaned forward and kissed her lips. "I'm glad you're staying." For a moment, he worried about what she would think of his prosthesis when they were naked. He'd only had sex once since the accident, and they'd both been drunk. Maybe Bailey wouldn't even notice his shin and foot.

"Me too." Bailey kissed him back. "We have work to do, but I won't be able to focus until we do this."

Garrett forgot about his leg and pulled her close. "Anything I can do to help."

CHAPTER 20

Bailey dressed quickly, eager to cover her aging body and get back to work. The sex had been terrific, surprising her with a powerful orgasm. She didn't always climax, because a lot of men simply didn't know what they were doing. That was part of the reason she hadn't dated or slept with anyone in a long time. It was more frustration than it was worth. But Garrett had been all about giving her pleasure. Because he was young? The men she'd dated in college hadn't been anything like him. Mostly drunk and selfish, she recalled.

"Hey, what's your hurry?" He hadn't moved from the bed.

"I have work to do." She tossed a pillow at him. "So do you."

Guilt flashed on his face. "You're right. My mother's life is on the line." He scurried to pull on clothes.

"It's okay to be human. Giving up pleasure won't save her."

He didn't respond.

Bailey slipped on shoes and grabbed her satchel. "I'll be in the living room, looking through your mother's computer." She moved toward the door.

"Wait," he called after her. "What did this"—he paused to search for a word—"this encounter mean to you?"

"It was terrific. Maybe the best sex I've ever had." Actually, she'd had a hookup in college that had been better, but she'd also been high on ecstasy and couldn't separate the two pleasures. It had also been the last time she'd experimented with drugs. She hated the loss of control.

He came toward her. "It was great for me too, but that's not what I asked."

Normally, she would say whatever her lover wanted to hear, but she didn't want to lie to Garrett. Or manipulate him. "I like you a lot. But we both know this is just a situational fling. I'm too old for you, and I'm married to my career, which keeps me on the move."

He started to say something that sounded like a counter-argument, then stopped. After a moment, he said softly, "Let's make the most of it then."

"We certainly will." Bailey kissed his cheek and left the room.

Downstairs, she warmed up some coffee and took it to the couch in the living area. She opened Dana Thorpe's laptop and turned it on. No passwords required. Or Agent Thorpe had already disabled the security. Her first focus was to search for any mention of the job offer Dana had received in early January. The email Garrett forwarded had mentioned relocating to Mountain View, but both Celltronics and ZoGo—and a zillion other tech companies—were headquartered there. She needed to nail it down. Celltronics' CEO had admitted to offering Nick Bowman a job, but claimed he'd laughed at the salary. Still, if Ziegler had tried to recruit both Bowman and Dana Thorpe, then he moved to the top of her suspect list.

After twenty minutes, she gave up. Neither of the companies nor the location had surfaced in her search, which included emails. The job offer had to have come by phone. Bailey called Agent Thorpe, and he answered quickly. "Did you catch a break in the case?"

"Maybe. Your ex was recruited by a Mountain View company in January. I'm trying to find that communication. It's not on her computer, so it must be in her phone records. I'd like access to them."

"What date in January? Our subpoena only asked for the last sixty days."

Not enough! "It was the fifth, so go back to the service provider and get all of January."

"I can't make that happen until Monday."

"Try anyway, please." Frustrated, Bailey hung up. She called Havi next, but he didn't answer. She glanced at the time. *Oh right.* It was Friday night, and he wasn't in the bureau. She left him a message: "Hey, Havi. I need your help with accessing phone records, and I mean the fast way. Call me, please." If he wouldn't hack the service provider for her, he would at least give her enough guidance so she could do it herself. She didn't have time to wait for Monday.

CHAPTER 21

Friday, March 20, 3:15 p.m., Washington, DC

Nam loosened his tie and tried to focus on the speaker. It was only polite to listen to other presenters at the symposium, but he desperately wanted to be outside, walking around the capital. This was his first trip to the United States, and he hated to spend the whole time inside a hotel, listening to lectures. *Defect.* The thought kept coming back to him. If he asked for political asylum, he could live here in DC and never go back to North Korea. The idea was so tantalizing. To live in this free country, where people did and said whatever they wanted—even criticized their own government! He'd learned that in the first few hours he'd been at the symposium.

If he were not alone in the world, he would never consider defection. But his parents had died young, and he was an only child. Sung, his beloved wife, had been eaten by cancer the previous year. So there was no one for Kim Jong-un to kill as punishment. Now was the time. Maybe the only opportunity he would ever have. Did he need to claim political persecution?

Nam glanced at his bodyguard beside him, a military policeman with handcuffs, a stun gun, and the legal authority to detain him. How would he escape him? North Korea's leader had allowed Nam to attend the symposium because the young dictator was thirsty for cutting-edge digital technology that could protect his secrets and keep hackers from opening up the internet to the North Korean people. He'd also sent Dukko Ki-ha, this unblinking military policeman, to keep watch.

Nam reminded himself he was fortunate to have only one body-guard. That meant Kim Jong-un trusted him, as much as he trusted anyone. Nam had never been anything but a good citizen and professor, and once he'd been ordered to work for Kim Jong-un's administration, he'd become a passionate encryption expert, now considered one of the best in the world. His country needed money, and Kim Jong-un was using him to help develop a variety of digital technologies he hoped to auction for millions each. Cyber security had many facets, and Nam was here to learn, as well as to give a presentation. But all he could think about was defecting.

What if he failed? He would disgrace himself and his country, then be sent to a work camp where his days would be filled with torture and backbreaking labor until he died an early death. The thought made his hands shake. Nam quickly pushed them under his legs. He must not draw attention to his behavior or seem nervous in any way. In his heart, he'd known since he'd risen that morning that this was his destiny—yet it had taken his mind all day to accept the risk. It was time to plan.

He would wait until they were out in the hall between lectures, then head for a bathroom. Ki-ha would stand outside the door. But how to distract him? Nam had no idea. A simpler plan seemed best. He would wait for an opportunity to disappear into a crowd of people—who were mostly men his age, all wearing suits. Then he would find a place to hide.

Ten minutes later, the lecture concluded, and Nam stood, still clapping. He had no idea what the presenter had said and he didn't care.

He was about to tear away from everything familiar and throw himself at the mercy of the American government. Heart pounding so hard he feared his guard could see the pulse in his throat, Nam grabbed his laptop case and walked toward the exit. Slipping his slender frame in between other attendees, he moved quickly, a wisp of a man who was light on his feet. The guard kept pace, though, and was right behind him as he entered the crowded foyer. Nam turned to Ki-ha and spoke in their native language, indicating he needed to use the facilities.

Nam hurried off, weaving through clusters of attendees all going the other way and talking excitedly. Maybe the restroom would have a vent he could slip into. Or should he just make a break and run? How far could the guard's stun gun reach? If he made it outside and hailed a cab, he could reach the State Department in ten minutes. But if he succeeded in defecting, Ki-ha would be punished, maybe executed. Guilt gripped him, and he lost his courage.

Don't sacrifice yourself. You have a lot to offer a new country. His wife's voice echoed in his head. Legs trembling, Nam pushed forward, unsure. Blood from his pounding heart overwhelmed his brain, and he couldn't think anymore. He spotted the bathroom sign and the familiar English words, and relief rushed over him. At least he could physically separate himself from his guard to think. Nam turned to Ki-ha and excused himself. The stoic man nodded and stepped back against the wall.

Inside the facility, Nam counted the stalls. The sixth one was empty. He hurried into it, bent over, and tried to calm himself. He could do this.

* * *

Harlan Romero watched the Korean tech guy go into the restroom. *Yes!* The other guy with him, who looked like a badass, stayed outside. Even better, the bathroom sat at the end of the hall, with double doors leading into the hotel's banquet kitchen. Harlan leaned toward Rocky and whispered, "We need someone to distract his guard. Then we chloroform the tech guy in the restroom and haul him out through the kitchen. It should be pretty empty at this point in the afternoon. The loading dock is right outside the kitchen doors."

Rocky shook his head. "He doesn't look very distractible. That expression could cut through steel."

"He's human. There has to be a way." Harlan racked his brain for a plan. He and Rocky had talked this through a dozen times, and even consulted with Shawn, but they never knew how it would play out until it did. The first two kidnappings had gone smoothly, but they'd had less time to plan this one and had spent more time traveling to get here. At least he'd been able to sleep on the flight. As the pilot, Rocky was exhausted and eating chocolate-covered coffee beans to keep going.

They were counting on the security-guard uniforms they'd acquired to make them look as if they were just doing their jobs by escorting an unconscious man out of the building. Rocky had wanted to wait until the North Korean was in his hotel room, but Harlan thought the bodyguard would be more of a risk in a private setting. The man walked like he was carrying, and Harlan didn't want to get shot.

"We could call in a bomb threat," he suggested.

Rocky shook his head again. "The hotel might go into a lockdown."

They were across the hall from the bathroom, facing each other, about fifteen feet from the bodyguard. Their faces were disguised with dark makeup, big noses, and glasses, but Harlan felt more nervous about this abduction than the first two. The conference crowd was way more public than the parking garage or the backstage area of the theater. Plus, this was the capital. FBI headquarters was across town. If the Korean bodyguard called the police, the hotel would be crawling with feds in minutes. But would he make that call? Or would he contact his own boss first?

Too bad the protesters out front were so peaceful. Their signs were a little hard to figure out, but he thought they were objecting to the government spying on cell phones. Or maybe it was the shortage.

"I've got it," he said, giving Rocky a gentle rap on the shoulder. "Go out there and tell the protesters that they're giving away free cell phones and computers in here. Lead a few down this hallway and point to the Korean bodyguard as the guy to ask."

Rocky blinked, then grinned. "That's crazy, but it just might work."

"Go," Harlan urged, still whispering.

While Rocky hurried down the long corridor, Harlan headed for the restroom. He needed to be in place and ready with the chloroform. Who knew how long Nam would be in there. What kind of name was that anyway? The crowd in the corridor had thinned out some as the attendees filed into big meeting rooms to hear more speeches. *Too bad.* The more people, the more chaos when the protestors pushed into the hotel and demanded free cell phones. Looting was happening everywhere now, and no one would equate this incident with a missing North Korean tech guy. Officials might even think he'd disappeared on purpose—so he didn't have to go back.

When Harlan walked by the bodyguard, he nodded, one security man to another. The North Korean didn't respond. *Fuck him.* Inside the restroom, a skinny young man stood in front of a sink, checking his face in the mirror. Otherwise the space was empty. Where was the tech guy? Trying not to be obvious, Harlan stepped toward the wall and looked down the row of stalls, checking for feet under the green metal doors. There, on the end. Dark dress shoes and black pants.

A commotion erupted on the other side of the wall. Thundering footsteps and dozens of people calling to one another with excited shouts. The preening guy spun toward the door, mouth open.

"You'd better clear out of here." Harlan couldn't resist using his fake authority.

The skinny guy bolted toward the exit. Harlan moved quickly toward the end stall, pulling the rag and chloroform out of his jacket pocket. Was the bodyguard preoccupied by now? Or would his instinct make him rush into the bathroom? Harlan prepped the rag with a heavy dose, just in case he had to use it on the guard too. The smell hit him hard, and he felt light-headed for a moment. Holding the rag at arm's length, he tucked the bottle away with his other hand and gave a quick rap on the door. "That goes for you too. We're evacuating the hotel."

The tech guy stepped out, a nervous twitch in his eyes. "I need your help."

Harlan made a quick decision, slipping the noxious rag into his pocket. "With what?"

"I want to defect from North Korea." His speech was stilted but his English was fine. "Can you help me get away from my guard and take me to the State Department?"

Oh boy. Sometimes luck swung his way. "Sure," Harlan said. "We'll go out through the kitchen." He slipped an arm around Nam's shoulders and led him to the door. The noise outside was raucous, and he heard Rocky shouting something. A wave of fear rolled over him. "Let me check the hall."

Harlan opened the door about four inches and peered out. The guard was right there, with his back to him. A group of three ragged-looking protesters were in the guard's face, demanding cell phones. Rocky was nowhere to be seen. The guard shouted back in a foreign language, then spun toward the restroom. Harlan pulled out his rag as he jerked open the door and shoved it into the guard's face. The protesters looked on open mouthed, then staggered back. One bolted. The Asian man brought up his arms and grabbed the cloth, but his knees buckled and he went down in a thump. Harlan jerked the rag from the downed man's grip, then reached back into the bathroom and grabbed the tech guy's arm. "Let's go."

Rocky was suddenly there, coming from the direction of the kitchen doors. "It's clear. I sent the dishwashing crew out through the banquet room."

Yes! They were going to pull this off.

One of the remaining protesters called out, "Hey! What's going on?"

Harlan started to respond, but another protestor knelt down and pulled a cell phone from the bodyguard's pocket. Two others leapt on him and tried to take it.

Rocky stepped to Nam's other side, and they walked him through the kitchen and out the back doors to the loading dock, leaving the chaos behind. Once they were in the stolen van, Harlan held the rag to the tech guy's mouth and he passed out. While Harlan secured him with duct tape and nylon handcuffs, Rocky started the vehicle and drove down the service alley.

Now they had to get him on the plane, but that seemed easy in comparison. Shawn would be pleased. After bungling Bowman's transport and failing to kill the FBI agent, Harlan needed a win. Shawn was hard to please, but very generous when he was happy. Once Harlan had the bonus money Shawn promised, he planned to get the hell away, maybe settle in Oregon or Colorado and open a pot store. He'd spent his whole life trying to please his friend, and he didn't know why. Shawn seemed to be headed for a meltdown, and it was time to move on.

CHAPTER 22

Friday, March 20, 2:30 p.m., Washington, DC

Jocelyn pulled into the underground parking garage at the new consolidated crime lab, eager to hear what the experts had to say about the microchip she'd dropped off earlier that week. She and her partner had made little progress on Zach Dimizaro's murder, and they were counting on the chip's data to give them a lead. She passed the morgue's entry and took the elevator to the cyber unit. Only one tech person was on duty, and he'd called her to come in. His workspace was surrounded by tall metal shelves loaded with electrical equipment that he used to access the data on cell phones brought in as evidence.

Despite his dreary cubicle, he seemed cheerful. "Mason Walsh." He shook her hand, then grabbed a chair from a nearby similar workspace. "We've made a copy and completed the hash on this chip, so you're free to take it with you. We don't store evidence here." He handed her a small pink plastic bag.

When she'd dropped off the microchip, she'd learned that a hash was a digital matching and copying process that guaranteed the files couldn't be tampered with. None of it would matter if she didn't find a perp to bring into court for Dimizaro's murder. "What's on here?" she asked, cutting to the chase.

"An encryption algorithm like I've never seen before."

"You mean you couldn't access the data?"

"No, I mean it's a software program that encrypts data and makes it totally secure."

It sounded like the same software that was on the prototype phone missing from DigSec, where the victim had worked. The implications for law enforcement were worrisome. "Could you break it if you needed to?"

Walsh shrugged. "I'm not an encryption expert, just a data extractor. The pros are still analyzing it."

That was always the struggle—finding good-guy tech freaks who were better than the black-hat coders. "So this software is valuable?"

"I would think so. Device makers and financial institutions, in particular, are always working to improve their security. One of them might pay handsomely for this software."

Was he implying that the tech team thought the encryption was unbreakable? "Now that you have the software, doesn't that give you the key?"

"Yes and no." He sighed.

"Never mind." She would give it to Ross to take to the FBI. "You don't have to explain. Just tell me who you think would kill someone for this chip." The software probably belonged to the victim's employer, but it was evidence now.

Walsh pursed his lips and gave it some thought. "I think it would work best in mobile devices. But the big companies already have encryption in place, which, by the way, is blocking our ability to access high-end phones when they come in as evidence. So I'm thinking that if a small company making the burner phones criminals use got hold of this, we'd be screwed."

Bailey could find those companies, but it would take time. He was the expert. "Can you name some of those businesses?"

"Celltronics, HiWire, ZoGo, Cricket." He shrugged. "Now that some of the metals for manufacturing are in short supply, the small companies will probably go out of business."

She asked him to repeat the names as she wrote them down. "Someone recently committed murder trying to steal this chip, so they must think their company has a future." Yet in that part of town, it still could have been a mugging. The victim could have been preparing to meet someone and not made it to the buy.

"Every company is looking for the best encryption available. Good luck."

He'd obviously told her everything he knew. "Thanks." They exchanged business cards, then Jocelyn headed out. Maybe she needed to turn the whole investigation over to the bureau. Once the FBI saw the software, they would get involved anyway.

Back in her car, her phone rang. "Larson, it's Murphy. We've got some kind of disturbance going on at the Presidential Plaza Hotel. Patrol units are handling it, but a foreign diplomat was knocked unconscious, and I need you to take the lead on the assault."

"What kind of disturbance?" Jocelyn started her car, adrenaline flowing.

"The group was out front, protesting a technology symposium, then suddenly rushed into the hotel and started grabbing cell phones from the attendees. Ironic, eh?"

The phone shortage was officially out of hand, and a hell of a problem for law enforcement. But why was she getting another assignment? Oh yeah, the rest of her team was overloaded with domestic murders and gang shootings, and her boss didn't expect her to solve the mugging or spend much more time on it. "Is the diplomat still at the hotel?" She pulled out into the street.

"I think so. But get over there and find out what you can before the feds take over."

Jocelyn almost laughed. Her husband was one of the agents who worked cases involving domestic terrorists and violent activists. He would probably be on the scene. "I'm on my way."

The Friday afternoon traffic was predictably heinous, and even using her siren, it was a bitch to clear a roundabout that wasn't moving. When she arrived at the hotel fifteen minutes later, she couldn't get anywhere near the lobby. Patrol cars had blocked off access to the front entrance and to the back alley loading dock. She parked at a nearby mall and power walked back to the hotel. It was better than running, but it still jostled her breasts to the point of discomfort.

She showed her badge to the uniformed officer at the perimeter of the yellow tape and kept moving. Inside the lobby, a dozen officers were standing guard over and questioning groups of protestors, who were all on the floor. Some were cuffed; others were lying facedown in protest. Because of all the minority deaths and lawsuits, cops everywhere had become more reluctant to use excessive or deadly force. Lawbreakers knew that. Jocelyn approached a patrol sergeant she'd worked with, trying to remember his name. Unlike hers, it was a common African American surname, as she recalled.

"Sergeant Johnson," Jocelyn said, offering her hand.

"Detective Larson." The corner of his mouth turned up in his version of a friendly greeting. "What can I do for you?"

"I need to see the diplomat who was knocked out."

"We're questioning him in the business center." The sergeant pointed to a room off the lobby.

"Thanks." Jocelyn kept moving. She needed to get to the victim before he got tired of answering questions and shut down.

Through the glass wall, Jocelyn saw that the room was bright with artificial light and held four computers and a printer-scanner. A formidable-looking Asian man in dark clothes sat in an office chair, his expression grim. A male patrol officer was seated across from him, leaning forward in a gesture of confidentiality, and a female officer stood near the entrance.

"Detective Larson," she said, pushing through the door. "I've been assigned this assault case."

Both officers turned to her. The man stood, clearly ready to hand it over. "Good luck."

She spoke softly, knowing the diplomat would likely hear and understand anyway. "What did you find out?"

"His name is Dukko Ki-ha, and he came here with Lee Nam, some high-value IT expert. They're from North Korea. That's all he would say."

North Korea? Good grief. Now she hated this case too. "I'll take it from here."

The patrol officers left the room, and Jocelyn sat down. She realized she was too close, and scooted her chair back. Intimidation wasn't her style. "Mr. Dukko." She assumed he'd given his last name first, the usual practice in most Asian cultures.

He nodded. "Officer Dukko."

"You're with the North Korean police?"

"Military special operations."

The military and the federal authorities were the same in North Korea. "Why are you here?"

"To protect Lee Nam, a cultural asset."

Protect? Or keep under control? "Why is he a cultural asset?"

"He's the best cryptographer in the world."

Encryption again. How peculiar. "What happened to you? To him?"

"I was drugged and he was kidnapped." His speech was choppy as he searched for the right words.

"By whom?"

"A thick man wearing makeup." Dukko hung his head. "I failed my country."

"What do you mean by makeup?"

He shrugged. "I'm not sure. He didn't look normal, but Caucasian faces are new to me."

"Would you recognize him again?"

"Yes. Was he with your government?"

God, she hoped not. "Please don't think that. We'll do everything we can to find Mr. Lee." Now that she'd won a little trust, she leaned forward. "Please tell me everything that happened."

"It was—" He stopped. "What is the word? Crazy? These people ran to me and shouted. They wanted cell phones. I didn't understand. The man with makeup came out of the restroom and shoved a rag in my face. I blacked out. That is all I know."

"Which bathroom?"

"Near the kitchen. I could smell the food they were making."

Two men in dark suits barged into the room. One was Ross, her husband. The other agent announced his name and authority. "We'll take this from here."

Jocelyn handed Dukko her business card. "Please call me if you need any help."

She smiled at Ross and left the room.

What the hell did the makeup mean? A disguise? Jocelyn headed for the kitchen to question employees. Someone had to have seen something.

CHAPTER 23

Saturday, March 21, 5:45 a.m., Seattle, Washington

Bailey woke early and quickly forgot her dreams, but was left with a
sense of unease. She rolled out of Garrett's bed, dressed, and went out
for a walk. Clouds as dark and brooding as her mood hung low in the
sky. She scanned the street, looking for dark vehicles or anything out of
place. The kidnappers wouldn't be stupid enough to try again, would
they? Bailey kept one hand on her weapon.

Keeping a brisk pace as she rounded the block, she analyzed every
aspect of her investigation and hit the same dead end. Frustration and
anger felt the same to her, and she wanted to punish someone for her
discomfort, for her failure. *A gym with a punching bag.* That's what she
needed. She circled the block until she felt calmer, then entered the
Thorpes' house.

In the shower, as she touched her own body, she thought about
the sex with Garrett. The second time had been even better. Because
it wasn't just sex, she realized. It was intimacy. They'd talked about
everything—but mostly music, politics, and their quirky, lonely lives.
Of course, she hadn't been completely honest with him, because it was

too soon, and she was never completely honest with anyone. But no one really was, even if they claimed to be. Relationships would never survive if people said what they were really thinking. *That mole is hideous. Your sister is hot! Your prosthetic is a little unsettling.* Nobody told the whole truth, because it was often too hurtful for the other person.

She held back too, not to protect her lover, but herself. That was just how she was wired. Although with Garrett, she actually thought about his feelings and wondered if he would be hurt when she left Seattle. More important, would she experience a sense of loss? She would soon find out—because it was time to leave. Staying here was accomplishing nothing.

She was still waiting to hear from the state's business office about real-estate transactions, and Garrett still had dozens of pharmacies to call. Maybe they would both score a lead today—one that brought their searches together and pinpointed where Dana Thorpe was being held. Bailey had until Monday before she had to call her boss and explain why she wasn't reporting to work in the DC headquarters.

Garrett was awake when she stepped out of the bathroom and into the bedroom. "Good morning."

"Hey," he said. "Come over here." His voice and expression were compelling.

"As tempted as I am, I'm not really a morning-sex person." She smiled to soften the rejection. That's what honesty cost. "Besides, we have to make progress on this investigation." She didn't mention his mother.

From the look on his face, she could tell his mind had gone there anyway. "We'll find her." Bailey didn't know if Dana Thorpe would still be alive when they did, but she hoped to locate the kidnappers before they dumped Dana's body in the woods, like they had with Nick Bowman's.

"I'll shower, make some breakfast, and start calling pharmacies." Garrett climbed out of bed and kissed her as he crossed the room.

Bailey grabbed her laptop and headed for the living room again. First, she would check the news and see what she'd missed in the last few days of travel and investigation. The top headline grabbed her attention. The story began:

> North Korean IT specialist Lee Nam was abducted from a technology-security symposium in Washington, DC. In response, North Korean supreme leader Kim Jong-un blamed the US government and threatened retaliation.

What the hell? She skimmed the rest of the story, then clicked a link that led to a new page with an embedded video. The heavyset dictator with the weird hair—who commanded one of the largest armies in the world—stood on an outdoor stage. The camera cut to Pyongyang's main square, where thousands of North Koreans with hand-lettered signs were shouting, "Crush America!" Some of the placards displayed crude drawings of missiles with *US* written on them.

Kim Jong-un held up a hand to silence the crowd. He spoke in Korean, and an aide translated for the media. "Our world-renowned cryptographer, Lee Nam, was kidnapped by the United States government when he visited their capital to attend an educational symposium. Last month, the US sent Jake Austin to spy and corrupt our citizens. Today, the court convicted him, and he will be executed in four days if America fails to return Lee Nam." The dictator shook a fat fist in the air. "America is a bully, but we are not intimidated! We have missiles aimed at its military bases in South Korea, and we will unleash a firestorm if the United States disrespects our sovereignty in this way again." The crowd burst into cheers, and the roar of fifty thousand angry people pulsed from her monitor.

Good god. Bailey shut off the video. The man was insane. Jake Austin was a ridiculous young Hollywood action star who seemed to consider himself an international diplomat. Kim Jong-un was—or had been, anyway—a big fan of his movies and had invited Austin to a private party and tour of the country. The actor had been foolish and delusional enough to go, thinking he could influence the dictator. It had taken him only two days to offend his host and be imprisoned. Three weeks of diplomacy hadn't secured his release. Now he was going to be killed.

Austin's fate meant nothing to her, but Kim Jong-un's follow-up threat was a concern. The dictator probably saw the kidnapping as an opportunity to display military strength, and the US bases in South Korea were definitely in range. No one knew for sure whether North Korean missiles could actually hit US targets, but military officials weren't foolish enough to assume they couldn't. Some experts believed that a combination of a mobile rocket launcher, a miniaturized warhead, and a long-range missile could make Los Angeles an accessible target. But hopefully, the situation wouldn't be allowed to escalate to that point.

Bailey picked up her phone to call her boss. The bureau had to be responding to the indirect threat, and she wanted to know what was being done and who was on the team. Even more, she wanted to lead the search for the North Korean tech guy. Preventing the execution of an American citizen and cooling off a missile threat could be a huge boost to her career. Yet she couldn't bring herself to abandon her current investigation. It just wasn't in a megalomaniac's DNA to stop until he got what he wanted. Other scientists would likely be taken. Even though she'd been pulled off the case, if she produced results, Lennard would get past it. The bureau rewarded agents who saved lives and put criminals away, particularly if the story made the media.

Bailey had a bizarre thought and put down her phone. What if her unsub had kidnapped the North Korean? Lee Nam's encryption specialty put him in a different category from either of the metallurgists, but his knowledge was still useful to cell phone and device manufacturing. In fact, encryption and security had driven major changes in the industry. The bureau often found itself shut out when they seized new phones as evidence, limiting their ability to access data at rest, as they called it. When the bad guys used anything but old-school communication networks, the FBI couldn't even wiretap those conversations, limiting their access to data in motion as well. So far, the bureau had failed to negotiate the access issue with device manufacturers, and Congress had failed to pass legislation that would force new communication networks to build in capture capability. All the bureau could do was hire the best hackers they could afford to keep breaking the new security codes. If the megalomaniac wanted to dominate the market, he needed cutting-edge encryption technology. The North Korean might be able to deliver that, and finding him might solve her other investigation.

She had to fly back to DC and gather all the intel she could. The trip would create an opportunity to chat up Agent Lennard, get updated, and convince her boss to give her a week off.

Garrett came into the room, hair still wet from the shower. "Anything new?"

The sight of him gave her a pang of emotion she didn't recognize. Then she realized that once she left here, she might never see him again. She pushed the thought away and told him the basics. "A North Korean tech expert has been kidnapped, and Kim Jong-un has threatened to execute Jake Austin."

"Kidnapped? By whom?"

"The little dictator has accused our government, but it's bullshit. I'm wondering if the same thugs who took your mom are behind this one too."

"Because the tech guy has some knowledge they want?" Worry lines dug into Garrett's forehead. He seemed to have aged in the few days since she'd met him.

"I'm flying back to DC to find out what I can. Keep calling pharmacies and send me any names, locations, or situations that involve anti-seizure meds."

He nodded. "I'll miss you." Garrett turned and hurried into the kitchen.

She would miss him too. But even if she never saw him again, their encounter had given her hope that she could care more deeply than she thought herself capable of. She might still have a long-term relationship someday. Bailey blinked back tears, called her favorite airline, and bought a ticket.

CHAPTER 24

Saturday, March 21, 8:30 a.m., Wanapum, Washington

Shawn went for a run along the deer trail at the base of the foothills. Even though the living space in the house near the mine was primitive compared to his California home, he rather liked being out here in the quiet open space. Such a change of pace from the traffic and constant chatter of Silicon Valley. And the air was amazingly clear and fresh. Yet he knew he would grow restless if he had to be out here too long. Thurgood's extraction process, specifically tailored to the Palisades Mine, was almost finalized.

The unknown factor was Dana Thorpe. She claimed to be near a breakthrough, but he didn't trust her to be truthful. She might have said it just to keep his hopes up. Or she could have already finalized the new material but, out of fear for her life, didn't want to tell him. Maybe he would have Thurgood evaluate her work. The Australian, who was staying in the mine's bunkhouse, knew she was down there, but was smart enough not to ask questions.

If Thorpe was simply stalling, what would motivate her to finish the work? Without the replacement material, he couldn't produce a new generation of cell phones on the scale he'd planned. He would stay in business while his competition struggled and failed, but surviving wasn't enough. He'd had a taste of what real success felt like, and he wanted more.

The trail sloped gently uphill, and his legs ached. Sweat ran down his back and temples, and he hated the feel of it. Running and swimming both worked his heart, but they were completely different exercises. Doing laps was a sophisticated gentleman's workout, while jogging in the wilderness felt primitive, like a hunter chasing prey. He would never get used to it, but he had to do something during this exile. Drops of moisture landed on his bare arms. From bad to worse. It rarely rained in Mountain View. Another good reason to wrap up this phase and get back home.

Shawn turned around and ran back to the house, passing an oversized metal shop before he got there. The property had been dirt cheap and it showed. The house was only eighteen hundred square feet, and he and Jia had to share a bathroom. The half bath next to the kitchen didn't count.

He stepped inside and cringed. The space even smelled bad. They'd pulled out the carpet as soon as they bought it, but the walls and vents still stunk of deep-fried food.

Let it go.

Once the kidnappings were old news, and his production line was running at full speed, they'd go back to California and buy a new home, one that was even more private.

Jia was setting up a workspace in an alcove next to the only big window in the house. She turned when he walked in. "How long do we have to be here?" His wife had arrived late the evening before, exhausted after a long day of driving, and hated the bungalow even more than he did.

"Three weeks at the most."

"I'll never make it that long. The kitchen is ridiculous!"

"You don't have to cook. We'll buy prepared food."

Jia rolled her eyes. She didn't like anyone's food but her own, plus a few high-end restaurants'. The nearest town was miles away and offered two diners and a pizza parlor. Jia would never try any of them. The mine, plus a few cattle ranches, was the main source of employment and revenue. People drove to Ellensburg or Moses Lake, sixty miles away in either direction, to shop and attend movies. He'd learned that during the two days they'd spent in the area when they bought the house and mine.

His wife put her hands on her hips. "Now that I've delivered your personal stuff, I don't see why I have to stay."

Keeping her here meant he could prevent her from being questioned by the FBI. He also knew her well enough to predict what she wanted to hear. "I need you to keep me company. I'd be miserable here without you." Her presence made little difference to him in this environment with everything he had going on, but he wanted to keep her away from probing FBI agents. Jia didn't know what he was up to, but she knew enough about his transactions to get him in trouble if she talked.

She smiled. "Well, I've always said I could work anywhere, so we'll see if it's true." She sat down in front of her monitor and opened a file.

Shawn showered, ate a breakfast bar, and got online. His first objective was to buy Aptiom or some other anti-seizure medicine for Dana Thorpe. She was becoming a real pain, but at least she wasn't violent like Nick Bowman had been. He'd been a terrible mistake. Shawn opened a website where he'd purchased OxyContin once after hurting himself waterskiing. His doctor, the prick, had only given him a three-day supply. He could order the medication under a different name, but the credit card could still be traced back to him. Another problem was that the pills wouldn't ship until Monday. And where would he have them mailed? He didn't want to use one of his real addresses either.

Dana Thorpe probably had a bottle of the medication in her home in Seattle. Could they get away with a middle-of-the-night break-in? With no ransom demand, the FBI agents had to be gone from her house by now. Harlan and Rocky weren't back from DC yet, so they couldn't handle this for him. But Harlan had called, and the grab of the North Korean had gone smoothly. They'd flown out of the Beltway area immediately afterward and would make the rest of the trip today.

Maybe he should just drive to Seattle and—*no*. Too risky. He might not find the medication in her house, and if he did, the bottle could be almost empty. If he was considering a smash-and-grab, why not just hit a pharmacy in Ellensburg? It would be closer and more of a sure thing. His pulse quickened at the idea. He could get there right before it closed, then bolt in wearing a ski mask, threaten the clerk with a gun, and demand a month's supply of Aptiom.

Crazy! But would it trigger any red flags? It might, if the FBI knew about Dana's prescription. So he would ask for OxyContin, Versed, and some other type of anti-seizure medicine. That way, the robbery—if the FBI even got wind of it—would look like it had been done by a drug addict desperate for a high. Shawn googled the phrase *anti-seizure medicine that produces euphoria* and came up with Lyrica. The drug had originally been developed for epilepsy, then had proved effective in treating nerve pain. But it also acted like a benzo, so some people took it for a tranquilizing effect. Good enough.

Could he pull this off? Shawn laughed out loud. After everything else he'd done lately, he could do anything. And the thought of the robbery actually excited him. Waiting for it to get dark would be the hardest part. He might as well drive up to the mine and see how things were progressing. He climbed into the truck he kept at the property, a silver Tacoma that looked like half the vehicles in the area, and headed north.

* * *

At the mine, he walked to the edge of the massive pit. Seeing the deep layers and busy earth-moving equipment calmed his nerves—and made him feel smart. He'd had the foresight to invest in producing his own rare earth metals. That bold move had caught the attention of venture capitalists, who'd pushed him to think even more boldly. The production facility, with its silos and feeders, was still a mystery to him, but that's what he paid a manager for. The mine's real secret, though, lay beneath the bunkhouse. He'd discovered the huge bomb shelter after he bought the property. When Max mentioned funding a research lab, the underground space had seemed ideal. Especially once he'd realized he might have to resort to kidnapping to get the personnel he needed.

The secret rooms were the perfect bonus to his investment. No one but him and his trusted crew knew they were down there. Maybe a few old-timers in the area might remember the bomb shelter being built before Palisades became a ghost town, but who would ever ask them? Shawn was tempted to visit Dana Thorpe and check on her progress, but he couldn't access the underground lab and then disappear for a while during the day without attracting suspicion from the manager. Besides, he needed to keep his contact with her to a minimum and mask his face every time if he hoped to let her go eventually. He still clung to the possibility of that outcome, but didn't spend much time thinking about it.

But he did need to check in about production. Shawn stopped in the office and found Tom Boxer, his manager, arguing with Milton Thurgood, the extraction specialist whose presence here was supposed to be a secret. They both turned to him.

"We need a bigger crusher," Tom said. His otherwise thin body sported a fat belly, making him look pregnant. Shawn had hired him for his résumé, knowing he wouldn't have to see him much.

"No, we don't," Thurgood argued. "We just need more highly skilled workers than these local half-wits." Thurgood's wild gray hair made him look a bit like Einstein. Shawn had researched him extensively and spoken with him on the phone several times before making the job offer. He'd learned that Thurgood wanted out—of his marriage and his university contract. A perfect fit for his plans.

"We'll do both." Shawn moved toward the computer on the desk. "I'll order the new crusher now." His investors seemed to have unlimited funding for equipment and believed in spending money to make it. Shawn patted Thurgood's shoulder on the way. "And you're right. We'll increase the wage so we can recruit people from out of state with recent mining experience."

"Good." Thurgood shook off his hand. "I've about done everything I can do here."

Shawn decided to order the crusher later. He turned and walked with Thurgood toward the back door. "Milton, I need you to stay out of sight as much as possible."

"I know the rules, but I'm leaving soon anyway."

That surprised Shawn. They had set benchmarks to meet first. "We'll have to review our agreement."

Thurgood scoffed. "Don't bother. I've almost met your terms, and I'll be out of here in a few days."

Shawn didn't have any leverage to stop him. Except to tell Thurgood's wife where he was headed. But he had bigger things to focus on. "I'd like you to evaluate the other scientist's work before you go."

"That would take more time and energy than I'm willing to give. G'day." Thurgood stepped out the back door and headed for the bunkhouse.

For a brief moment, Shawn imagined himself following him out and shooting him in the back of the head. That would guarantee Thurgood's silence forever. He shook off the thought. There would be the body to do away with and Tom Boxer to mollify. Besides, Thurgood wasn't quite finished, and the Australian planned to head for the Cayman Islands when he left, so Shawn wasn't really worried about anyone ever questioning him.

He turned around in the narrow hall and stepped into one of the cluttered storage rooms. From a canister, he grabbed the ski mask he kept handy for his visits with Dana Thorpe and stuffed it into his pocket. He'd already chosen the pharmacy, looked at photos of the area on Google Earth, and taken a booster dose of dextro. He was ready.

CHAPTER 25

Back in the truck, Shawn checked the glove box. The Colt was there, as usual. He kept it there for safety against bears and rattlesnakes, but now decided he should start keeping it on his body at all times. On the way out of town, he called Jia. "I'm headed to Ellensburg for supplies, so I'll be home late. Do you need anything?"

"Yeah, I need to get the hell out of here. Why didn't you come by and pick me up?"

"Sorry, I didn't think you'd want to make the drive after your long trip getting here."

She didn't have a good comeback. After a moment, she said, "Fresh fruit, please. Mangos and cherries, if you can find them."

He would pick up a few things at the market in Wanapum on his way, just to cover his tracks. "I'll look, but don't count on it. See you later." He hung up before she could add to her list.

Even with the stop at the store, the trip to Ellensburg took less time than he'd thought, so he drove around the small city for a while killing time. It had been raining off and on all day, and the streets were sloshy and nearly deserted. Finally, he stopped behind a tire store and took off his license plates. At seven forty-five, he drove past Decker's Pharmacy on Pine Street, parked a half block away, and pulled on the ski mask. In that moment, the risk became real and his pulse thumped in his neck. So far, he hadn't seen a single police car, and he hoped that in this Podunk town, the two cops on duty were taking turns napping at the station.

Shawn charged toward the little drugstore tucked in between an antique shop and a bakery, both of which were closed. A bell jangled when he jerked open the door, surprising him. But no cameras that he could see. He trotted down the narrow aisle to the counter in back. The clerk, an older woman with short gray hair, let out a little scream when she saw him.

He pulled out the gun, leaving the safety on. "Be quiet, don't be stupid, and you won't get hurt."

"We don't keep much cash here."

"Just get me some OxyContin and Lyrica. A big stash of both." He'd forgotten the third drug, but it didn't matter.

"The pharmacist left already, and I don't know where anything is back there." Her voice trembled with fear.

"Find it fast!" A rush of intense pleasure flooded his brain. He hadn't known how much he would enjoy making someone fear him.

She moved toward a narrow door behind the counter and fumbled with the lock.

"I said fast!" Despite the thrill, he worried about getting caught.

The clerk finally got the door open and went straight for the back wall. Shawn stood in the doorway, watching her, then glanced back at the front door. The shop was about to close and he didn't expect anyone, but still, he had to stay alert.

Plastic containers covered the back shelf, and the clerk picked up a few before she said, "Got it. This is oxy." She turned to him with a large white bottle.

"I need the Lyrica too. Now!"

Panic rippled across her face. "I don't know where it is. We don't get much call for it."

"It's a tranquilizer. Find it!" His pulse raced as if he were running for his life. Was it pure adrenaline or the amphetamine in the dextro?

She turned to the partition beside her and started grabbing bottles off an upper shelf. "I don't see it."

Shawn rushed into the cramped back room, put the gun into his waistband, and searched with her. A few minutes later, he found it next to the prednisone. He grabbed two bottles, stuffed them into his pockets, then snatched up the OxyContin she'd tried to hand him earlier.

"Get on the floor and don't move for twenty minutes!"

He turned and bolted through the narrow door, past the counter, and down the aisle. No one had come into the drugstore. He sprinted for his truck, jumped in, and gassed the engine. If the old woman stayed down long enough for him to get out of sight, he could pull this off. When he took the freeway entrance a few minutes later, he let out a howl, then burst into laughter. What a rush! He almost wished he'd participated in the kidnappings. After a life spent carefully monitoring his behavior and doing everything expected of him, it was exhilarating to break the rules!

On the drive home, Max called. Shawn answered, feeling upbeat. "Things are under control," he reported. "We just grabbed the best cryptographer in the world, the mine has doubled its capacity, and Dana Thorpe is on the verge of finalizing the new compound."

"We have another problem."

The chill in Max's voice made his gut tighten. "What is it now?"

"Rocky's been identified by the feds."

Oh fuck! "How did that happen?"

"Obviously, he was careless during Dana Thorpe's abduction. Deal with him."

"I'll make him lie low for a while."

The pause unnerved him. Finally, Max said, "If he's arrested, they'll offer him a sweet deal, and Rocky will turn on you."

"We're out at the mine now, we're done picking up resources, and Rocky will be fine."

"You don't understand." The deadpan tone had shifted to menacing. "I don't like it either, but Rocky has to be silenced. We're the majority stakeholders, and we make the decisions. Just do it and don't look back."

Shawn's gut fluttered, and he closed his eyes for a moment. But he forced himself to focus on driving and thinking. The unspoken threat was that the venture capital company would pull their financing or take over his company. He had to tell his backers what they wanted to hear. "Don't worry. I'll handle it. I won't let anything stop our plans." He couldn't ask Harlan to do this. He and Rocky had become friends. But Shawn didn't know if he could pull it off. "How soon?"

"Tomorrow."

A lump formed in his throat. "I'll try."

"This isn't something you try. Just get it done and hide the body well."

"Yes, sir." Shawn hung up, deeply troubled. The man who'd fired him early in his career he hated with a passion and could easily kill without guilt. But Rocky, the pilot he'd gotten to know and come to depend on? There had to be another option.

CHAPTER 26

Sunday, March 22, 10:00 a.m., Washington, DC

Bailey had the cab driver drop her off at the Presidential Plaza, where the North Korean had been abducted. She knew better than to stop at her home in Brentwood. She would want to swap out her travel clothes, cook a decent meal, and pick up the Nikola Tesla biography she'd been reading—and there was no time for any of that. The hotel was back to operating as if nothing had happened, and she didn't spot any agents or patrol cops. She left her suitcase at the check-in desk, showed her badge, and asked where the cryptographer had been abducted.

"I wasn't here Friday, but it was at the end of the corridor that dead-ends at the banquet kitchen. By the restroom." The clerk pointed to a hall leading off the massive lobby filled with paintings of presidents.

"Thanks. I'll check it out. While I'm doing that, alert your security department that I want to see the video of the abduction."

"You really have to ask them yourself. They're on the second floor."

The bureau probably had a copy of the video, but she hadn't seen it. Nor did she know if they would include her on the new kidnapping-incident team or share the intel. Especially if her boss suspected she was being noncompliant. Bailey had no intention of letting them think that. She would show up at her unit's next meeting and see how it played out. Her boss would simply think she'd come back to DC as ordered. Tomorrow could still be a problem. Depending on what she found out about the North Korean's kidnapping, Bailey expected to head back to the West Coast. She still hadn't decided what to tell her boss about her absence. Illness? Death in the family? She could always use her father's arrest as a valid family-crisis excuse.

At the end of a wide hotel corridor, she entered the men's restroom. An odd mixed smell of urine and baking cookies hung in the air. She startled an old guy at the sink. He opened his mouth to complain, but she flashed her badge. "FBI. This is an investigation."

He finished washing his hands and left. Bailey looked around for a vent or possible escape route and didn't find any. The food smells unnerved her. It was just wrong for a toilet area. She started for the exit. If the kidnapper had waited in here, he'd come in through the door. The bureau's forensic technicians had likely combed every inch of the area and picked up any trace evidence, so there was no point in searching. She just needed to see the scene and put herself in the mind of the abductors. The tech guy had probably not been alone. North Korea didn't send important people out of the country without babysitters who made sure they came back. So where had his bodyguard been? Outside the door?

Bailey stepped out of the restroom, looked around, and spotted the double doors at the end of the hall. The hotel desk clerk said it led to the banquet kitchen, which explained the cookie aroma. The kidnappers had probably gone out the back, a short, safe route. She hurried into the kitchen area, where a full crew bustled around, and walked straight back to the loading doors. She could question the staff, but the abduction had happened while a different crew was working, and she didn't have time to waste.

The kidnapping had not been a US federal job, regardless of what Kim Jong-un said. She'd never worked for the CIA or NSA and could only speculate, but if she were required to kidnap someone as part of her job, she would have chosen a more private venue, perhaps even gassed his hotel room, knocking out both him and the guard. Her government had time and resources. This operation had been done hastily and at great risk. Desperate men at work. But why Lee Nam? And what was the rush?

The surveillance video was key, but it would save her time and the hassle to view it at the bureau, where she was headed anyway. She would crash the meeting, as if she belonged, silently daring them to exclude her. If that didn't work, she would use Agent Lennard's password to access all the files. Long ago, Bailey had snooped and found it when she needed more intel than she'd been given access to. She walked out to the loading dock, inhaling the exhaust fumes of the last truck that had parked there, and made a call. Havi, her analyst buddy, would be able to tell her what time the team was gathering. If they had the bodyguard in custody, she might even be able to meet with him.

Havi took forever to answer and his voice sounded strained. "Hey, Bailey. Where are you?"

"I'm here in DC. Briefly." She didn't understand his discomfort and didn't have time to find out. "I need to know when the North Korean incident team is meeting."

"I'm not in that loop, but I'm sure it's happening today."

"Lee Nam had a babysitter, correct? Is he in custody?"

"Dukko Ki-ha, a military police officer, and no, he's not in custody." Havi clanked something in the background, then continued. "Dukko has been questioned, but he refused to come into the bureau. No one wanted to exacerbate the situation with Kim Jong-un by detaining one of his officers."

"Do you know where Dukko is?"

"No. Why don't you just ask Lennard?" A pause. "I heard you were pulled off the other kidnappings. What's going on?"

"I think all the kidnappings are connected, but I'm not sure the AD wants to hear that, so please don't repeat it." Impatient, she walked down the service alley, planning to grab her luggage and catch a cab. "Can you find out about the meeting? Or where the North Korean police officer might be?"

"I'm not in the office, but I'll see what I can do."

Now she understood his irritation. "I'm sorry to bother you at home. Thanks for your help."

"No worries."

They hung up. Bailey decided to go straight to the bureau. Everything she needed to know was in that building. Her only worry was that her boss would tell her she couldn't investigate the new kidnapping, then give her some bullshit assignment. In which case, everything she did after that would be insubordination. That didn't bother her, except for the potential consequence of losing her job. This career held too much power, prestige, and protection for her to ever let it go without a fight.

As she exited a cab in front of the bureau's headquarters, Havi called back. "The team is meeting in an hour in the small critical-incident room. Lennard is running it."

"Anything on the bodyguard?"

"No, sorry."

"Thanks, Havi. You're the best. Let me know if I can return the favor." She enjoyed making people happy, as much as an empath would. She was just more calculating about it.

The halls were even emptier than usual. Despite the number of people who worked at headquarters, it was often a quiet place, even during the week. Field agents like her were rarely at their desks, and analysts like Havi were always at their desks. Very little meandering or socializing went on. Bailey hurried to her own workspace and turned on the computer.

The screen blurred and her body sagged at the same time. She was exhausted, but she didn't have time to make coffee. She closed her eyes, focused her brain, and willed herself to find a reserve of energy. A little food would help. She hadn't eaten anything since the crappy little snack on the plane six hours ago.

Bailey got up and hurried down the hall to Kepner's office. She was the public relations liaison and made a point of being friendly to everyone. She also left her office unlocked and kept food in her drawers. Bailey slipped in, found a chocolate protein bar, grabbed it, and left. Kepner would have given it to her if she'd asked.

Back at her desk, Bailey logged into the system and keyed in search words related to the North Korean incident, hoping to find the hotel video of the kidnapping. The bureau gave all major cases a code name, and sometimes the moniker was logically connected, and other times it wasn't. She got lucky on her fifth guess: *interview*. Kim Jong-un had recently been the butt of a comedy called *The Interview*. She'd also tried *Fat Boy*, because that's what some agents called him.

The file was locked, so she used her boss' password to get in, giving her a jolt of pleasure. She could always bullshit her way through the conversation if Lennard ever found out. Bailey could have asked to see the file and might have been allowed. But why risk being told no? Especially when the thrill of rule breaking was too seductive to resist.

The video clip was only a few minutes long and had been taken from a camera across the corridor about twenty feet away. Still, she got a decent look at the kidnapper coming out of the bathroom, the victim behind him, and the guard, who seemed to look straight at the camera for a moment. The unsub wore black pants and a white button-down shirt with a security badge. The thin, nervous Asian man behind him did not appear captive in any way. The presence of three unknown people—hotel guests?—surprised her. They came at the guard and seemed to shout questions. Then the fake security man shoved a hand into the bodyguard's face and he went down. Chloroform? Even after his guard was knocked unconscious and accosted by the three intruders, Lee Nam didn't appear disturbed or afraid, and he left with the two men willingly. Bailey wasn't even sure she'd witnessed an abduction.

The second unsub had entered the scene from the side, with only his profile showing. Still, under the makeup and the oversized nose, she thought she recognized Jerry Rockwell's broad face. He was the right height as well. She looked for the dark birthmark on his cheek, but didn't see it. Was that the point of the makeup? The theatrical disguises would probably throw off the facial recognition software, and Rockwell was at least thirty pounds heavier than he'd been in his mug shot all those years ago. Still, logic indicated these were the same guys who'd kidnapped the scientists.

The tech guy had watched the security person knock out his fellow North Korean and hadn't reacted, so they must have convinced him they were somehow helping him. Lee Nam wanted to get away from his guard. Was he defecting? If so, the kidnappers could have been government agents after all. *Oh hell.* Was it possible the CIA was responsible for the other abductions too? The agency did whatever it wanted as long as someone thought national security was the end game. But why would metallurgists, with different specialties, be important to national security? Unless the CIA needed the scientists to develop some kind of weaponry. An image of Nick Bowman's naked, battered corpse played in her brain. His kidnappers had pushed him out of a helicopter or plane. Would the CIA murder an American civilian? It seemed so unlikely. Bailey set aside the idea but didn't dismiss it outright.

She opened the initial report filed by the agents who'd responded to the hotel kidnapping, and skimmed through it. Pages of interview notes revealed almost nothing she didn't already know, except that one kitchen worker had witnessed "an Asian man leaving out the back dock with two security guards." She also learned that the military bodyguard, Dukko Ki-ha, had said very little during his interview. Bailey glanced at the time on her monitor. The task force meeting would start soon. She logged out of Agent Lennard's account and logged back in with her own, leaving the computer running.

The maze of hallways leading to the Critical Incident area was complex and frustrating for someone with her directional challenges, and she had made dozens of wrong turns in her first year in the building. By now, she knew them well, but as tired as she was, she recited her left-right memorization just to be sure. She wished again for a cup of coffee.

The smaller CI room held ten tables with computers, monitors, and other digital equipment. While an incident was unfolding, Lennard, the unit's director, called in the field agents and analysts with the expertise needed for the case and instructed them exactly where to sit and who to interact with. This current scenario was unique, and only six people were in the room. Two analysts showed signs of having been at their back-table station for hours—jackets off, empty coffee cups, watery eyes. Special Agent Lennard stood at the front of the room with Assistant Director Brent Haywood—the two people who'd given her the original assignment. Markham and Trent, two male agents who worked domestic terrorism cases, sat together at a table in front.

"Bailey!" Lennard looked surprised, but not upset, to see her. "When did you get back?"

"Today." Bailey breezed in and sat at a table next to Markham and Trent's. "I saw the news about Lee Nam's kidnapping and thought I should be here." She gave a small shrug, implying casualness. "Just in case the two investigations are linked."

"That certainly occurred to us," the AD said, making eye contact. "But with all the intel gathered, we've decided the North Korean incident is distinctive and unrelated."

Seriously? Bailey locked her jaw to keep from arguing. She needed information, and the best way to get it was to listen.

"The abduction was staged," Markham said, next to her. "Lee Nam went with the two men willingly. We think he plans to defect."

"Or at least disappear," the assistant director added.

Again, Bailey held her tongue. They didn't know she'd seen the video, and it wasn't in her best interest to indicate she had. Hadn't anyone seen the resemblance between the kidnapper at the hotel and Jerry Rockwell, the man identified by a witness as Dana Thorpe's abductor? The thought of Garrett made her heart flutter. Bailey focused on the bigger issue and finally spoke up. "If Lee Nam is defecting and doesn't want to be found, how do we placate Kim Jong-un? If he's crazy enough to execute the head of his military for dozing off at a meeting, he won't hesitate to kill an American actor. He might even be wacko enough to launch a missile."

"We either find their cryptographer or we pretend we have," Lennard said. "We'll patch together a video or audio statement if we have to." Lennard looked like she'd been awake and at work since the North Korean's kidnapping.

Bailey didn't mean to sound skeptical, but she was surprised they thought they could pull it off. "Is there enough available digital recording of Lee Nam to splice together an intelligent statement?"

Lennard's shoulders slumped. "We're still searching for public statements he might have made and combing the symposium's footage." Her boss gestured at the analysts working the back table. "It would have helped if Lee had made his presentation before he checked out."

"Have we heard anything else from KJU?"

The AD shook his head. "His silence is more disturbing than if he were making more public threats."

Lennard cut in. "If we don't make progress or if KJU makes another missile threat, I think we should start evacuating our military personnel from the South Korean base."

The AD gave her a dismissive glance. "That's premature and not our call, in any event. The game will change if he follows through with his threat to execute Jake Austin, of course."

If the group had business to discuss or reports to share, they didn't seem to be in a hurry. Or maybe she'd missed the bulk of the meeting. Bailey wanted to question Dukko, but no one had mentioned him. "What about Lee's bodyguard? Can he help us placate Kim Jong-un? Do we have him in custody?"

"We've questioned him," Lennard said. "And released him. He wasn't forthcoming at all."

When? And where was he now? She couldn't ask without seeming too pushy. An agent had to be tailing him. "What can I do to help?" She wanted to be kept in the loop, but she didn't really want an assignment. She intended to keep searching for Dana Thorpe, and when she found her, Bailey half expected to find Lee Nam working right beside her in some hidden lab. Averting a North Korean crisis bumped the stakes of her success to a whole new level. Since the AD didn't believe the cases were connected, it seemed unlikely his team would get the job done.

"We've got it covered," Lennard said. "In fact, you should go home and take a few days off. You look tired."

Fuck you. Bailey stood and smiled. "Thanks. I think I will."

CHAPTER 27

On the street, Bailey bought a cup of strong black coffee from a vendor and tried to form a plan. The agent tailing Dukko would have to report his location, and she had to access that information. But how? Lennard would be the recipient of the reports, and if they were oral, her boss might not even make notes, especially if Dukko checked into a hotel and stayed there.

Time to get moving. She stood on the curb to hail a cab. The symposium hotel was the best place to start, and the bodyguard might have only been released in the last hour or so. Dukko probably had a room at the Presidential Plaza and might not feel inclined to change locations, unless he'd been involved in the kidnapping or was operating under an assignment from KJU. In which case he might not return to the hotel at all, even to grab his luggage.

The wind picked up as she waited, and Bailey gulped her hot coffee to stay warm. She tried to put herself into the bodyguard's frame of mind. He had to be worried. He'd failed his mission and disappointed his psychopathic leader. Kim Jong-un had to be on the far end of the spectrum. No nurture versus nature debate with him. Genetics and bad parenting had worked together to create a freak. Dukko was probably afraid to go home without Lee Nam, and if he was a policeman, he might even try to find his missing charge.

A taxi pulled up. After she gave the driver the hotel's address, her phone rang. *Garrett!* Her feelings for him surprised her again. Yet, as much as she'd wanted to experience a real, lasting love affair, she didn't want it to be with a twenty-three-year-old who lived across the country. *Why not?* If most relationships were doomed to fail, what difference did his age make? The location could be a problem, though.

This call was probably about the case, so she put in her earpiece. "Garrett. What's going on?"

"I'm just taking a break from calling pharmacies and asking the same questions over and over." A pause. "I miss you."

She couldn't say it back. Keeping their intimacy going could get her fired. With his father's connection to the bureau, the risk was real. She almost laughed. Garrett would never tell his father, and she was hard-wired to be a risk taker. "I'll be back soon. I have a witness to question, then I'll catch the next flight."

The cab pulled into traffic.

"You must be exhausted." Garrett was such an empath.

"I am, but I can sleep on the plane."

His voice perked up. "You said 'witness.' Do you have a lead?"

"Don't get your hopes up. Our best bet is still to find the pharmacy and link it to a device-manufacturing business or mineral mine within a fifty-mile radius." The damn Washington State business licensing office hadn't given her a list yet. If her interview with Dukko didn't pan out, she would call Havi again and get his help hacking into the business registry. Waiting for information drove her crazy.

"Is the North Korean kidnapping connected to my mother's abduction?"

"I think so, but the bureau doesn't, so we're still on our own."

"I trust you."

"I appreciate that, but I have to get back to work." Bailey hung up, feeling surprisingly awkward. The social skills she'd carefully cultivated over a lifetime failed her around Garrett. What was happening to her? Relationships had always been on her terms, with her in control. With Garrett, she couldn't predict, control, or calculate with any effectiveness. She felt emotionally vulnerable for the first time in her life, and the new experience was exhilarating. Even unexpected or negative emotions were better than boredom and loneliness.

A few minutes later, the cab pulled up in front of the hotel, so she paid the driver and hurried inside. At the front desk, she showed her badge again—to a new clerk—and asked which room Dukko Ki-ha was registered in.

As Bailey stepped out of the elevator on the tenth floor, she caught sight of herself in a lobby mirror. Her makeup had disappeared, her hair was disheveled, and she had a small coffee stain on her white sweater. She realized she hadn't showered or changed clothes in nearly twenty-four hours. The thought of going home for a few minutes to freshen up was overpowering, but the trip across town would be too time consuming. She had clean clothes in her travel bag, and this hotel was full of showers. She just had to find an empty or temporarily unoccupied room. But not yet.

Bailey stopped in front of 1010 and knocked softly. Dukko's body language in the video clip had projected rigidity and abrasiveness, but his hair, which was a little longer than most male officers', suggested he might be vain and susceptible to flattery. She didn't fully understand how North Korean men viewed women, but it seemed safe to assume he wouldn't react well to female aggressiveness.

Footsteps, then a pause. Was he pulling a weapon and readying himself? Bailey touched her gun under her sweater. She would have preferred to have it in hand, but she wanted to put him at ease.

"Who is it?" he called out.

"Andra Bailey. I'm a private investigator." The lie had come to her at the last second.

"What do you want?"

"I can help you find Lee Nam."

"I don't need your help." Even through the door, he sounded abrasive.

"You don't have all the facts."

A long moment of silence. Finally, the door opened and he looked her over.

Up close, he was more attractive than she'd first thought, but he also had a nose that had been broken and never reset properly. He also had the most distrustful eyes she'd ever seen.

"Thank you. May I come in?"

"I don't need your help."

Yet he'd opened the door. "I think I know who kidnapped your encryption expert. You have information I need too. Let's work together."

An almost imperceptible nod, then he stepped aside and gestured for her to enter. A packed suitcase lay on the foyer table. The rest of the small room was free of personal items. Dukko was preparing to leave. Hairs tickled the back of her neck. No one knew she was here—in a private hotel room with a man who had diplomatic immunity. She had a flash of herself bloody and dead in the bathtub. Bailey sat in one of the soft chairs and forced herself to appear relaxed.

Dukko perched on the edge of the other chair, and his jacket opened a little to reveal a stun gun strapped to his side. "Why do you carry a weapon?" he asked.

"For the same reason you do." She gave a charming smile. "I know this is a sensitive subject, but I need to know if Lee Nam was preparing to defect."

Dukko leapt to his feet. "You insult me and my country. Leave now."

Oh hell. She'd blown it first thing. "I'm sorry. I didn't mean to offend you. But I watched the video of what happened. Mr. Lee left with the men voluntarily."

His expression tightened. "They must have tricked him."

"Probably. Had you ever seen the men before? Do you know them?"

"No." He shook his head. "You said you know who took him. Before I answer more questions, you have to tell me."

"I'm pretty sure it wasn't our federal agents." Bailey thought about Milton Thurgood and his car left at the airport. "I think Lee Nam may have been offered a job, rather than actually kidnapped. Do you know anything about that?"

"No." He stood. "I don't think we can help each other."

Dukko wanted her to leave. Whatever he knew about Lee Nam, he wasn't prepared to share. "Thanks for your time." Bailey headed for the door.

She sensed his sudden movement behind her and instinctively lunged sideways, but a blow struck the side of her head and she staggered, landing on the bed. She grabbed for her weapon just as he landed on her back, pinning her down.

CHAPTER 28

Sunday, March 22, 5:55 a.m., Palisades Mine, Washington

Dana woke with another headache but didn't care. At least she could feel it, which was better than the numbness that had set in. She lay on the narrow bed and couldn't bring herself to get up. A brittle darkness had settled into her soul, and she felt dysfunctional. Worse than the depression was the indecision. She'd finally had the epiphany that could push her research to a fruitful outcome. But if she stabilized the compound and gave them the formula, she would no longer be necessary and they would kill her.

Once she was dead, her keepers would have the synthetic dysprosium and be able to do whatever they wanted with it. That worried her. She'd just discovered that with a minor tweak, the compound was highly explosive. If her keeper was crazy or evil enough to abduct and imprison her to get his hands on the material, then he was evil enough to make bombs with it. She would rather let the knowledge die with her than give it to a madman. So she wouldn't go into the lab again, which meant the day of her death was coming soon.

The need to pee finally drove her from the narrow, uncomfortable bed. As she urinated, cramps made her cringe in pain. Oh no, not again. But the blood was coming. Once the flow started, she was a mess for days, often afraid to leave the house. Fibroids were the culprit, but rather than surgery, her doctor had her taking birth control, hoping that menopause would resolve the issue soon. But she hadn't taken her pills in days. Now she was bleeding in a basement, god only knew where, with no tampons or pads or Midol for the cramps. A bitter laugh bubbled from her throat, and sobs quickly followed. Once she was under control, Dana made a pad from folded toilet paper, but it wouldn't last an hour. Maybe her blood would disgust them, and they'd put her out of her misery. The sight of it could be frightening, even for her.

Could she use the blood and its visual effect to her benefit? Dana washed her hands and splashed cold water on her face, thinking it through. If she smeared the blood on her neck or wrists, would they think she needed medical assistance? Or take her to a doctor if they thought she was dying? No, of course not. The keeper had brought her Lyrica for her seizures, but that didn't mean he would seek outside help. Still, if she could get him to focus on the blood, maybe she could steal the key while he was distracted. Or disable him somehow. She would have to think it through.

Dana paced the small room, feeling more alive than she had in days. Scenario after scenario played out in her mind. Using the blood here in her room, waiting for the keeper to check on her, then locking him inside and running. Waiting until she was in the lab, then faking an accident with broken glass. Each possibility made her nervous, yet she wasn't afraid to try. What did she have to lose? She probably only had one chance at this, so she had to be smart and make it work. She didn't feel smart. The lack of sunlight, the isolation, the hopelessness—it was all combining to create a mental fog. Her research had been impeded by weird mistakes the day before, and now she struggled to predict the possible pathways and outcomes of each escape scenario. The biggest concern was which way to run. What would she find outside these walls?

Dana heard the keeper's heavy footsteps coming down the stairs. He was probably concerned that she hadn't knocked for him yet. Her pulse escalated just thinking about escape. She'd never be able to wait until she got down to the lab. It had to be now!

She pulled the toilet-tissue pad out of her pants and smeared the dark menstrual blood on each wrist. It was obviously not fresh, oxygen-rich blood, but maybe a man wouldn't know the difference. She moved quietly toward the door and lay down on her back, letting her face fall away from the entrance.

Several loud pounds. "Are you ready?"

She took long, slow breaths.

Another knock. "It's time for the lab."

Eyes closed, she counted slowly just to keep calm.

"Dana? Are you okay?"

A key turned in the lock and the keeper stepped inside. Cold, damp air from the hall oozed in, and she could feel the weight of him looming nearby.

"Oh no," the big man cried out in what sounded like concern.

Dana felt a whoosh of air brush her neck as he squatted down. *Now!* She sat up and shoved both hands against his bent knees. Caught off guard, he rocked back and landed on his butt. She leapt to her feet and charged through the open door. The thought of him coming after her made her ill. She grabbed the door handle, slammed it shut behind her, and charged down the hall—in the opposite direction of the lab.

She passed through a wide foyer-like area filled with dusty boxes and junk, then charged through another metal door. A tunnel! *Please let this be the way out!* Dana kept running, but began to fear she'd gone the wrong way. Soon, the tunnel widened and she spotted stairs. She pounded up the steps, her breath ragged. At the top was a trapdoor in the ceiling. She grabbed the latch and pulled. It didn't budge. *No!* She tried again, yanking with all her strength. The keeper's footsteps came down the tunnel, moving fast. He wasn't locked in her room! She'd hit a dead end. Dana turned, prepared to fight.

CHAPTER 29

Sunday, March 22, 2:05 p.m., Washington, DC

Dukko pressed his knees into the woman's back, then pinched the vagus nerve in her neck. Her body went limp. He pulled plastic handcuffs from his pants pocket and secured her wrists. His belt served as a restraint for her ankles. She wouldn't be unconscious long. She was a fighter—he could tell. He reached under her sweater for her weapon and removed it. What if she screamed?

He put the gun on the dresser, then unzipped his travel bag and grabbed a sock. He wasn't an interrogator, and what he was about to do made him uncomfortable. Especially because she was a woman. But he had to know why she was looking for Lee Nam and what she knew about his disappearance. Kim Jong-un would execute him, along with the American actor, if Dukko failed to bring Nam home. The United States was pretending to look for Lee Nam, but Dukko didn't trust the FBI, and he wasn't convinced they hadn't helped Nam defect.

Impatient to be done with it, he rolled the woman over and slapped her face. She opened her eyes, blinked, and started to say something. He shoved the sock into her mouth.

"No screaming or I'll have to hurt you."

She nodded, hatred blazing in her strange green eyes.

"Sit up!"

He didn't have to tell her. She was already scrambling to get upright on the bed. Maybe she thought he was going to rape her—a heinous act that would be unworthy of him. To put that fear out of her mind, Dukko dragged her to the chair she'd just occupied, surprised she didn't fight him. *Smart.* Saving her strength for when it might be constructive. He pulled the other chair up close so he could manipulate the sock in her mouth.

Her eyes were suddenly calm, as if she had accepted her fate.

"If you answer my questions truthfully and quietly, you won't get hurt." He prayed that she would. Assaulting her would be shameful, but it was his duty. "Who are you and why are you looking for Lee Nam?" She'd called herself a private investigator, but he didn't understand that term. With two fingers, he pulled the sock from her mouth, careful not to get bitten.

"I'm a federal agent," she said, without emotion. "The hotel clerk knows I'm in this room, and you're in a shitload of trouble."

She was lying to save herself. She had to be.

"My badge is in my satchel. Outside zip pocket. You really need to rethink this."

He shoved the sock back into her mouth and reached for the bag on the bed, but he knew the badge would be there. *Shibal!* What now? If he were arrested and jailed, North Korea would be shamed, and he would rot in an American prison. The only other option was to kill her. Or go on the run as a fugitive in America.

She tried to talk around the cloth, but he didn't understand her words. It couldn't hurt to hear what she had to say. Dukko removed the sock.

"There's another choice."

This strange, fearless woman knew what he'd been thinking. "What do you mean?"

"We both want the same thing, so let's work together. Yes, I'm pissed that you assaulted and restrained me, but I'm more interested in finding the kidnapping victims than sending you to jail." She gave him a knowing smile, with a little shrug. "I've done the same thing to people I wanted information from. Although I've never used a sock."

Was she mocking him? It didn't matter. She was offering to let him go unpunished. "Why?"

"I'm trying to prevent a crisis between our countries."

The implication was that his motive was less noble. "That is my goal as well."

"So untie me and tell me everything you know."

He let out a harsh laugh. "You first. Who are the kidnappers?"

"We think one is named Jerry Rockwell, but he's just a hired hand. I don't know who the mastermind is, but I think it's someone who makes cell phones or plans to start making them."

This was about cell phones? "What companies?"

"I don't know. I've been traveling constantly just to keep up with the abductions and haven't had time to do enough research."

She showed no signs of lying, and she looked like she'd been on a plane for a week. "What other abductions?"

"A scientist with a specialty in synthetic metals."

What? He didn't understand the connection to Lee Nam, an encryption specialist. "Who else was kidnapped?"

She hesitated, and he watched her eyes as she calculated how much to tell him. "A scientist named Nick Bowman."

"Is Lee Nam with him? Where are they?"

"I don't know."

He assumed she had an idea or a plan to figure it out. He would follow her when she left the hotel. If she got on a plane, so would he. She seemed more determined and flexible than the agents who'd questioned him after Lee's kidnapping. They had been convinced that Nam was a defector and that Dukko had to be a conspirator. Lies and nonsense. He'd been charged with protecting the coding genius, and he'd failed. What if the abductors tortured Nam for information, then killed him? "Is Lee Nam's life in danger?"

"Maybe."

"How can the North Korean people know that your government didn't plot this?" Frustration made him gesture, something he rarely did.

"Why would we? Call Kim Jong-un and tell him to back down. Buy us some time to investigate."

"I can't do that without proof that Nam is alive and not a hostage of the American government."

"Then let me go so I can get back to work."

He didn't trust her not to have him arrested. "I'll leave first." He jumped from the chair, shoved the sock back into her mouth, and grabbed his luggage. "I'll call the hotel in twenty minutes and tell them to release you. Please report that this was a joke." Was that the right word? She seemed to understand. Near the door, he turned back. "I don't care if the American actor is killed, but I may be the only person who can stop it—and whatever comes next. If I go to prison, I'll never make that call to Kim Jong-un."

CHAPTER 30

Sunday, March 22, 11:05 a.m., Seattle, Washington

Garrett poured another cup of coffee and sat back down in the recliner. How did detectives and agents do this? Calling business after business looking for information—it was mind numbing. Yet it was obviously part of the job. His father had complained about occasional drudgery a few times back when he still lived with them.

Garrett couldn't imagine Bailey having the patience for this. He didn't know her well yet, but she seemed to be constantly thinking, moving, and planning. Her intelligence was a huge part of his attraction to her. And her fearlessness. He wished he could be more like her—logical, decisive, and unconcerned about how people would react. He often put himself in the other person's frame of mind, and that could be confusing and counterproductive. But despite Bailey's unemotional nature, she also had an uncanny ability to anticipate his needs and moods. She was a mystery. He was falling in love.

The thought startled him. This was supposed to be a casual fling with a woman who would leave town in a few days or weeks, never to be seen again. *Infatuated* was a better word, he decided.

He grabbed his tablet and logged into Contra, his current favorite video game and the closest he would ever come to carrying a gun. But after a few minutes, guilt made him put it down and go back to his pharmacy list.

He still had twenty-six drugstores he hadn't contacted yet and another twelve follow-up calls to businesses that hadn't been open or had said to call back. Yesterday's effort had been cut short by a windstorm and a power outage, and he'd started late this morning. He was determined to finish today, leaving only the follow-up calls for the morning.

Just as he started to make a call, he heard an engine in the driveway. He got up and hurried to the window. His father was here. But why? Garrett's gut tightened. This had to be about his mother. *Please don't let it be bad.*

He opened the door, stepped back, and waited. A moment later, his father's massive body filled the frame.

"Garrett. Is everything all right?" His father looked surprised, but he stepped in.

"I'm fine. Any update on Mom?"

"No. I'm sorry. I just thought I'd see how you were doing. Maybe take you to lunch."

Garrett didn't invite him to sit or close the door. "Thanks, but I'm busy."

"Doing what?"

He couldn't tell him about the pharmacy calls for several reasons, and he wanted to get back to them. "Catching up on my class assignments. Maybe we'll go some other time. After we get Mom back."

"I hope you mean that. I'd like to spend more time with you."

"Sure." Garrett just wanted him to go.

His father slipped his hands into his pockets, not going anywhere. "Maybe we'll try bowling again. We used to enjoy that."

That was a long time ago. Before he'd lost his foot. His father had been out of town on assignment when it happened and hadn't visited him in the hospital. A decade-old anger surfaced. "Why now? Why not when I was a kid and needed you around?"

His father shook his head, his expression a little sad. "You didn't want to see me, remember? You were mad."

That was a lame excuse. "I was a teenager. You shouldn't have given up."

"You're right. I shouldn't have. But your mother put up barriers." They were both still standing in the foyer, and his father stepped toward him. "Let's put it behind us now."

"What barriers?"

"No matter when I called, she'd say you weren't home. When I offered to take you somewhere, she'd say you had plans."

Was that true? Why would his mother let him think his father didn't care enough to contact him? "Mom's not like that. You're exaggerating. And this is a bad time to be saying shit about her." Garrett reached for the edge of the door. "Please go. I'm busy."

His father looked crushed. "When we get your mother back, we'll all sit down and discuss this. She won't deny it if I'm there." He turned and walked out.

Garrett knew his father was telling the truth. He had many flaws, but he'd always been painfully honest. At the time, his mother had probably thought she was protecting him. But still, he felt betrayed. What else would he learn about his mother during this incident? He pushed it all out of his mind. First, he had to find her, then he could confront her. He sat down again and found his place on the list.

The day before, he'd worked his way through all the big cities in the western part of the state and started calling pharmacies in central Washington. In the cities, many drugstores were part of a larger grocery or retail business, and it had taken longer, often several transfers, to get connected to someone who could answer his questions. He'd been relieved when he reached businesses that only had one or two employees and he could get right to it.

He dialed the next number and waited.

"Rite Aid," a young woman chirped into his ear.

"This is Agent Bailey with the FBI. I'm working a kidnapping case, and I need to ask about a prescription that might have been picked up." He'd perfected his spiel to elicit the least amount of surprise and questions. Most of the clerks he talked to had been women, and they were happy to help him—but they were often inquisitive and chatty.

"A kidnapping? Here in Wenatchee?"

"No, but we think the victim might be in your area now. Has anyone new or unusual filled a prescription for Aptiom within the past few days? Or some other kind of anti-seizure medicine?"

"Oh goodness, the poor woman. What was the name of that medicine?"

"Aptiom. But there are about twenty anti-seizure medicines, and I'd like to know if you've filled a script for any of them."

"I'm not the pharmacist, and I can't keep all the drugs straight. Let me ask."

He overheard her conversation with another woman in the background and almost didn't wait for the clerk to return.

"I'm sorry, but we haven't. We have a regular customer who picked up her medicine early last week, but that's it."

"Thanks anyway. If someone new comes in and asks about anti-seizure medicine, will you please call me?" Garrett gave her the number of a cheap little phone Bailey had given him in case anyone called. So far, no one had.

He gulped some coffee while it was still hot and made another call.

"Decker's Pharmacy. How can I help you?" An older woman this time.

Garrett repeated his lines, sounding more deadpan and unhopeful than he intended.

"What are you asking?"

"Has anyone new or unexpected filled a prescription for Aptiom since last Thursday? Or some other kind of anti-seizure medicine?"

"The kidnap victim has epilepsy?" She sounded puzzled and worried.

"Yes, and if her abductors have picked up medicine for her, we need to know where."

"That is so odd. Just a minute, I have to deal with a customer, then take this call into the back." He sensed excitement in her tone. But he'd encountered that a lot. Pharmacy clerks didn't get many inquiries from the FBI. He'd stopped feeling guilty about the deception after the first five calls. He was Bailey's proxy.

The clerk put him on hold and was gone for five minutes. Garrett picked up his video game and shot a few bad guys while he waited.

"Sorry that took so long. Mr. Crane is damn near senile and I had to repeat everything." The clerk sounded a little rattled now.

"It's all right. Take your time." Garrett paused to let her collect herself. "Do you have any information that could help me?"

"I think I might." The woman pulled in a shallow breath. "We were robbed last night. I was here alone, and a man in a ski mask came in, waving a gun. Scared me half to death."

Garrett waited, a tingle running up his spine. *Don't get your hopes up*, he reminded himself. She might just be crazy or bored.

"The robber demanded OxyContin and Lyrica, which I thought was a little strange."

He knew oxy was a powerful pain medication that addicts sometimes burglarized pharmacies for, but he didn't know anything about the other drug. "What is Lyrica prescribed for?"

"Typically, it's used for rheumatoid arthritis and fibromyalgia. It calms nerve pain. But it was originally developed for seizures." She took another breath. "I've learned a few things about medication working here."

His hopes fizzled a little. The robber was probably an addict look-ing to get high. Still, it was the only lead he had. "The guy asked for the Lyrica by name?"

"Yes, and I didn't think we had any. He was insistent and helped look for it."

That didn't sound like an addict. Someone just wanting to get high would have been more interested in fentanyl or Valium or any number of other drugs. "Tell me what he looked like." Garrett glanced around for his scratch pad and found it on the floor. He snatched it up and scribbled notes as she talked.

"He was wearing a ski mask, so I don't really know. But he was about five-nine and thin. He wore all-black clothes, and his leather jacket looked expensive."

"Anything else you remember?"

"Not really. I was pretty scared."

"Did you file a police report?"

"Of course. My nephew is a patrol sergeant, so I called him."

"They didn't happen to arrest the guy, did they?"

"No." She seemed disappointed now. "By the time I had the nerve to get off the floor and go to the window, he was gone. I'm sorry. I hope you find that poor kidnapped woman."

That poor woman was his mother. "I think we will. Thank you!" Garrett hung up, eager to call Bailey and tell her the news. While her phone rang, he looked up the address of the pharmacy and found it in Ellensburg, a town right in the middle of the state.

CHAPTER 31

Sunday, March 22, 4:17 p.m., Washington, DC

As the door clicked shut, Bailey sprung into action. The North Korean officer might call the front desk to release her—or he might not. She wasn't going to sit idly, waiting to find out. She dropped to the floor on her side and curled into a ball. With her hands still behind her back, she worked the cuffs over her butt. Thank goodness she hadn't developed a midlife spread. Still, the damn sock in her mouth blocked her oxygen and made her jaw ache. She cursed Dukko for leaving it there.

Once she had her hands behind her legs, she felt even more trapped. She pulled up a knee and began the strenuous task of working her leg through the loop her body formed. Once it straightened out on the other side, she knew she was home free. The second leg was easier. When her hands were in front, she reached up and pulled the gag out. Although still bound together at the wrists, her fingers were functional, so she bent over and loosened the belt around her feet. Bailey rolled it up, walked over to her satchel, and shoved the belt inside. If she were contained in the trunk of a car or a shed in the middle of nowhere, her next step would be to find something—a string, a piece of wire—to saw against the plastic cuff until she cut through it and freed her hands. But fortunately, she didn't have to waste thirty minutes with that tedious effort.

She picked up the old-style phone and called the front desk. "This is Agent Bailey. I'm in room ten-ten, and I need you to send a bellman with a sharp knife or box cutter."

"Our bellmen are busy helping other guests with their luggage, so it could take twenty minutes."

"I've been handcuffed." Bailey searched for a plausible excuse. "As a training exercise. But I need help immediately. I also need the luggage I left at the desk earlier. So have someone bring it up too."

"Yes, ma'am."

She scrambled from her lotus position on the bed and opened every drawer in the room, just in case Dukko had left something behind. But he hadn't. Nor did she find anything in the bathroom that would cut through the plastic ties. Kneeling on the floor, she used her still-bound hands to rummage through the little trashcan. He hadn't been in the hotel long enough to leave anything but a used tissue and the plastic cover to a disposable razor. None of it mattered. She wasn't going to search for Dukko. She had other people to find. For now, she just had to wait for the bellman to show up.

She sat on the bed, shut down her mind, and tried to get into a meditative mode, like she'd had to do when she'd needed an MRI after a motorcycle accident. She'd experienced a lot of injuries in her first twenty-five years—the inevitable by-product of her impulsive and fearless nature. To relax, she let go of her thoughts and imagined herself lying in a meadow, surrounded by wildflowers, staring up at a blue sky, feeling the gentle warmth of the sun. Then a bear walked into her meadow looking for lunch.

Someone knocked on the door, and Bailey jumped up. Out of habit, she picked up her weapon from where Dukko had left it, but with her hands bound she wasn't able to put it back into its holster. The gun might startle the bellman if no one had warned him she was FBI. But it might save her life if Dukko or one of the kidnappers was on the other side of the door.

A giant young man in a blue blazer stepped inside. "Whoa!" He dropped her suitcase and held up his hands, still gripping something in his palm.

"Relax." Bailey laid the weapon on the bed. "Bring that box cutter over here." She held out her bound wrists.

After giving her a quick once-over, he stepped forward. "Who did this to you?"

"Another agent. It's part of our training. But he didn't know my luggage was still at the front desk."

The bellman grabbed the plastic cuffs with a giant hand. "Is this cheating?"

Bailey laughed. "The point is to get free, and there are no rules."

The young man cut carefully through the ties, then handed her the plastic pieces. "Good luck with your training."

"Thanks." She dug a ten-dollar bill out of her purse and handed it to him. "Please never mention this to anyone."

"No worries." He flashed a bright smile and left.

Even though she was desperate for a shower, she had to buy a ticket to Seattle first. Dukko had a twenty-minute head start, but she hadn't told him about Dana Thorpe's abduction, so he might be headed to San Jose. She still believed that a remote rural area in Washington State was logically the most likely place to serve as a hideaway. She made the call to the airline, then took a quick shower, wishing she could spend more time in the hot water. But her flight was leaving in seventy-three minutes, and she had to keep moving. Her badge would get her quickly through airport security, but it couldn't move traffic along.

When she was dressed, she called the front desk and asked them to arrange a cab. She wasn't a guest in the hotel, but who cared? Dukko had paid for the room and its services. What an odd man. She admired his loyalty to his country and his willingness to risk his own freedom to accomplish his goals. But assaulting her without first checking her ID had been reckless. Almost any other agent would have the bureau looking for him already. Bailey reasoned that Dukko was more beneficial in the field, where he would continue to search for the people who abducted Lee Nam—and might even find them. She believed Dukko when he said he would never call Kim Jong-un from a jail cell to stop the execution.

While she waited in the lobby for her cab, she checked her phone. Two missed calls—one from her father and one from Garrett. She called her father back, because he hadn't left a message.

"Hey, Andra. I thought I'd let you know I'm out of jail."

"Good to hear. Any update on the charges?"

"Nothing's changed, except I have a court date in two weeks to enter a plea."

"Are you going to fight it?"

He chuckled softly. "If you send me ten grand for a retainer. My lawyer won't take my case without it."

Because her dad was financially irresponsible, guilty as charged, and would be unsympathetic on the witness stand. "I can cash out some stocks and loan you the money, but I want you to get to anger management counseling."

He burst out laughing. After a moment, she laughed too. "Hey, you made me go."

"You were thirteen and still somewhat malleable. I wanted you to have a better life than I did."

He'd done all right for himself. Except for finances. And relationships. And controlling his temper. "You helped me a lot. Once I accepted the truth of what you were telling me about myself."

A long pause. Neither of them was good at small talk or sentimental reminiscence. "Are you dating anyone?" he finally asked.

"Sort of. It's probably temporary, but I've connected with him in a way I've never experienced." He would know what she meant.

"Then hang on to him for as long as you can. Or you'll end up alone, like me."

"We'll see." Thinking about Garrett made her want to check her message. "I have to get going, but I'll wire the money soon." She knew it was a waste of time, but she added, "And it's a loan. I expect you to pay it back."

"Of course. Thanks, Andra." Her father hung up.

Bailey called her voice mail, happy to hear Garrett's voice: "I have good news. I think. A pharmacy in Ellensburg was robbed last night. The thief asked for OxyContin and Lyrica. They're both pain meds, but Lyrica is also an anti-seizure medicine. Oh, and she described the robber as five-nine, thin, and dressed in all black. He also drove away in a truck. Call me when you can."

The intel was fascinating. OxyContin indicated an addict had committed the robbery. But the Lyrica was not a first choice for euphoria, and it was so specific that it had to serve some other purpose. She calculated that the chance of the pharmacy robbery being connected to Dana Thorpe's kidnapping was about fifty-fifty. She started to call Garrett back, but her cab arrived.

As the driver loaded her suitcase into the trunk, she directed him to Dulles Airport. Physically exhausted, she climbed into the vehicle, hoping to put her head back and rest for a moment. But first she googled *Ellensburg, Washington* on her phone and found it in the middle of the state. A further search revealed that north of it was mountainous terrain known for its past mining operations. The odds for the robbery-kidnapping connection jumped another 25 percent.

* * *

From his spot behind the coffee vendor, Dukko watched Agent Bailey walk to the cab. He heard her say "Dulles Airport" to the driver. She was leaving DC—after saying she'd been traveling to investigate previous kidnappings. Was she going back to her other cases? Or did she have a clue about Lee Nam's location? If government agents had taken him, Nam was probably still somewhere in the capital. But if this incident was really about device manufacturing, then getting Nam out of Washington, DC, would be a smart move for the kidnapper.

Dukko decided to follow Bailey. She seemed intelligent and determined. As soon as her cab pulled away, he ran to the curb and watched for another one. This city was so different from Pyongyang. Busier and louder, and the people were so diverse. Every size and color and race. At times, he felt overwhelmed. But he'd been chosen for the assignment because he knew English and had come to the States once before on a college trip. He spotted a yellow cab and threw his arm into the air.

A few minutes later, he was on his way. He looked up ahead for Bailey's taxi but didn't see it. He leaned toward the front seat. "My girlfriend just left in a cab, and I need to catch up with her. Can you hurry?"

The driver looked back at him and raised one eyebrow. "Have you seen the traffic here?"

"Please try. She is on her way to the airport and she left her—" Dukko tried to think of the word. "Wallet."

"Dulles or Ronald Reagan?"

"Dulles."

"That helps. But I need a hundred dollars up front for that fare."

He paid the driver and mentally counted his remaining cash. He could access more, but it would be complicated, and he didn't know where Agent Bailey was headed. America was a big country, and he'd heard that parts of it were still uncivilized. They still didn't see Bailey's cab on the expressway, but it didn't matter. He just had to figure out where she was going.

While his driver took him to the United terminal, Dukko pulled out his cell phone. She had mentioned Nick Bowman, a scientist who'd been kidnapped. He searched online and found that he lived in San Jose—or had. He'd also been murdered. Bailey obviously wasn't looking for a dead man. Who else had been kidnapped? Another search for missing scientists produced a news report about Dana Thorpe, who'd been taken from Seattle and was still missing. Should he buy a ticket and find Ms. Thorpe's house? Or would that waste his time and ultimately leave him stranded in this crazy country?

Without Lee Nam, he couldn't go home. He wasn't afraid to die, but torture or life in a prison camp intimidated him. Would the Dear Leader hurt his family to pressure him? Dukko knew the answer. Failure wasn't an option.

CHAPTER 32

Sunday, March 22, 1:35 p.m., Wanapum, Washington

Shawn paced the house, anxious about everything. He'd gone for a run and read through a pile of manufacturing reports, but nothing could take his mind off the situation he was in. Max's phone call the night before demanding that he deal with Rocky had him on edge. And now he had another captive to deal with. But at least Lee Nam wanted to be in hiding until he could establish new identification, so he was being cooperative and pleasant.

For the first time, he thought about what Dana Thorpe must be feeling. Obviously, what was happening to her was unpleasant. But he'd also created the perfect circumstances for her to excel and do something amazing in the advancement of technology. Her sacrifice would be worth it. He still wanted to let her go, but thinking through the potential consequences and scenarios created too much stress. Meanwhile, resisting the urge to watch her work or ask questions was challenging, but it was still best to minimize his contact and keep his identify unknown. He couldn't afford another Nick Bowman incident.

Yet there was Rocky to deal with. How many deaths would he be responsible for in pursuit of his goals? He was so ready to move past this phase of the plans.

His phone rang from the kitchen table and he ran to check the caller: *Max.* Shawn didn't pick up. His financial backer would ask if he'd dealt with Rocky yet, and he didn't want to talk about it. In his gut, he knew Max was right. If Rocky was ever arrested and charged— even years from now—he would tell them everything to cut a deal for himself. They couldn't leave that loose end.

Shawn took another of his focus pills, then went to the freezer, pulled out a bottle of cherry vodka, and took a gulp. Just enough to take the edge off.

"Are you drinking in the middle of the day?" Jia had come into the kitchen behind him.

"Just a sip. I'm bored and frustrated here."

"While I'm writing and testing code nonstop." Her eyes pinched in anger, then she softened again. "I'm sorry I haven't come through for you. I know you're up against the rollout deadline. Why don't you hire a real cryptographer?" She slumped her shoulders, defeated.

Shawn touched her arm. "You've done your best, and I'll get someone else on board." Lee Nam was already at work in the underground facility, so maybe it was time to send Jia home. One less risk of exposure.

"You don't have to stay." He pulled her in for a hug and stroked her hair. "I love your company, but there's no reason for both of us to be here in this godforsaken place. Especially now that Harlan and Rocky are here." They'd arrived with Lee Nam late the day before and were now staying at a motel in Wanapum, the nearby town.

"I told you I'd stay a week," Jia said. "I'm more worried about you than me."

"I'm fine."

Jia drew back and looked deep into his eyes. "There's something you're not telling me, but I know you will eventually." She kissed him and went back to her workspace near the window.

Shawn sat down to map out the timeline for rolling the new-generation phones off the production line. The encryption was the only real holdup now. Dana Thorpe claimed to be moments from producing a viable synthetic dysprosium. Shawn's phone rang again. This time it filled him with dread. He looked at the ID: *Uncle Tai*.

He had to take it. "What's going on?"

"The lady scientist knocked me down and tried to escape this morning. Now she's lying on her bed and won't get up. I don't know what to do."

Escape? Shawn leapt from his chair and hurried out to the porch so Jia wouldn't overhear. "How could she possibly escape?"

"Don't worry, she didn't get out. But she says she won't work anymore."

Goddammit! He'd robbed a fucking pharmacy to get her medication and now she was going to quit on him? The little bitch. He would have to handle this himself. "I'll be there in a bit." Shawn hung up, hands shaking. *Keep calm.* It could still all work out. Shawn stepped back into the house and headed for the vodka in the freezer.

"What's wrong?" Jia was behind him again.

He spun around and snapped, "Stop looking over my shoulder!"

His wife recoiled, lips trembling, but didn't walk away. "What's going on that has you so worried?"

"I'm sorry." He scrambled to tell her something plausible and partially truthful. "I'm having trouble recruiting the tech people I need to meet our deadline for the new phone rollout."

She cocked her head. "So push back the deadline. You haven't promised consumers anything yet."

But he had.

"Have you?" She crossed her arms.

"The media campaign kicked off two days ago. We have to condition the market." Shawn hated having to explain himself, but he owed it to Jia. "Yes, the shortage will drive a lot of consumers to us, especially since we're encouraging them to buy extra phones as a precaution against the future shortage. But people who love their iPhones and high-end Androids might still buy a used familiar product rather than switch."

"But in time, they'll have to come to us."

"Unless China starts exporting again, or Apple or another major player comes up with their own new production material. Our competitors aren't going down without a fight."

Arms crossed, Jia hugged herself.

"Don't worry. Maybe I'm just not offering enough salary to prospective employees. I'll go back to the financiers and see if they'll increase their equity." He was still surprised that Bowman had refused his initial offer. A half million dollars for a month's work? But the metallurgist hadn't wanted to give up the intellectual property rights to his discovery—or the public acknowledgment. Shawn wanted the credit for himself, so he understood that.

"I'll do my best to master the encryption code before the deadline." Jia gave him a worried smile and went back to work.

Shawn checked his pulse. Over eighty again. He took another sip of vodka and hurried to the bedroom closet to dig out the ski mask he'd worn during the robbery. He pulled on a light jacket, stuffed the mask in a pocket, and headed out to his truck. He would visit Dana Thorpe in person and convince her to get off her ass and get it done. If money didn't motivate her, he knew what would.

At the mine, he drove to the back and parked beside the bunkhouse. He didn't want to see the manager or deal with any production issues today. He especially didn't want to hear any complaints about working on Sunday. There wouldn't be any days off until the mine was producing at full capacity. He hurried inside the old wooden building and went straight back to the laundry room that contained the hidden trapdoor. After a glance around, he lifted the iron basin sink, stepped down onto a small landing, and yanked the trapdoor closed after him.

He pounded down the stairs, then hurried through the dark connecting tunnel, the cool air clinging to him, its dampness tangible. He hated being down here and had a flash of guilt for keeping the experts underground. But it was no worse than many other windowless labs and workspaces, and at least they didn't have emails or irritating coworkers to distract them. They weren't being abused, and in the end, he would reward them with cash. Once he'd worked through all that, Shawn's visceral response to the situation faded, and he was ready to do whatever was necessary to accomplish his goals.

At the door to the old bomb shelter, he pulled on his ski mask, unlocked the entrance, and stepped inside. The dark concrete interior was as suffocating as always. He remembered his excitement when he'd discovered it, but that had worn off. Shawn stopped at the first door, stuck a key in the lock, and braced for the unexpected. Dana Thorpe had assaulted Uncle Tai that morning in an attempt to escape. She might try again. He opened the door and waited. But from the hall, he could see the woman on her narrow cot. She was on her back, unmoving except for the shallow rise and fall of her chest.

Shawn stepped in and closed the door behind him. "Dana?"

She sat up, perhaps surprised by the sound of an unknown voice, then recoiled at the sight of him.

The ski mask. He'd simply meant to hide his face, but it would serve to intimidate her as well.

"Who are you?" Her voice held a note of resignation, and her face looked almost white against her dark hair.

"It doesn't matter. What matters is that you finish the work. You said the synthetic was only a few days from being ready. Why hold back? I'll let you go as soon as it's working."

"I can't let you have it. I don't trust you."

Taken aback, he sat down on a wooden stool, just out of her reach. "I just want to make electronics. What is there to trust?"

"The new compound is so much more than that. We both know that's why I'm here."

Shawn didn't know what she was talking about, but he couldn't admit it. "You have no choice. Do yourself and your son a favor. Get up and get to work."

Her eyes widened. "Leave my son out of this."

"I'd be happy to. But if you won't produce what I need, I'll bring your son here as motivation." What was he saying? Another kidnapping? The thought unnerved him. But they'd gotten away with all of them so far. Now the FBI was so focused on North Korea, probably no one was looking for him anymore. Even if they were, none of the Washington properties, including the mine, were directly in his name. A holding company within a holding company that was based in Mexico. Nearly impossible to trace back to him.

"No!" Dana Thorpe began to weep and lay down again.

He wanted her up and working. "Do you need anti-depressants?"

The scientist didn't respond.

Maybe he should bring her son here, just to invigorate her. "What do you need? Music? Lighting that mimics the sun?"

"Just let me go." She didn't move.

"I can't do that until the compound is ready and I have the data to reproduce it."

Dana was silent.

Her refusal to finish would really fuck up his plans. Rage reached into his chest and squeezed. "Get up!"

Still on her back, Dana flinched, then rolled away from him.

The little bitch. She didn't believe he would kidnap her son. She didn't understand the importance of what he was trying to accomplish. He would show her.

Shawn strode from the room, hands shaking as he struggled to lock the door. He needed to calm the fuck down. After a deep breath, he rushed to the lab, wanting to see the sample she'd created but claimed wasn't ready. On her workbench lay a thin two-inch strip of a silvery-green material that looked like water. He touched it and felt that it was solid. But then the color where his finger had pressed it started to change. That must be what Dana meant by "still a little unstable." All right, so she had to perfect the formula. And if that meant using her son, he would. He was too close to making it all happen the way he'd envisioned.

Shawn hurried back out of the lab. As he climbed the stairs to the bunkhouse, he remembered the call from Max. *Oh fuck,* he had to deal with Rocky too. What if he combined those things? He could take Rocky with him to kidnap Dana Thorpe's son. They already knew where to find Garrett. Only this time, Rocky would get shot during the abduction, and Shawn would protect all of them by dumping his body. Harlan would buy that, wouldn't he?

Dana Thorpe would get back to work when she knew her son's life was at stake.

CHAPTER 33

Monday, March 23, 8:15 a.m., Denver, Colorado

Bailey found a row of empty seats at a quiet gate and plopped down. She plugged in her laptop, got online, and searched for Ellensburg again. Her two-hour layover had turned into a six-hour layover because she'd missed her connection after her first flight had been delayed. She'd already had a meal, taken a walk, and napped for a few minutes. Frustration wouldn't get her to Seattle any faster, so she might as well get some work done.

She read for an hour, learning everything she could about the area, but nothing helped her pinpoint a location where a megalomaniac might keep people captive—while also possibly providing them with research space. Milton Thurgood was either long dead or voluntarily employed. Dana Thorpe might have already shared her research data and been eliminated as well. But Lee Nam, the cryptographer, was probably still alive, coding as fast as he could with a figurative gun to his head. But even if he was dead, she still needed to find the kidnapper and provide evidence that her government hadn't been responsible for Lee's abduction and death. Kim Jong-un's deadline was only thirty-six hours away, and on every TV screen she saw, the media had an expert yammering about Jake Austin's impending execution, with some neocons using it as an excuse to pound the war drums, saying that a nonresponse would be a "show of weakness."

Her phone rang, and she hesitated. It was probably Garrett. She hadn't returned his call yet and she wasn't sure why. But it could be her boss too, so she checked the screen. A Washington State number she didn't recognize. "Agent Bailey."

"This is Nolan Fredrick from the Washington State business licensing office."

Finally! "I hope you have information for me."

"I do. I worked through the weekend to pull together a list of recent real-estate transactions in the three categories you specified. I just emailed you a file with the complete list."

"Thank you."

"I summarized my findings in the email, but I wanted to call and share the critical transactions with you in person."

Great. She waited.

"There are two that seemed significant. Two months ago, a radio manufacturing company called WireWorks sold to Everett Digital Enterprises, and last September, the Palisades Mine sold to a company called JCC Holdings."

Both gave her a jolt of hope. "Where are they located?"

"The radio factory is in Yakima, and the mine, which had been shut down for years, is also in central Washington, near Wanapum."

Google Maps was up on her laptop's screen. Both locations were within easy driving distance from Ellensburg. "What do you know about the buyers? Are those two companies connected?"

"Not as far as I can tell, based on the paperwork filed."

"What else can you tell me about the company that bought the mine?"

"It's owned by another holding company, C&M Investments, based in Mexico. So I don't have access to the owner's name."

Damn! "I may call back with more questions." Eager to extend her research, Bailey hung up.

The holding companies didn't surface in any online search. The owners wanted to remain anonymous. She called Havi. "It's Bailey. I need your help again."

"Hello. What can I do for you?"

His tone confused her, but she didn't have time to process it. "I need to find out everything I can about JCC Holdings and also C&M Investments, which is based in Mexico. I've searched online, but nothing comes up."

"I'll see what I can do, but this may require a call to the Mexican government."

Oh hell. "That could take too long."

"Let's see what I can find. Where are you, by the way?"

"The Denver airport, waiting for a connecting flight."

"Do you have a new lead?"

She hesitated, her secretive nature kicking in. "Only the companies I just mentioned."

"Lennard thinks you're taking some time off."

"I am." She gave him a plausible line in case he was forced to reveal her whereabouts. "I enjoyed Washington State so much when I was there, I'm going back to spend a few vacation days."

"Right. Talk to you soon."

Bailey stood and stretched, glancing around the airport terminal. It was still the cool season, but she noticed that people west of the Rockies wore a lot more color than those back east, where airports in the winter were a sea of black coats. In her scan, she also noted Asian men, but none were Dukko. She'd thought another cab might be following hers on the way to the airport, but once they were on the freeway, it seemed to disappear behind them. Still, she'd kept a vigilant watch. The bastard had gotten a jump on her once and tied her up like a trussed turkey. *Humiliating!* That was as close as she ever came to feeling shame or regret. But it wouldn't happen again. They both wanted to find the kidnapper, but she would beat him to it. Giving him one of the victim's names had bought her his trust and maybe her life. If Dukko was a sociopath, which he almost had to be to carry out KJU's directives, killing her might have been an easy choice for him. The fact that he hadn't done it meant she was more beneficial to him alive. So he might have tried to follow her.

Bailey spotted another woman eyeing her seat near the electrical outlet, so she plopped back down. She spent a few minutes online trying to find a Northwest-based device manufacturer she could have missed in her earlier efforts. Either of the CEOs she'd questioned in Silicon Valley could have sent hired thugs to kidnap Dana Thorpe and Lee Nam, but she was more convinced than ever that it was a Washington State–based operation. Someone had to be watching and feeding the victims—if any were still alive—while Lee Nam was snatched in DC. Plus, someone had committed the pharmacy robbery in Ellensburg in the same time frame.

Her phone buzzed in her ear. It was Havi, calling back. "Sorry, but I couldn't access anything on either of the holding companies. No website, no public corporate meetings, no SEC filings."

"Well, damn. There has to be some paperwork filed somewhere."

"Yes, but it's not public. And if C&M is based in Mexico, good luck with that office."

Unacceptable! "Can you hack into it?"

A pause. "Yes, but no."

That meant he had the skills but didn't want to take the risk. She'd done a little hacking, which sometimes was as simple as sending an email with malware that copied and sent the person's password the next time they used it. "Can you walk me through it?"

"Yes, but let's do this on my private cell phone. I'll call you back."

A tremor of excitement rippled through her body, erasing the exhaustion she'd been struggling with. She loved breaking rules and going anywhere she didn't belong. Plus she was moments away from finding out who was responsible for the kidnappings. Or hours away. Or days. Depending on what kind of hack they used. Bailey glanced at her phone. She still had plenty of time before her flight.

Havi didn't call back for ten long minutes and sounded a little rattled when he did. "I emailed you a file with some code to embed, along with the name and address of someone at the Mexican business registry. The message is coming from a private account. You remember how to embed the code?"

"Yes." They'd done this before. Havi was a rule breaker too. Many in law enforcement were. That was part of the draw. The power to break rules and get away with it. "Anything else I need to know?"

"When you get the password, use all caps, no matter what it looks like. Then get in and out quickly." He talked rapidly in a barely audible whisper. "I don't think the site has much security, but it will recognize that the user is logging in from a different computer. If you do something unexpected, the system may shut you out after a few minutes."

"Why do you sound nervous? Is someone standing nearby?"

"The AD is on the warpath."

"What's going on?"

"I don't know yet."

"Keep me posted."

Abruptly, Havi hung up. Bailey's off-the-books mission now felt riskier. If she failed to find any of the victims or to arrest the unsub, she could end up getting canned. But only if she used her FBI credentials when she was supposedly off duty. *Screw that.* She would use every resource she had and not stop until she succeeded. She was too close now to give up.

Bailey checked her little-used dummy Yahoo account and found the email with Havi's code. She couldn't use her own laptop, so she left her spot by the window and backtracked through the airport to an alcove where two public computers were available. A young woman using one of them ignored her until Bailey flashed her badge and asked her to vacate. The girl wasn't happy about it but she complied.

Bailey shoved her luggage against the wall and sat down at the little desk. She opened her Yahoo account and created an email addressed to the manager in the Mexican government's business registry. Embedding the malware took a few tries, because she hadn't done it in a while. After reading over the message a few times and double-checking her work, Bailey clicked Send. *Please let the woman be working today and open her email.* Once Bailey discovered who owned C&M or JCC, she could locate every property he or she was connected to. The one closest to the pharmacy would be the first place she would search.

CHAPTER 34

Monday, March 23, 8:05 a.m., Seattle, Washington

Garrett woke suddenly and checked his phone on the nightstand. He hadn't overslept, and there was no message or text from Bailey. Was she stuck on the tarmac somewhere? Or maybe just busy working the case. Still, he'd expected her to call back after getting his voice mail about the pharmacy in Ellensburg. Maybe she hadn't received it. Should he call again? He didn't want to seem obsessive. A terrifying thought hit him. What if the kidnappers had tried to kill Bailey again? A surge of panic drove him out of bed. Because she was traveling, she was probably safe, he reasoned. They couldn't get to her unless she came back to Seattle, to this house. Maybe when she finally returned, they should both go stay in a hotel.

He headed for the shower, thinking about the day ahead. Maybe it was time to get his life back to some kind of normalcy. Bailey had encouraged him to keep up with his university assignments. But it felt so wrong to just go about his life with his mother missing. Yet, as a university professor, she would want him to attend class, rather than sit at home worrying. But he couldn't go to campus yet. Even though he wasn't ready to focus on his studies, he had another obligation he could meet if he got moving right now.

Garrett dressed, stuffed his phone and wallet into his pockets, and headed out. He had just enough time to make his Monday morning shift at the St. Paul Kitchen where he volunteered, usually peeling vegetables or loading canned goods into boxes. Two hours a week wasn't much, but he'd been doing volunteer work since he was a kid, and would feel better if he didn't miss his shift.

The drive over took only ten minutes, and the woman who ran the kitchen greeted him with a hug. "Any word on your mom?"

"Not yet." They walked back to the food-prep area.

"You don't have to be here, but I'm glad you are." She patted his shoulder.

"If I get a call, I may have to leave early."

"No problem. A high school group will be here in an hour, so you can take off then."

Relieved for the short shift, he picked up a plastic apron and got to work.

On the way home, he bought coffee and a bagel, and checked his phone again. His father had left a voice mail: "Want to join us for dinner tonight? It would be good for you to get out of the house." He hated when his dad announced what was good for him, but still, the offer made him smile.

Garrett pulled into the driveway and parked on the far right out of habit. His mother kept her car in the garage, and she needed to be able to back out past his. There was room for both vehicles inside, but he never parked in there. Even with the covered walkway between the buildings, it was too much hassle. His mother's little car was just sitting in there, waiting for her to come home. He hurried up the wide front steps, picked up the newspaper from the porch, and went inside.

The faint smell of cigarette smoke surprised him. A rush of movement from the living area made him spin left. A stocky man in a ski mask shoved a hand in his face. Garrett ducked and swung wildly, clipping the attacker on the chin. The contact hurt, but it was nothing like the blow to his own nose that followed. The pain vibrated into his eye sockets, and he shouted a curse. Someone gripped his elbows from behind as blood ran from his nostrils. The first man shoved a rag over his mouth, and the medicinal smell made him gag. Dizziness overcame him, and his body went limp.

CHAPTER 35

The young man collapsed like dead weight, and Shawn couldn't hold him up. Now Garrett was sprawled on the floor.

"Not the plan!" Rocky squatted, obviously irritated. "You only had to keep him upright for a few seconds while I got into place."

Shawn squatted too. "Let's just do this quickly." He put both hands under one of Garrett's armpits.

Rocky did the same. "Ready? Lift!"

They stood up together, then scrambled to get their arms around the young man's shoulders and waist—before they dropped him again. Garrett's head lolled sideways on Shawn's shoulder, blood dripping from his nose.

"Why did you punch him?" Shawn said. "I've got his blood on my jacket now."

"Reflex. He hit me first." Rocky steered through the archway and into the kitchen.

They were headed out to the garage, where their van was parked. So far, the abduction was going more smoothly than Shawn had expected. They'd watched Garrett drive away earlier and discussed following him. Rocky had wanted to see where the kid was going and watch for a more secluded spot to make the grab. But Shawn had felt certain Garrett wouldn't be gone long and that their original plan was still the safest. Rocky's universal remote had opened the garage, and they'd driven in and closed it again. The neighbors' line of sight was blocked by tall hedges on either side of the property, and the park directly across the street was empty this early on a Monday morning, so it seemed likely no one had seen them enter. Shawn had bought the used vehicle that morning with cash, so it wasn't registered to him, and he could easily abandon it if things went badly. He would dump it after the mission anyway.

Inside the house, they had simply waited for the young man to return, then chloroformed him when he walked in. Now they had to get him into the van and secure him before he regained consciousness. Then get the hell out of the garage before anyone else showed up. Max's informant at the bureau had assured him the local field agents had left the Thorpes' home days before and that Agent Bailey had returned to DC. So they should be fine. Still, he was eager to be outside the city and on the road east.

Rocky opened the side door, and they lifted their cargo as far into the space as they could reach. Shawn climbed in over the unconscious man and dragged him the rest of the way in. Rocky wrapped rope around Garrett's legs and a bandanna around his eyes, while Shawn tied their captive's hands behind his back and duct-taped his mouth, looping it around his head to be sure.

Seeing the young man trussed like that overwhelmed him for a moment. Disgust with the victim for being so easily overpowered. Disgust with himself for participating in such lowlife activities. Then a brief moment of pity for Garrett, who would be terrified when he woke up. But still, he was proud of himself for having the courage to pull it off. He'd come a long way from the timid, nerdy kid who'd been picked on in grade school. He'd proved to himself he wasn't too effeminate for the dirty work. Too bad he couldn't brag about it to the people who'd doubted his toughness over the years, especially his cousins who'd laughed when he'd run from dogs and school bullies.

"Do we need to tie a rope between his ankles and hands?" Shawn asked.

"I don't think so. Let's go."

Shawn scooted into the driver's seat, and Rocky came around the van and got into the passenger's side. Shawn clicked the universal door opener. Nothing happened. "What the hell?" He clicked it again with the same result.

"It should open manually too." Rocky looked back at the closed garage door.

"Go find out. And look in the other car for the owner's door opener." The setback was annoying, but would be temporary. If necessary, he would gun the engine and bust right through the wooden door.

As Rocky searched for a manual lever, Shawn kept clicking. Suddenly, the door began to rise. Rocky rushed back and jumped into the passenger's seat. Shawn put the van in reverse and pressed the gas, almost hitting the car parked in the driveway behind him. "Shit!" He slammed on the brakes and took a moment to collect himself. He hoped no neighbors had heard the squeal.

He backed around the Jeep and into the street. No one was watching them, and no police cars were coming their way. He pulled off his ski mask and drove out of the neighborhood, making turns every two blocks to cover his tracks. A few minutes later, he hit the main artery and headed out of town.

On the drive east, Rocky asked, "What happens to the kid when it's over?"

Shawn had given it some thought. "After I use him to motivate his mother, I'll let him go. As long as he never sees any of our faces or knows where he is, this shouldn't come back to bite us."

"I don't know about that." Rocky gave a slow shake of his head. "I think he'll be trouble. More so than the woman. You might want to rethink leaving any of them as loose ends."

Shawn knew he was right but couldn't face that. More important, the pilot had just given him permission to do this ugly but necessary thing. He would apply Rocky's advice to Rocky first. "I'll think about it."

"What about the woman? Is she going to produce the material?"

"I think so."

"How long?"

"Three more days." Shawn felt confident Dana would soon hand over a usable sample and formula that his engineers could replicate and scale up. Just knowing he had Garrett and might hurt him would motivate her. When it was over, he would drop Dana and her kid off at the edge of Seattle somewhere, leaving them blindfolded.

They were on I-90, surrounded by fields that turned to forests in the distance. Shawn watched for a side road to turn down.

"What happens with the North Korean?" Rocky asked.

Shawn laughed. "I'll think I'll adopt him."

He was keeping Nam in a separate basement room, because the coder didn't need any lab equipment and Shawn didn't want him to know about the others. Nam didn't seem to mind his predicament and had offered to trade his skills for new identification and a real job somewhere. He wanted to defect and start over in the United States. Once the others were gone, Shawn would work something out with Lee Nam.

The road climbed slowly, and the fields disappeared entirely. An occasional orchard appeared between thickets of oak and pine, then the fruit trees phased out. Garrett had woken up in the back, so they'd had to stop talking. Rocky put on earphones to listen to music, and Shawn was glad for that. He needed some emotional distance to get this done. He'd already been through the guilt phase, then Rocky had given him permission, so Shawn felt calm and ready. He glanced over his shoulder at their passenger. He'd shifted positions again, but didn't seem to be making any moves to free himself.

Shawn spotted a turnoff, then passed it, because it had sign markers indicating camping spots. Five miles later, another side road appeared. He slowed and made the exit.

"Piss stop?" Rocky asked.

"Yep." After a short uphill drive, Shawn pulled off onto a dirt road and coasted a hundred yards into the woods. He turned off the engine and touched the gun under his jacket. He'd never fired it at a person before. He climbed out and looked over at Rocky. "You coming?"

"I'm good."

Shawn walked up the road a few feet into the trees and relieved himself. It was even better to shoot Rocky in the car. He wanted his blood on the seat so Harlan would believe that he'd carried Rocky to the car after the kid had shot him during the kidnapping. He had his story all worked out. He would say he planned to drive Rocky to a hospital, but then he died very quickly. Then he'd wanted to bring him back to the property near the mine so they could have a service and bury him, but the risk had been too great. What if they got stopped? Or one of the miners spotted the grave? No, he'd had to dump him in the woods, and it broke his heart. Harlan would buy that. He would tell Jia something else entirely.

Shawn zipped his pants and walked back to the van. As he neared, he moved toward Rocky's side, smiling as if he had something funny to share. When he was near parallel with the door, he slid the gun out and clicked off the safety, keeping his movements below Rocky's line of sight through the truck window. With his free hand, Shawn gestured for him to step out of the truck. "Hey, you've got to see this." Would Rocky see how hard his heart was pounding?

Shawn hesitated. He hadn't known Rocky long and didn't have a real emotional connection to him. But still, to shoot a man at close range. He had no choice. His financier thought it was necessary to protect them all. Rocky would understand that.

The pilot looked annoyed, but opened the door and started to climb out. "What is it?"

He hadn't thought that through. "Some kind of animal bones. Maybe a mountain lion." Shawn nodded toward the trees where he'd just been and took a step back, hoping to keep the blood off his clothes.

Rocky closed the truck door. "I've seen it all, but I decided to piss anyway." He looked up at Shawn, noticing the gun.

Shawn swung it into position and fired two shots into Rocky's chest. His mouth opened to speak, but only blood came out. Rocky staggered forward two steps, then collapsed.

Good god. He'd just taken a man's life. Before he could get overwhelmed, Shawn locked his emotions away, sending them deep into the vault. It was all for the best. Rocky didn't want to end up in jail, and Shawn's own plans were too important to sacrifice. He looked past the dead man at Garrett in the back of the van. The kid had rolled up against the side and was shaking. At least he would take him seriously now and make his mother do her job.

Shawn knew he should drag the body into the woods, but he couldn't bring himself to do it. With one hand, he smeared some of Rocky's blood on the passenger seat so Harlan would see it. After that, he would clean it up, then dump the vehicle somewhere. Before leaving, Shawn bent down and closed the man's eyes, relieved it was over.

CHAPTER 36

Monday, March 23, 12:17 p.m., Seattle, Washington

The plane touched down, and Bailey woke from a restless sleep. She was finally back in Washington State! This investigation had pushed her to her limits. Traveling wasn't as much fun as it used to be. It was time to do whatever it took to get the promotion to run the Critical Incident Response Group. It was the only position that would give her the constant excitement she craved without forcing her to travel or do undercover work. She wanted to be on the SWAT team but was too lazy to do the training. Resolving the North Korean incident would put her in the running if Lennard moved up, but she also had to make a connection soon with the assistant director, or maybe even the director.

By the time she rented a car and got on the road, she'd worked out a plan to ingratiate herself with the AD and make him see her as the only logical choice for the CIRG position. She considered, briefly, staying in a hotel for the professionalism of it, then laughed at the idea. Garrett Thorpe was a possible victim who needed protecting, so staying there was the right thing to do. Fortunately, it suited her personally too. She wanted more time with Garrett and had no reason to deny herself the pleasure. He was an adult who made his own decisions. It wasn't her responsibility to protect him from emotional harm. Yet the thought of hurting him when she walked away made her uncomfortable—a new experience.

When she pulled into the Thorpes' driveway and parked behind Garrett's Jeep, she noticed the garage door was open. That was odd. The garage had never been open before. Garrett parked in the driveway, and Dana Thorpe wasn't here to drive her car. A bad vibe rolled up her spine. Bailey jumped out of the rental and ran into the garage. Nothing seemed out of place. She stepped toward the covered walkway leading into the house. Was that a drop of blood on the cement floor? Bailey knelt down and looked more closely. *Maybe*. The dab of dark liquid had mostly dried, so it was hard to tell.

If it was blood, Garrett had likely hurt himself in the garage and gone into the house to get a bandage. That would explain why the overhead door had been left open. Occam's razor. The simplest explanation was likely true. She hurried into the house anyway, watching for more blood, just in case she was dealing with a crime scene. She spotted another drop in the kitchen, a dark spot on an otherwise clean white-tile floor. Bailey took a picture with her phone to preserve the record. Where was Garrett? He must have heard her come in.

"Garrett!" She called his name as she trotted from room to room, looking for him.

He was gone. But his Jeep was in the driveway. She repressed a shiver of panic, forcing herself to work through it logically. There was blood, but very little, so he hadn't been shot or stabbed. There was no sign of a struggle, so maybe he'd only scratched himself or had a nose-bleed. He could have left with a friend or gone out for a walk. But why was the garage door open? She called his phone, and after seven rings, heard his voice mail greeting. Bailey hung up, not knowing where he might be receiving the call and not willing to leave her name.

Had the kidnappers taken him? Considering the previous events and his mother's circumstances, she calculated the odds were pretty high, maybe 70 percent. But why? Garrett wasn't a scientist or a tech expert. He was only useful to them as leverage. A way to make Dana Thorpe do what they wanted. *Oh hell.* Anger and worry settled in her heart, and indecision bounced around in her head. The anxiety was annoying, so she focused on making a decision. She had a solid lead for the general area where she might find all the victims, and she might as well drive there now.

Without any proof a crime had been committed, there was no point in reporting Garrett missing to the Seattle police. A young man could have simply left his house on foot, accidentally leaving the garage door open. But she had obligations to the bureau, and those were a little stickier. Reporting the incident directly to her boss wasn't an option. She'd been ordered to discontinue her investigation and let the local field agents handle the kidnappings.

She would hedge her bets and split the decision down the middle. Bailey grabbed two bottles of water from the fridge and a box of crackers from the cupboard, saving herself a stop at a store. She hurried back out through the garage, leaving the front door locked and the garage door open, as she'd found both.

Once she'd made it through Seattle's traffic and was on I-90 headed southeast, she called Agent Thorpe. "Bailey here. I was just at your son's home. The garage door was open and Garrett was gone, but his Jeep is still in the driveway. I thought you'd like to know."

"You don't sound worried."

She rarely did. "I called Garrett and he didn't answer. There's a drop of blood, but no sign of a struggle, so I'm not sure what to think." No longer true.

"I'll head over there now. Let me know if anything develops."

"I'm on my way to central Washington. I have an idea about where Dana might be held, and I'm following up on it."

"What lead?"

Bailey told him about the pharmacy robbery in Ellensburg and the sale of the Palisades Mine. "It just came together for me today."

"What does a drugstore have to do with this case?"

He didn't know about his ex-wife's epilepsy, and she wasn't supposed to tell him. "Dana needs medication, and I think the kidnapper was getting it for her."

Thorpe hesitated, then scoffed. "That's pretty tenuous."

"I know. That's why I'm not asking any local agents to spend their time on it until I know more."

"When you have something solid, call me. I can be in that area in ninety minutes. Don't go in without backup."

"I won't." Unless she had to. There was no reason for him to know she wasn't technically assigned to the case anymore. "If you hear from Garrett, let me know." She hung up before he could ask questions she would have to lie about.

On the drive to Ellensburg, it rained steadily, and she hated every dark and dreary minute. The crackers kept her stomach from growling, and she checked her Yahoo email on her phone every ten minutes, hoping to find a bounce-back message from the malware email to the Mexican business registry. Once that came in, she would stop and find a public computer—if there was such a thing out here in the sticks.

The farther she drove, the more rural the landscape and the more she worried about internet access. Even through the rain, she could see the forests thin out and become scrubbier. The undergrowth changed too, from lush ferns to ugly little bushes. Once she was over the Cascades, the clouds parted and the rain stopped. Thank god. As the sun peeked through, she got her first decent look at the midstate landscape. A wide, flat plateau, with patches of desert pine trees and more mountains in the distance. The occasional house appeared along the frontage road, often with a truck parked in front. It was a habit to notice details and take mental pictures of everything, but she could barely concentrate on her surroundings. She called Garrett again, but still no response. She couldn't help but think he was out there in the mountains somewhere, locked in some shitty space, maybe being tortured occasionally to frighten his mother into working faster or revealing more.

Bailey shook it off. If that was what empathy felt like, she was glad she didn't experience it with anyone else. Besides, he'd only disappeared that morning, so she was right behind the kidnappers. She only hoped she didn't regret driving out here before she had all the information she needed. If she couldn't access the internet, she could call Havi. Bailey noticed a sign announcing that Ellensburg was only ten miles away. She would stop for coffee and, hopefully, a little hacking.

A few minutes later, she drove into Ellensburg, a quaint mix of old brick buildings and newly built franchise eateries, with a river bisecting the town. She used her phone to find a Starbucks and was soon in line for coffee and wifi—the lifeblood of a field agent.

At a corner table, while she waited for her grande Italian roast to cool, she checked her Yahoo email. The bounce back from the malware had landed. *Yes!* But she couldn't open it on her own laptop or do any snooping from here. That could come back to bite her. She needed another public-access computer. A library. She asked for directions and found it five blocks away, with only one wrong turn.

An older building with a musty smell, the library was nearly empty and she had the tiny technology room to herself. Bailey signed into her Yahoo account and opened the bounce-back email, which contained the password *Octavius91703*. Probably the birthday of the clerk's son. The email included a link, which she clicked, and it took her to the business registry database. A dialogue box appeared, and she logged in with the hacked password. Depending on the level of security employed by the

Mexican government, she might get frozen out immediately because the system didn't recognize the computer or she might only have a few minutes before it demanded she answer some security questions.

From the landing page, she clicked *Foreign Corporations*, then keyed *C&M Investments* into the search bar. A single page loaded with basic information in rectangular fields. The owner was listed as Jia Chen. Who the hell was she? Bailey's grip tightened around her coffee cup. She'd been so sure she would find one of the executives of the startup phone companies. She googled the name *Jia Chen* and came up with only a few sites and images, none of which seemed connected to her investigation. Was the name an alias? Jia, or someone, had gone to considerable trouble to mask the purchase of the mining company. But why? Antitrust laws? Or was he or she hiding something at the property and didn't want to be associated with it on paper?

Havi didn't answer when she called, so Bailey sent him a text: *Find a Jia Chen connected to this case. Criminal record? Marriage license? Anything!*

She scanned back through her call log and reconnected with the number from the state business office.

"Nolan Fredrick. How can I help you?"

"Agent Bailey again." She kept her voice down, not wanting to draw the attention of the librarian on duty. "I found the owner of the holding company. Jia Chen." She spelled out both names. "Does she own any other businesses in Washington?"

"Give me a minute to search."

Bailey finished her coffee while she waited, and the acid burned in her stomach. She needed real food, and soon.

"Sorry," Fredrick said, "but she doesn't."

"What about personal property?"

"I'll have to get into the property tax files, and that could take a minute. Can I call you back?"

"Please do."

Nervous that her lead could turn out to be a dead end, Bailey kept busy while she waited. She clicked on the first Google result for *Jia Chen* and discovered she was a prolific porn actress. Bailey quickly closed the site and opened the next one, a Facebook page for a student at a Florida university. Bailey's phone rang and she clicked her earpiece to silence it. "Havi?"

"Of course."

"What did you find?"

"The most famous Jia Chen is a porn star with a specialty in bestiality."

She ignored his amusement. "Yeah, I discovered that. Any others who might be connected to metallurgists or device manufacturers?"

"I found a marriage license for Jia Chen and Shawn Crusher. Now she goes by Jia Crusher but uses the same social security number."

Score! "That's it. Thank you."

"What's the connection to the kidnappings?"

"Shawn Crusher is the CEO of ZoGo, a burner phone manufacturer based in Mountain View, California."

A pause while Havi processed it. "Does the mine produce the rare earth metals he needs?"

"Probably. Or at least he believes it will. Can you find out where Shawn Crusher is? Maybe track his credit cards or cell phone?"

"You know you need a warrant for that."

She wasn't on the case and couldn't produce one. "We don't have time. I just need a general location."

Havi sighed. "I'll try. But the AD has me looking for safe houses where the North Korean cryptographer might be staying. That has to be my priority."

"I think Crusher has Lee Nam too, so helping me is just as critical."

A moment of silence. "You're seldom wrong, so I'll toggle back and forth."

"Thank you!"

She hung up and called the manager at the state business licensing office. "Hey, Bailey again. I just discovered that Jia Chen also goes by Jia Crusher, so please look for any personal property she might own."

"I have a meeting in a few minutes, so I'll get back to you." He abruptly hung up.

Had she pissed him off or was he just busy? It didn't matter. She had to find the Palisades Mine and covertly check it out. If the property had a building that could be used to house people, she figured it had an 80-percent chance of being the location of the victims.

Logistic and legal questions came to mind. Would she call Agent Thorpe for backup? Did they need a search warrant to go in? What were the consequences if she or they didn't find the victims on the property? Bailey would work around whatever was thrown at her—she always did. But what about Dana and Garrett Thorpe? She couldn't fail them. She'd connected with Garrett in a way she'd never experienced before, and she wanted to see how it played out. Not to mention that Dana and Garrett were good people and she wanted them to be alive in this world. After seeing the body of Nick Bowman, she knew their survival odds decreased rapidly every day. Maybe every hour.

The clock was ticking on Lee Nam and Jake Austin too. As a North Korean prisoner, Austin was probably doomed. The actor was an idiot for traveling there, regardless of his motives. On the other hand, Lee would probably survive the longest of the megalomaniac's captives. But if they couldn't find him in time, or convince North Korea that the US government wasn't responsible, what would Kim Jong-un do next? Bailey checked the time on her phone. How many hours did they have left?

CHAPTER 37

Monday, March 23, 12:55 p.m., Washington, DC

Jocelyn wiped the sweat from her forehead, put on her jacket, and headed out of the studio. Salsa dancing during her lunch hour three days a week was a new routine, but so far, she loved it. And she'd lost five pounds. If only she could stick with it. Her job would get in the way eventually, though. A noon meeting, a lead that had to be followed up immediately, or simply getting behind on paperwork. They could all sabotage her efforts. But she was determined to not let a single slipup derail the whole effort.

In her car, she changed back into her sensible black work shoes and checked her hair in the mirror. Not that anyone else could tell the difference between her good hair days and bad ones. She opened a granola bar and pulled out into traffic, hoping she'd given herself enough time. After five calls over the weekend, she'd finally connected with Zach Dimizaro's roommate and set up an interview with him for this afternoon. She didn't want to be late and give him an excuse to blow her off.

* * *

At the Georgetown apartment, she pounded on the door, trying to be heard over the music playing inside. At least it was classic rock and not something that made her want to scream. Finally, she pushed open the door and yelled, "Detective Larson, DC police!"

A twenty-something man jumped up from the couch as if he'd been hit with a cattle prod. He reached for the laptop he'd just shoved aside and clicked off whatever he'd been watching or listening to. "Jesus, you scared me."

"Sorry. You're Noah Cramer?"

He nodded.

"We have a meeting scheduled, remember?"

He cocked his head, then laughed. "Actually, I'd forgotten."

Sheesh! Did anyone under thirty respect the police anymore? "Can we sit down at the table? I have some questions for you."

"Sure." Cramer shuffled toward the small dining area, his body even shorter and thicker than hers.

"Do you work in technology too?" She followed him and sat down.

"Of course. I'm an app designer with Zion. That's where I met Zach."

"How long have you known him?"

"Three years." Cramer's expression shifted, and his voice got quiet. "I can't believe Zach's dead."

Time for the main event. "Where were you Sunday night, March fifteenth, between six and eight p.m.?"

Cramer's mouth dropped open. "Are you kidding me? You think I killed Zach?"

"It's certainly possible. Where were you?"

The roommate rolled his eyes. "No, it's not possible. I've never hurt anyone. I don't even like to kill bugs." He pulled a cell phone from his pocket. "But I'll check my calendar."

Jocelyn suspected the gesture was staged. She'd searched Zach's bedroom two days ago with the manager standing by. The apartment held a collection of mismatched furniture, minimal cookware, and some action-movie posters. No women lived or visited here, and Cramer probably didn't have much of a social life.

"I had dinner with my parents that night," he said after a minute. "I was there from five thirty to eight thirty or so."

Jocelyn asked for their contact information, then moved on. She would circle back to his possible involvement after she checked the alibi. "Did you see Zach Sunday?"

"Yeah, we were both here for the afternoon, then left around five. We've been working overtime for months."

"Did Zach mention where he was going or who he was meeting?"

"He said he was having a drink with a potential investor."

Someone connected to the chip? "What investor?"

"I think Zach referred to him as Max, but I don't know his last name."

Jocelyn wrote it down. Her first real lead . . . and it wasn't much. "What kind of business deal did Zach have going?"

"He wanted to start his own app business." Cramer took a sip of the coffee he'd brought to the table. "Zach was a brilliant cryptographer, but he was bored with security. His real passion was financial apps for amateurs."

"He and his work were well known, then?"

"Oh yeah. He gets recruitment offers all the time." Cramer flinched. "I mean he did. But like I said, he was tired of encryption."

"What exactly was he working on?"

"At DigSec he'd coded an unhackable algorithm for mobile devices." Nothing new there. "Who would want him dead?"

The young man sat back and shook his head. "I have no idea." After a moment, he continued. "I mean, someone might kill to get their hands on the encryption software, but it wasn't his. Everything he produced at DigSec belonged to the company."

Time to be blunt. "Would Zach steal it to sell?"

A long pause while he stared down into his cup. "A year ago, I would have said no. But things changed for Zach after the DEA tried to recruit him."

"The DEA?"

"They needed someone with mad skills to crack open drug-dealer cell phones they'd confiscated. Coders who create security software make the best security hackers."

"But Zach turned them down?"

Cramer cocked his head again, then scoffed. "Some hackers who've been busted and owe the government go to work for the alphabet agencies, but most coders aren't interested in putting people in jail."

Had he forgotten who he was talking to? "Did the DEA pursue Zach, or pressure him?"

"No, they just moved on."

"So why did things change for him after that job offer?"

Cramer kept his eyes on the coffee cup. "Zach realized he hated encryption and wanted to do something else. So he started working on a financial app and looking for investors."

The roommate was holding back—something connected to why Zach might have stolen the software from his employer. "What else? Was he in financial trouble?"

Cramer shifted in his chair. "To test his app, he bought and sold stocks and tried a few other risky investments. Zach lost money and got into debt with one of the online traders." He sighed. "He needed cash, *and* he was desperate to quit his job so he could work for himself."

"Who would he sell the encryption software to?"

"I don't know. Zach didn't talk about it."

"What about the investor you mentioned? Would he buy it?"

Cramer shrugged. "Maybe. But he said the meeting was about starting his company." The roommate suddenly jumped up. "I don't want to discuss Zach anymore. I'm starting to think I didn't really know him, but it's weird to talk shit about him now that he's dead."

"I'm trying to find his killer. You want justice for him, don't you?"

"Yes, but I don't know what else to tell you. His funeral is tomorrow, and I have to go pick up his mother at the airport."

Jocelyn was glad she hadn't been the one to make that call. Telling parents their child was dead was the worst. She stood and handed him her card. "I hope you'll call me if you think of anything helpful."

Heading out, she wondered who she should call at the Drug Enforcement Administration. It would be interesting to find out what the DEA knew about Zach Dimizaro and to learn more about why they'd tried to recruit him.

At the door, she stopped cold. All those recruitment offers Dimizaro had received. What if he'd accepted one of them? Had he been secretly working for another agency or company?

CHAPTER 38

Monday, March 23, 1:30 p.m., Palisades Mine, Washington

Dana's mind drifted in a dreamlike state, but she couldn't sleep. She'd had another seizure that morning while brushing her teeth and woke up on the bathroom floor with a significant bump on her head. The medication they'd provided wasn't working, but she didn't care. She almost wished she'd died from the head trauma. She would not finalize the synthetic or give the creepy masked man the formula. The risk was too great that he would tweak it and use it for bombs—or sell it to someone even more evil.

She remembered his threat to kidnap Garrett. Would he really do it? More important, would she give in to save him? How could she rationalize possibly letting thousands of people die just to save one life? If they brought him here, Garrett was just as doomed as she was. Her captors' facial coverings were her only hope that they might still let her go. Yet she knew that hope was an illusion. They wanted her to believe it, to be willing to do whatever it took to gain her freedom.

The sound of footsteps coming down the hall made her involuntarily curl into a ball. She cursed her own weaknesses. But depression wasn't something she could control or override. The footsteps came closer. More than one set. Someone was with the keeper! *Please, don't let it be Garrett.* As the key turned in the lock, she rolled over to face the door. It wasn't the keeper. The thin man in the ski mask stepped into the room, then moved to the side. In the doorway stood Garrett, hands bound behind his back and a gag over his mouth. His eyes were filled with shame and anguish.

It was all she could do not to charge the masked man and assault him. He was smaller than the keeper but more dangerous. She could tell by the intensity of his eyes. "Let him go!" she shouted, her voice weak. "He's not involved in this!"

The masked man spoke softly, his voice cold. "I told you I would bring him here. Next, I'll hurt him and make you watch. Are you going to give me the final data?"

The bastard! Would he really torture her son? She hadn't considered that possibility, and she couldn't let it happen. His pain was her pain. Only more so, because her son was an innocent, and she was responsible for him. "You win. I'll finish the final process. But you have to let Garrett go."

"Not until my engineer has the material and says we're ready to manufacture."

"But that could take days or a week."

"Then you'd better get busy." The bastard turned and shoved Garrett out into the hall, then spun toward her. "I'll be back to take you to the lab."

Dana fought her tears. She had to finish the process and hope like hell the synthetic metal worked in devices the way it did in the lab. The kidnapper's engineer might not even have the skills to handle the material. But at least the testing process might buy her and Garrett time. The FBI had to be looking for them. Her ex-husband might not care about finding her, but he would search for Garrett until he took his last breath. Her son had pushed his father away out of loyalty to her—and she'd let it happen. But his father loved Garrett and had never given up hope of rebuilding their relationship. But would he get here in time?

Dana knew she couldn't count on it. She'd almost escaped once, and she would try again.

CHAPTER 39

Bailey drove north on I-90 toward Wanapum, mentally wired from the coffee, yet physically exhausted from constant traveling. The Palisades Mine was listed at 1050 Meadow View Road, and according to Google Maps, the tiny town of Wanapum was the nearest junction of civilization. What little daylight the day had held was fading fast, and she was skeptical about looking for the mine in the dark. The listing didn't show up when she keyed the name into her GPS, and with her topographical dysfunction, she might not find it without help. She would check into a motel, take a brief nap, then discreetly ask around about the mine.

Soon after passing the town's welcome sign, Bailey spotted the Sagebrush Inn blinking in the dark with green and red neon lettering. It would do. She just needed a place to sleep and brush her teeth. She parked and headed into the office, glad to stretch her legs. The middle-aged woman at the counter seemed happy to see her and asked if she wanted a room with a view of the town or the countryside. Bailey almost laughed. "Whichever is the most private."

"I'll put you on the end, facing the mountain."

"Sounds good." Bailey dug out a credit card and started to ask about Palisades, then changed her mind. A hotel clerk was in a position to gossip. She put her credit card away, took out cash, and gave the clerk a phony name. The kidnappers had tried to kill her once, and if this was their territory, they might try again.

"If you're hungry, the Woodsman next door gives a nice discount to our guests. Just tell them Kay sent you."

Bailey found her room and tossed her suitcase on a dusty chair. The tacky landscape paintings made the small room even more unpleasant, but it didn't matter. The hot water in the shower was plentiful, and it revived her enough that she decided to skip the nap. The diner next door might be a good place to ask about the location of the mine.

As she dressed, her phone rang. She snatched it up, but it wasn't Garrett. His father instead. "Agent Thorpe, what have you got?"

"Nothing. We processed the house as though it were a crime scene and didn't find any trace evidence. Except a few drops of blood. Garrett might be hurt."

"That's why I'm pushing forward without much bureau support," Bailey admitted. "But I've made another connection that might justify a search warrant. Hang on." She put down the phone, pulled on a sweater, and located her earpiece. "The Palisades Mine was purchased six months ago by a holding company whose owner is Jia Crusher, the wife of Shawn Crusher, CEO of ZoGo, a startup phone manufacturer. He's been at the top of my suspect list all along."

Thorpe cleared his throat. "You're saying he bought the mine before the shortage and crisis, then after it got bad, kidnapped a metallurgy specialist to—" Thorpe stopped midsentence. "It's a long shot, and even if you're right, you have no evidence linking Crusher or his mine to the kidnappings."

"But we have an eyewitness ID of Jerry Rockwell as one of the kidnappers. There has to be a way to link Rockwell to Crusher." Bailey paced the room, worried that Thorpe would want to wait for a search warrant.

"I'll get an analyst to do a search of Crusher's employees and recent transactions." Thorpe made scratching noises in the background. "I'll get a subpoena going too, in case we find some evidence to substantiate it. Where are you now?"

"Wanapum. The mine is around here somewhere, and I'm going to find it."

"Wait for me. I'll drive over tomorrow morning, and we'll do this together. As a federal agent, my hands may be tied by legalities, but as a father, I'll do whatever it takes to find my son."

"Get here early. We're running out of time on North Korea's execution threat, and I believe Lee Nam is up there too." She hung up so she wouldn't have to explain her thinking. Thorpe was skeptical enough.

Bailey walked next door to the diner. The sky had cleared, revealing a blanket of stars, and the cold evening air smelled like Christmas. Feeling more upbeat than she had all day, she treated herself to a steak dinner and began to feel human again. She still needed a good night's sleep, but she thought she'd drive out to Meadow View Road first, just to see if she could find the property. As she paid her bill, she asked her waiter if he knew anything about the Palisades Mine.

"Oh sure. My cousin just got hired. When it reopened, it was a great thing for this town." The guy was in his late twenties but still had a youthful enthusiasm.

"Do you know the owner?"

He furrowed his forehead. "Nobody does. The employees have to sign an agreement not to talk about their work."

Crusher sure was a secretive bastard. "Where is it located?"

"At the end of Meadow View Road. But the property is fenced off, and they don't let anyone but employees in."

"Why the security?"

"I heard that the stuff they're bringing out of the ground is very valuable. Are you going up there?"

"Probably."

"The road splits a few times, and you have to remember the pattern." He scrunched his face while he worked through it. "I think it's left, left, right, left."

Bailey committed it to memory, left him a ten-dollar tip, and hurried back to the motel. She had planned to check her email, then go out again, but exhaustion overwhelmed her. As worried as she was about Garrett, she knew it wasn't logical to drive around in the dark to find a property with a security fence that she didn't plan to scale. She took off her clothes and crawled into bed, leaving her phone and her weapon on the nightstand.

She woke to a beeping sound and sat up. What time was it? How long had she slept? The sun wasn't peeking through the curtains, so it couldn't be that late. She grabbed her phone and looked at the screen. It was six thirty a.m., and Havi was calling. "Bailey here."

"I woke you, didn't I? I forgot about the time difference."

"It's fine. What have you got for me?" She struggled out of bed and looked for her pants.

"Jia Crusher bought a piece of property in Douglas County, Washington, about six months ago. A house with two acres on Quincy Road. It's about five miles from the Palisades Mine. I'll text you the address."

"Excellent. It's probably where I'll find Crusher and his thugs."

"You're not going there alone, are you?"

His concern was sweet but misguided. "Don't worry. An agent from the Seattle field office will be with me. Did you find anything on Crusher? Or Rockwell?"

"Neither purchased airline tickets, but Rockwell is a pilot, so they probably don't fly commercial. One interesting thing. Rockwell rented a vehicle in Seattle the day before Dana Thorpe's disappearance."

Yes! "That's the break I need for a search warrant."

"Don't get your hopes up. It was a bronze-colored Honda Element, which doesn't match the description the witness gave."

She wasn't surprised. "We knew they'd stolen a vehicle for the kidnapping. That one ended up in the lake. But the rental proves he was in the area, which is not coincidental."

"But that's Seattle, which is not connected to either property in central Washington. And you still haven't linked Rockwell to Crusher. You need more for a judge to sign."

Fucking rules! A flash of rage possessed her. "To hell with it! I don't need the damn paperwork. I know those people are up there!"

"Give me a little more time," Havi soothed. "I'll come up with something."

Her plans wouldn't change. "Thanks, Havi."

She texted Thorpe the information, then went out for a quick morning walk. Still half-dark, the town's streets were deserted, except for an occasional truck or beat-up car heading out of town. Were they going up to the mine? Bailey averted her face when the vehicles passed, just as a precaution. She grabbed a quick breakfast at the diner, then checked her email. Nothing from Thorpe yet. What if he didn't show up? His supervisor might have other directives for him.

Too restless to sit around, Bailey got into her rental and drove it across the street to buy gas. Inside the little store, she looked around for supplies she might need and picked up a pair of binoculars and a couple bottles of water. After paying for everything, she headed in the direction of the mine. The highway was nearly empty, and she passed a field of sheep, an abandoned lumber mill, and a couple of mobile homes. She slowed as she approached a junction. Sheep Canyon Road. That was the turn. From here, she had to drive about twenty miles, find Meadow View Road, then follow the directions the waiter had given her.

It proved more difficult than that, and she had to backtrack at least twice. But an hour later, she spotted a wide clearing in the distance—with a few buildings perched at the edge of what appeared to be an asteroid-sized crater. A six-foot iron fence ran along the road, blocking access to the property. Bailey pulled over, shut off the car, and grabbed the binoculars. She spotted the gravel entrance but didn't see any guards. Just a gate with coded security. That was worse. Without the code, they would have to scale the fence to get in. Unless someone was monitoring the gate and decided to let them in. Not damn likely.

She itched to charge through the trees, scale the fence, and search for the victims. But once she was on the mine's property, there was no cover, just wide-open space. She'd be an easy target if a guard in one of the buildings decided to take a shot at her. That had been the point of her recon, though—to see what she and Thorpe would be up against. She forced herself to turn the car around and head back into town. She'd spent her whole adult life trying to override impulses, but it never got any easier.

CHAPTER 40

Back in her hotel room, Bailey studied the Google Earth view of the mine's property. The iron fence ran for about two hundred yards on either side of the gate, stopping at a rock outcropping to the north and a ravine to the south. The ravine likely had water this time of year, but it probably wouldn't be deep. Maybe they could enter the property that way. *If* they didn't have a warrant or permission from the owner to enter. She still hoped they would be able to search without breaking the law or using violence, but she was prepared to do both. More than prepared. Her primal nature wanted to go all Rambo on the scene. She craved risk, adrenaline, and dominance. Sometimes, she needed to feel her fists strike a pliable object—which was why she pummeled the punching bags at the gym whenever she could. But her job and her quest for social acceptance usually kept her from acting on those desires.

Restless again, she called her backup, but Agent Thorpe didn't answer. Was he on his way, driving and out of cell phone range? Or was he not coming? *Damn!* This wasn't just about saving a few lives. If Lee Nam was up at the mine, they could prevent a potentially horrific incident with North Korea. Kim Jong-un was a freaking lunatic. Bailey tucked her weapon back into her body holster and stepped outside. The covered walkway shielded her from the morning sun, but not the wind. The click of a latch caught her attention. She glanced left and saw a man step out of a room two doors away. She didn't recognize him, but she averted her face anyway. Crusher and his thugs were likely staying at the house near the mine, or maybe at Palisades itself, but she still had to be careful. She started to get into the rental car, then her phone rang. *Agent Thorpe. Finally!*

"Where are you?" She didn't mask her irritation.

"At the gas station across from the Sagebrush Inn."

The tension left her shoulders. "Great. I'm at the motel, around back. You can leave your car here, and we'll take mine."

"I'd rather drive."

She wouldn't waste time arguing. "Either way." She hung up and waited for him to cross the highway.

Thorpe pulled up a few minutes later and she climbed in. "Any luck with a search warrant?"

"I left it with another agent to take to a judge. Hopefully, the motel can receive and print faxes." He sipped a container of coffee and gave her a look. "*If* we get a signature. I'm not counting on it." Thorpe shifted to face her. "Have you located the mine?"

"It's about twenty miles from here." He wasn't going to like the next part. "The property has a security gate and a long iron fence that blocks easy access. We can't even get close unless someone opens the gate or we cross a ravine that likely has some water in it, and then hike a short ways."

"Well, shit." Thorpe slammed his palm against the wheel.

"I want to go in anyway."

He was silent for a long moment. "What about Crusher's home? We've got the address. Let's stop there first."

"No! I don't want to warn him that we're here."

"He probably won't be at the house. So we can search it, maybe find a key to the gate. Or some evidence that will support a search warrant." Thorpe shifted in his seat. "We might even find my ex-wife and son."

Now that she thought about it, Bailey liked the idea of breaking into the megalomaniac's hideaway. "What if Crusher is there?"

"We'll strong-arm him into taking us to the mine."

Thorpe was ballsier than she'd thought. "It's a plan."

She keyed the residence address into her phone app again and directed Thorpe to drive north on the main highway. They took a turn onto Sheep Canyon Road, the same exit she'd taken earlier on her way to the mine. After that, the routes were different, and fifteen minutes later, they pulled down a private dirt driveway that crossed a field before disappearing into a small grove of aspens. Inside the cover of the trees, Thorpe stopped and shut off the car. Bailey pulled out her binoculars and trained them on the rural home. No vehicle was in the driveway, but the small attached garage was closed, so she couldn't be sure the house was empty.

Movement inside caught her attention. She focused on the gap in the front curtains.

"See anyone?" Thorpe asked.

"Yes, but I'm not sure who yet."

A minute later, a woman passed through the living room. The quick glance revealed that she was young, dark-haired, and maybe Asian. "I think Crusher's wife is in there."

"What do we know about her?"

"She's a techie too. She creates apps for mobile devices. No criminal record."

"But is she involved in the kidnappings?" Thorpe was musing out loud, rather than asking her directly.

"Maybe we should go find out." Eager to get moving, Bailey opened her car door. "I'll do recon first, if you'd like."

"We're in this together." Thorpe reached for his weapon under the seat, climbed out, and holstered it under his jacket.

They jogged to the edge of the grove and looked around. Nothing but an open space between them and the house. A building off to the side looked like an oversized shed with a smaller structure nearby that could be a well house.

Bailey said, "The woman passed through the living room both times I saw her, so she's not hanging out there. And it's the only room with a direct view of us." She turned and grinned at Thorpe. "Let's just go for it."

He didn't argue, so she took off running across the field, a flat area of short wild grass that was starting to turn green. Thorpe sprinted after her. They stopped at the porch and stepped gently onto the wood platform. Training kicked in, and they both flattened themselves against either side of the front door. The house and its occupant remained still. The woman hadn't heard them. Bailey gestured that she would move around to the side of the house. Thorpe nodded.

A wide dirt path surrounded the exterior wall, so no landscaping got in her way. The house and yard looked like they had been neglected for a long time. Bailey rounded the corner and spotted a bay window that jutted out from the main wall. She eased up next to it and listened. The faint sound of keyboard clicking seeped through. After a moment, the woman muttered something foul. Bailey listened for a full three minutes and heard no indication that anyone else was in the house. She took a quick peek through the window and didn't spot any weapons or danger signs, so she moved back to the front door and signaled that they should knock.

Thorpe rapped on the door, then jumped back again. Muffled footsteps came toward them across the living room.

"Who is it?" a young female voice called out, sounding wary.

"UPS," Bailey said, before Thorpe could announce they were feds.

The door opened, and Bailey stepped into the woman's line of sight. "Jia Crusher?"

"Yes. Who are you?" Mrs. Crusher was delicately beautiful, with mixed Asian and European facial features.

"Agent Bailey, FBI. Can I come in?"

Mrs. Crusher's lips trembled. "Why are you here?"

"We have questions about the Palisades Mine." Bailey wanted to ease into this. If she began by accusing her husband of kidnapping, the woman might shut down.

Thorpe stepped out so Mrs. Crusher could see him too.

Her eyes narrowed. "I don't know anything about it. You'll have to talk to my husband."

"Where is he?" Bailey asked.

"Up at the mine. If you'll excuse me." She pushed the door to close it.

Bailey stuck her foot into the space and pushed back. "Are you aware that several scientists are missing?"

Jia Crusher blinked rapidly and backed up. "No. What does that have to do with me?"

"We'd like to come in and explain." Bailey leaned against the door and the woman stepped back into the house, allowing Bailey and then Thorpe inside. Bailey resisted the urge to pull her weapon. She assumed Thorpe had his in his hand.

"I'm going to call Shawn and ask him to come down here." Mrs. Crusher turned toward the desk near the bay window.

"No, you're not!" Bailey shouted. "Sit down!"

The woman spun back, eyes wide with fear.

Bailey pointed at the couch. As Mrs. Crusher eased onto it, Thorpe moved behind Bailey and stood where he could see out the front window.

"We need your help," Bailey said, as she pulled out the coffee table and sat on it. "People have been kidnapped, and it's possible they're here on this property somewhere. Or maybe at the mine."

"That's just crazy." She shook her head. "Why on earth would you think that?"

"One disappeared from San Jose, very near your hometown of Mountain View. Another disappeared from Seattle, just over the mountains from here. We have a lot more evidence suggesting your husband is responsible, but I can't share it with you."

"No." Mrs. Crusher shook her head vigorously, just like a little kid would. "You don't know Shawn. He's ambitious, but he's a good man. He donates to charity and treats his employees very well."

Who was she trying to convince? Bailey pressed on. "Do you know Jerry Rockwell?"

Her face lost its color. "He worked for Shawn recently as a pilot."

"Worked?" Bailey needed clarification. "Past tense?"

"He died very recently." Mrs. Crusher rubbed her hands on her legs and wouldn't meet Bailey's eyes.

Jerry Rockwell was dead? Bailey's pulse quickened. *What the hell happened?* "How did he die?"

"He went home to Alaska for a family funeral and had a heart attack."

Bullshit! "Your husband told you this?"

"Yes."

"We'd like to look around." Bailey needed a moment to process the new intel. She didn't believe the heart attack story for a minute. Rockwell had died in a way that Crusher didn't want his wife to know about, and that meant Crusher had probably killed him. But why? The only logical reason was that he knew Rockwell had been identified. But only people inside the bureau had that information, so someone had leaked it. *What the hell?* She hadn't felt this betrayed since high school. Bailey stood, shook off her discomfort, and focused her mind. Who was working against her? No one she knew in the DC headquarters came to mind.

Instinctively, she looked at Agent Thorpe. Was it him or someone else in the Seattle field office? Thorpe also had inside knowledge of his ex-wife's research and schedule, so he could have facilitated her kidnapping. But his own son? What was in it for him? Maybe Thorpe hadn't known Crusher would go that far. But still, when you made a pact with the devil . . .

Thorpe gestured that he would search the bedrooms. Bailey turned back to Mrs. Crusher. "Is there a basement?"

"I don't think so. I've only been here a few days. Before that I only saw the place when we bought it."

She tried to calculate whether the woman would run or try to inform her husband. Bailey strode over to the desk and scooped up Mrs. Crusher's phone. "Sit on the couch and don't move until we're done."

The woman bit her lip but sat down again. Bailey hurried into the kitchen and moved quickly through it to the garage. A big black SUV and not much else. She glanced inside the car and didn't see anything, not even a scrap of trash. The door was locked, so she let it go for the moment. Crusher had probably been smart enough not to use his personal vehicle for any of the crimes, and Bailey was looking for captive human beings. She spotted a few packing boxes on the cement floor, but they were empty. A quick search of the floor and perimeter indicated there wasn't an access point to a basement. Back in the kitchen, she opened all the bottom cupboards, most of which were also empty. She felt around each one, looking for latches or places where the wood or drywall might give a little. Nothing. Bailey knelt on the floor and inspected it the same way. The vinyl was worn and faded, but it didn't have any obvious trapdoor openings. Mrs. Crusher hadn't moved but tears ran down her face now. Bailey headed for the bedroom, where she heard Thorpe opening drawers.

Thorpe turned as she walked in. "I can't find any hidden compartments."

"The victims aren't here. They're at the mine." Bailey was sure of it, as she had been since she'd connected Palisades to the drugstore robbery. The question was whether she trusted Thorpe to go with her. What if he was working with Crusher? Maybe that was the only reason he'd agreed to come here with her. If she brought him along, would she end up dead and buried at the mine?

Bailey went back to the living room and Thorpe followed. Mrs. Crusher stood when they entered. "I'm sure this is all a misunderstanding. Why don't I take you up to the mine? You can look around and talk to Shawn, then go find the real criminal."

A surge of relief washed over Bailey. With the wife along as a witness, neither Thorpe nor Crusher was likely to move against her. Still, if Thorpe was a traitor to the bureau, she couldn't trust him to do a real search. She would have to search everything herself and be prepared to kick ass if she found anything. "Great. Let's go."

CHAPTER 41

They followed Mrs. Crusher's big black vehicle up the mountain. She wouldn't be calling ahead to warn her husband, as Bailey still had her phone in her pocket.

Bailey wanted to confront Thorpe about the leak of Rockwell's identification, but it would serve no purpose. If he was a mole, he would simply lie. She needed a way to test him. But she wouldn't have time before she searched the mine. So their trip was mostly silent.

At the gate, Mrs. Crusher got out and Bailey followed her, then watched over her shoulder as she punched in the code. The woman didn't try to hide her number selections, so Crusher would probably change it at the first opportunity.

"I wish you would let me call Shawn and let him know we're here," Mrs. Crusher whined. She'd asked for the phone as they left the house, but Bailey hadn't even bothered to respond. Nor did she now.

The heavy gate retracted as they got back into their cars. On the other side, the clearing was massive and stark compared to the forests and mountains beyond it. The pit itself came into view a moment later. An ugly, tapered crater that spanned the size of ten football fields. Ahead to the right was a gravel parking area filled with some of the same trucks and beat-up cars she'd seen leaving town that morning. Beyond the vehicles was a series of buildings, including a giant structure that looked like a convoluted set of silos and conveyor belts. The task of searching the property suddenly seemed overwhelming. Bailey wished she had a team of agents.

Even if she did, Crusher could still turn them away. Without a search warrant, they would be trespassing. She didn't care about the legality, but if Crusher and his employees had weapons and tried to defend the property, the technicalities could get sticky later in court. Especially if they failed to find the kidnapping victims.

Mrs. Crusher parked and scurried toward a small building in front. Thorpe shut off his engine and said softly, "How far are we going to push this?"

He'd either been thinking along the same lines or wanted her to back off.

"Let's see how Crusher responds and whether he has weapons."

"I don't expect that. If Dana and Garrett are here, Crusher will either turn us away or run."

Bailey reached for her door handle. "Let's go find out."

The first building, a mix of cedar and corrugated metal, looked like an office with a window that viewed the crater. Mrs. Crusher had already hurried inside. Bailey picked up her pace, weapon at her side. She climbed the short wooden steps and pushed through the door. A forty-something man with a potbelly was standing up behind a messy desk. He glanced at her gun as Thorpe came in the door behind her. Mrs. Crusher stood off to the side, looking uncertain.

"What's going on?" The man's hands came up, open palmed.

"We're FBI." Bailey holstered her Glock and stepped toward him. "Who are you?"

"Tom Boxer. I'm the manager. What do you want here?"

"Jia Crusher has given us permission to search this facility."

"For what?" His sweaty brow crinkled, and he glanced at Mrs. Crusher, then back at Bailey. "She's not the owner, and I can't let you wander around here without his permission."

"JCC Holdings is the registered business owner, and Jia Chen Crusher owns the holding company. So why don't you step outside and take a break."

Mrs. Crusher spoke up. "Where's Shawn?"

"I'm not sure," the manager said. "He went to check out the new extractor, but that was an hour ago."

"His car is still here." The wife's worried face seemed to tighten with every new development.

"Shawn is probably visiting with his uncle in the caretaker's cabin." The manager grabbed a pack of cigarettes from his desk and bolted out the door they'd just come in.

Mrs. Crusher trotted down a short dark hallway, and Bailey followed. As she walked across the room, Bailey called over her shoulder to Thorpe, "Search this building. I'll stay with her."

If Thorpe was the leak, she was screwed no matter what happened. But if he wasn't, they had to split up and move quickly, or they might not find Crusher before he headed for the hills. His wife passed two small rooms, both with open doors. As Bailey hurried by, she glanced in. Storage spaces stuffed with crap—tools, machinery, coveralls, boots, and paperwork. Was that a box of dynamite? Typical for a mining operation, she realized. Still, she hoped Thorpe would do his job and search both rooms thoroughly.

They exited out a back door and crossed a small dirt area that held a chicken coop and a greenhouse. To the left, several hundred feet away, was the processing plant she'd spotted from the parking lot. An unlikely place to hold captives, especially if they needed facilities to work in. Several recreational vehicles sat alongside the tall silo: two quads, a dirt bike, and an old black Jeep with no top. Straight ahead was a narrow building with peeling horizontal siding that looked like a bunkhouse for workers. Ahead of her, Mrs. Crusher knocked on the door and called out, "Shawn!"

Bailey stayed right behind her. She wanted to see how Crusher reacted to the news of FBI agents on the property—in the moment it happened, not after he'd had a chance to prepare. If he'd kidnapped four people and killed two, then he was probably a psychopath, on the extreme end of the antisocial spectrum. Or possibly a rare empath who'd gone off the deep end, pushed by stress or greed or raging jealousy to ignore his conscience and commit heinous acts. Mothers who killed their children came to mind.

The door to the bunkhouse opened and Shawn Crusher stood in the frame, looking puzzled and alarmed. He also seemed older than she remembered. When his gaze focused on Bailey, his expression froze, then hardened. After a second, he forced a smile. "I know we met last week, but I can't remember your name."

Bullshit. "Agent Bailey."

"What's going on? Why are you here?"

"Your wife gave us permission to search the property. Please step aside and let me in." Bailey wanted to cuff him to a chair, but she had no real reason to yet. Her priority was to find the victims, and she might need his cooperation. As soon as she located them or their holding cell, a single call would bring in local agents, cops, and the sheriff. Or, if Crusher bolted, she would have to trust them to track and apprehend him.

"Search for what?" Crusher asked. "This is a legitimate mining operation."

"Kidnapping victims—as you well know."

He forced a laugh. "That's crazy."

"Step aside." Bailey glanced over her shoulder to see if Thorpe was coming along—either to help or to hinder.

"My wife doesn't have the right to give search permission, and I'm telling you no."

"Yes, she does." Bailey cited the ownership paperwork again.

Crusher grabbed his wife's arm. "Jia, tell her to leave. This is ridiculous."

Mrs. Crusher jerked free. "If nothing is going on, prove it, Shawn, and be done with it for good."

Five long seconds passed while he weighed his options. Finally, Crusher stepped back, clearing the door. "I have nothing to hide."

His wife walked into the bunkhouse and Bailey followed, keeping her eye on Crusher. A big family room with fake wood paneling and scarred pine floors. Bailey glanced around, determining where to start. Her weapon was still in her right hand, and she had to keep it ready. Searching with one hand would be a pain.

A big Asian man walked into the room. Midfifties, she guessed, with dull eyes. He must be the uncle someone had mentioned. She stepped toward him. "Who are you?"

"Tai Ming. I live here."

Was he the one watching and feeding the prisoners? "Who else is here? Are you hiding some people?"

He blinked and shook his head. "I don't know what you're talking about."

"Have a seat, please. I'll have more questions for you later." She gestured with her weapon.

The big man complied. Crusher and his wife stood close together in the middle of the room, whispering. The scenario felt out of control, with her outnumbered. Where was Thorpe?

Keeping one eye on the group, Bailey walked around the room, knocking on walls and listening for hollowness or a change in tone. Nothing surfaced. She visually inspected the floor and found no seams or hidden latches. After moving a TV and coffee table, she made Tai get up from the couch so she could pull it away from the wall and search behind and under it.

As she finished, Thorpe came through the door. "There's nothing significant in the office."

"Keep an eye on everyone while I search the rest of this building."

"Will do." Thorpe turned to Crusher. "If you have my son, I'll put you away for life."

She wasn't a good judge of emotions, and anyone could lie, but Thorpe sounded sincere. She holstered her weapon and moved down the hall, knocking on paneling and looking for seams in the floor. The building was smaller than it had looked, with only three bedrooms and a large locker room–style bathroom and shower with an adjacent laundry room. She went through the whole space quickly, looking for the obvious, then returned to the first bedroom for a more thorough pass. *Damn!* She needed a whole team with crowbars to pull up the floorboards.

After another ten minutes, Mrs. Crusher came into the room. "I think we've proved there's no one else here. I'd like you to leave now."

Oh hell. How to handle this? Be assertive or appeal to her humanity? Bailey stood up. "What if they are here? What if your husband kills them later today to cover his tracks? How are you going to feel when we find the bodies later?"

Mrs. Crusher's lips trembled, but then her eyes flashed with anger. "You're wrong about Shawn! Leave now or I'll sue you for harassment."

Negative consequences rarely deterred Bailey, and every nerve in her body wanted to keep searching. Garrett was here! Her heart could feel it. But Bailey couldn't risk losing her job. She would leave, but she wasn't giving up. She would think of a way to manipulate everyone into leaving the property so she could come back secretly with a crowbar and tear the place apart. She couldn't resist throwing another threat at Crusher's wife. "You'll be charged as an accessory when this blows up in your face."

Mrs. Crusher stood her ground, faithful to her husband. "Leave the property now."

Bailey wanted to smash her gun through the tiny bedroom window, just for the pleasure of hearing the glass shatter. She resisted, but the impulse gave her an idea. "Go ask your husband how Jerry Rockwell really died. We know for a fact he didn't buy a plane ticket to Alaska or log a private flight there."

Mrs. Crusher glared, then hurried from the room. Bailey turned to the ancient window, unhinged the latch, and slammed her gun against it—so it wouldn't lock again. With any luck, no one would even check it. She made a few loud tapping sounds with her weapon against a dresser to cover the first noise, then gave the room another once-over. A stained pair of pants on the floor looked too small for Uncle Tai. Who was staying in this room? She picked up a magazine from the desk. *International Journal of Minerals, Metallurgy, and Materials.* She couldn't imagine Tai reading that. Had Milton Thurgood been in this room?

Mrs. Crusher burst back in. "I want you to leave. Now!"

Bailey shook her head. "Big mistake." She strode down the hall, mentally cursing her failure. In the living room, Thorpe stood watch, stiff legged and silent, like a solid agent. She still didn't know if she could trust him. "I guess we're out of here."

He gave Crusher one last menacing stare, then they headed out the door. Thorpe didn't speak or look at her as they walked. When they neared his car, he finally said, "It looks like you were wrong about them being here."

She wasn't wrong! "We just didn't have the time and manpower to do a thorough search. We still need a warrant and a team to take this place apart."

"No, what you need is more evidence." Thorpe grabbed his door handle but turned and met her eyes. "I have to get back to the Seattle field office. If you come up with something tangible, call me."

That would be too late. She climbed into the car, wishing she'd brought her own vehicle. "Remember the Jeffrey Dahmer case? Or Marc Dutroux in Belgium? Police officers went to both serial killers' homes, then walked away. In the Dutroux case, they had a warrant, and a team searched his house twice. But they didn't find anything, so they left. The little girls who were chained in the basement at the time died of starvation." She told the story without emotion, only as a reminder of why they shouldn't give up too soon.

But her throat constricted when she announced her intentions. "I'm staying here in Wanapum, and I intend to find Garrett, with or without your help."

CHAPTER 42

Shawn's pounding pulse slowed as he watched the agents walk past the office and head for their car. That had been too fucking close. The rage he'd been holding in finally erupted. "Goddammit, Jia! Why did you bring them here? I don't need this stress right now."

She cringed and shrank back. "They came to the house and accused you of kidnapping. I was scared and confused. But I wanted to show them they were wrong."

His wife was obviously distressed, but that wasn't his priority. He had to wrap up his basement-lab project and figure out where to move the cryptographer, who wasn't done coding yet. Shawn didn't trust the feds not to come back for another look around.

"They are wrong, aren't they?" Jia grabbed his hands and held them to her own chest. "Tell me you didn't do it!"

"We just talked about this!" He jerked free. "That you could even doubt me."

"What about the North Korean? You asked me who was the best. Then I gave you his name, and a week later he was kidnapped."

Why was she doing this now? He thought he had her support. But he had an answer ready. "Everybody in the personal-device business talked about Lee Nam when they heard he was coming to the symposium. And nobody believes he was really kidnapped. Our government helped him fake that so he could defect."

Jia was quiet for a minute. "I need to talk to Uncle Tai."

Not a chance in hell. "Please don't. You'll just confuse him. He's already distressed about the agents coming here." Shawn had sent him back to his bedroom as soon as the feds walked out. Now he had to get Jia off the property and out of town. They would use his wife as leverage, like the weak link that she was. He deeply regretted bringing her here, but he hadn't counted on Bailey finding his facilities. How the hell had she connected everything? He'd been so careful. Steering Jia toward the door, he said, "Why don't you go back to Mountain View? You didn't want to be here more than a week anyway."

"I think I will." She left without looking at him.

That was one fire put out. Two, actually. Milton Thurgood had left that morning, the moment he'd confirmed the hefty cash deposit in a bank account in the Cayman Islands, which was where he was headed to start a new life. Shawn would move Lee Nam to a rental he owned in Mountain View to finish coding the algorithm. That left Dana Thorpe and her son. He'd checked on Dana that morning, and she said she would complete her project that day. Once Shawn had the compound and the data, she and her son probably had to die. The thought sickened him. It wasn't what he'd planned, but now the risk of releasing them was too great. But how? He didn't think he could kill a woman with his own hands. Maybe Harlan would handle it. Where the hell was he anyway?

Shawn yanked out his cell phone and called him, but Harlan didn't pick up. *Damn!* Could he count on anyone? He left a brief message: "Harlan, I need you up at the mine. Right away."

Shawn left the bunkhouse, crossed the space to the office, and entered through the back door. His manager stood at the window, watching the parking lot. Tom turned and asked, "Everything okay?"

"Yeah, I think so. The feds want this mining operation, but they can't nationalize it, so they're trying to use civil forfeiture to take possession." Tom would buy that. His manager hated the government. Shawn needed everyone off the property to wrap up his project here. "Let's shut down early today. The crew could use a break."

"Sounds good." Tom shuffled his feet but didn't move. "I won't be back. This job was already stressful before the FBI showed up. You're pushing us all too hard."

He was *quitting?* "Hey, just take a couple days off while this blows over." Finding a new manager would be a pain in the ass. "I'll give you a raise."

"I don't know. We'll see what happens." Tom grabbed his coat and headed out.

"Give everyone tomorrow off, and I'll see you on Thursday," Shawn called after him.

Tom didn't look back.

Damn! What was wrong with people that they were so afraid of hard work? Shawn paced the office, hoping to hear from Harlan before he went underground and couldn't get a signal. He called again, and his special-ops man finally answered. "What's up?"

"Where are you?"

"I'm at the motel, resting, like you said I could."

That was yesterday! "Two federal agents were just here at the mine. They searched the bunkhouse."

"Holy shit! But they must not have found anything, or we wouldn't be talking."

"I'm worried they'll be back. Or at least Agent Bailey will. The bitch has been dogging me for a week, and I don't expect her to give up. You need to take her out."

Harlan made a small grunting sound. "That didn't work so well last time."

"So be more prepared for it. She could send us both to prison for life if she comes back up here and finds the people we kidnapped."

A long silence. "If I do this, I want a huge bonus. Then I'm done. This has gotten too crazy for me."

Shawn would talk him into sticking around, but he didn't have time now. "You've got it."

"Where is she?"

"Probably in town somewhere. Maybe even the same motel you're in."

"I'll need your help," Harlan whined. "I can't just shoot an FBI agent in the motel room. We'll have to plan something and lure her out of town. It's time to get your hands dirty."

"I have my hands full!" Shawn's patience snapped. "Jia's going home, and Tom just quit on me. You need to step up."

"I'll find the agent, then I'll call you to help with the rest. I'm not doing this alone." Harlan hung up.

The prick! Shawn didn't want to leave the mine and its underground guests. But Bailey was the one person he actually wanted to see dead. If he had to make a trip into town to help get rid of the agent, he would. Depending on how much more time Dana Thorpe needed.

He hurried out the back door and crossed the grassy space again. He would give Uncle Tai some time off too. He didn't want anyone around for what he had in mind. Except Harlan. But he needed his special-ops man to take care of Bailey first.

Inside the bunkhouse, Uncle Tai was in his bedroom packing. His expression was sheepish when he looked up. "I don't want to work here anymore."

"I understand that you're worried about the federal agents, but they're gone now." Shawn patted the older man's back. "But go ahead and take some time off."

"I'm going home to San Jose to stay with Mom."

Tai was cutting and running too. *Lazy fucking cowards!* Pain and humiliation roiled through Shawn's chest. They were just as bad as the bullies and sunny-day friends from grade school. Another worry landed on his chest. Would Jia be at their home when he got back to California, or would she abandon him too? Shawn walked out of the room, found a chair, and sat down. With long, slow breaths, he focused on his pain and fear. He visualized boxing it all up and sending it down a long tube into a vault. Feeling calmer, he headed for the laundry room at the back. Time to check on Dana's progress again.

The bunkhouse had been built in the fifties, and the room still contained two side-by-side giant iron sinks that were attached to the wall. The eight legs all ended in round floor casings that were secured down. When they'd checked out the property, he'd accidentally discovered the basement bunker by leaning on the left sink. Something had clicked, and he'd felt the sink shift. He'd grabbed the edge and pulled, and a square section of the floor had come up with the basin, revealing an opening below. Shawn repeated that motion now, eased down the first few steps to the landing, and closed the trapdoor behind him. He made his way downstairs with the motion-sensor light he'd installed, then strode down the narrow tunnel to a door about ten yards away. He unlocked the metal closure, stepped into the old bomb shelter, and pulled the ski mask from his pocket.

The shelter had been meant to house several families during a nuclear event, so the electrical and water systems had already been in place. Transporting the equipment for the lab had been challenging—until he'd discovered a second entrance that opened at the edge of the woods. But the mine had been shut down when he bought it, so he and Harlan had had the place to themselves when they carried in the microscopes, grinders, and all the other things required to outfit the lab and holding facilities.

Shawn passed the sleeping rooms, knowing Dana would be in the lab, where he'd left her earlier. He unlocked the door on the right. The big room had been divided into separate workspaces, where two metallurgists could work on different projects. From the beginning, he'd been prepared to pay them well for putting up with the harsh environment, whether they came voluntarily or not.

Dana looked up from her computer and shook her head. "I told you I needed time to organize the data so your engineer can replicate my work. And I need to synthesize a larger sample."

Was she stalling? Did he need to threaten to hurt her son again? Shawn crossed the room, but still kept his distance from her. "Don't lie to me. It's almost over, and I'll let you both go."

"Just give me another four or five hours. Honestly. I want this done more than you do." Her voice cracked at the end.

"Can I bring you anything? Coffee or food?"

"No. I have water, and I ate this morning."

"All right. I'll see you again soon."

"Garrett might need food," she called out as he walked away.

Shawn stepped back into the dark concrete hall and locked the door behind him. Garrett could go hungry. He wasn't contributing anything to the project. As Shawn hurried back out, he thought about what it would have been like to live down here after a nuclear bomb. Would anyone have survived the radiation? Was the shelter really that well sealed off?

Sealed well enough. An idea came to him for how to silence the mother and son, a painless way for them and himself. Once he was in the tunnel, part two of the plan popped into his head. A few sticks of dynamite from the storage room would collapse the passageway, and no one would ever know the basement lab had existed.

CHAPTER 43

Tuesday, March 24, 1:00 p.m., Washington, DC

Jocelyn's homicide unit gathered in the conference room for the weekly update. Each two-person team reported on their investigations and asked for help if they needed it. Her partner announced a breakthrough in the domestic murder they were handling, a confession and plea deal from the boyfriend who'd killed his male lover. Relieved to put that one behind them, Jocelyn updated everyone on the mugger homicide she was point person on.

"I finally identified the victim as Zach Dimizaro, a software developer, and our digital technicians analyzed the computer chip from his mouth. They found a program that encrypts personal devices so the communication is inaccessible to law enforcement."

A few detectives groaned and one cursed. Jocelyn continued, "I gave a copy of the chip to the FBI, and they're investigating the source. They're also looking at who would be in the market for the software. The consensus is that the homicide wasn't a mugging, that the killer wanted the chip but failed to find it on Dimizaro's body."

The sergeant raised an eyebrow. "So essentially, the feds have taken over the case?"

"Pretty much. I still have flyers posted in the bars and restaurants in the crime-scene area, asking for people to come forward. If we get lucky and connect with an eyewitness, the call will come to me, and I'll interview them. So I'm still on the case."

"What about the victim's financial and phone records?" her boss asked.

"The only suspicious activity was a series of phone calls from a burner phone. Just a number and no identification." Jocelyn had spent the night before staring at those files and had called the phone company that morning. "The service provider is trying to track the locations of where the calls were made from."

"Anything else?" Sergeant Murphy was ready to move on.

"Not for that case. But you also sent me to the hotel where Lee Nam, the North Korean tech guy, was kidnapped. I interviewed his bodyguard." She glanced at her notes. "Dukko Ki-ha claims he was chloroformed by a man wearing thick makeup."

"What?"

"That's what he said." She hadn't seen the security video. "I talked to the kitchen staff, and one person saw Mr. Lee going out through the loading dock with two men. Voluntarily."

Her boss scowled. "You're saying he wasn't kidnapped?"

The incident had been covered relentlessly by the media, and the speculation was rampant. "I don't know. The FBI took over that case too."

The sergeant gave her a half smile. "Talk to your husband, find out what you can. I like to be kept informed of what's happening in our jurisdiction, even when we're not running the cases."

Ross had been working all weekend, and she hadn't heard from him. "I'm having dinner with him tomorrow, and I'll get back to you."

The meeting adjourned, and Jocelyn stopped by the kitchen to retrieve a cold can of soda before heading to her cubicle. Her desk phone was blinking when she arrived, and she listened to the voice message: "This is Amy Charles. I noticed the flyer asking about the guy who was murdered. I think I saw who killed him." The young woman recited her number and hung up.

Holy cow! Jocelyn's heart skipped a beat. Cynicism kicked in next, but her gut told her the young woman was sincere and sane. Jocelyn called back, excited when the witness picked up. "Amy, it's Detective Larson. Give me the details. Where were you and what did you see?"

"I was in a cab. I had just left the Dog's Head Tavern, and we were moving . . . west, it would be. We'd only gone a few blocks when we passed two guys on the sidewalk. One was Zach Dimizaro, the guy from the flyer. I don't know him, but I'd seen him in the bar a few minutes earlier. The other man was bigger and older and walking toward him."

"What did he look like?" Jocelyn had her pen and tablet ready.

"Long dark coat, knit cap, brownish skin. Maybe African-American. About six-two and heavy. Not fat, but thick. He also had a wide nose and a weak jaw."

Wow. Enough detail to create a composite. Where had this witness been all week? "Can you come into the department and work with a sketch artist?"

"When?"

"Right now."

"Uh, sure. I need to postpone something, but I can be there in twenty or thirty minutes."

"Thank you." Jocelyn gave her the address and reiterated how important the sketch would be. Nerves jumping, she hurried toward her partner's desk in the open workspace, but he wasn't there. Still wanting to share the news, she almost called Ross, but decided to call the sketch artist first, then wait until she had something to show. Once she had an image, she would send it to the patrol department, the FBI, and maybe the media.

Amy Charles didn't show up on time, and Jocelyn paced the department, resisting the urge to interrupt other detectives just to take her mind off waiting. Maybe the girl was just another quack, one of the nut jobs who wasted law enforcement's time with fabricated stories just for the attention. They got a dozen calls a day like that. But Amy had sounded so serious, so specific. Jocelyn walked up to the front desk to chat with the duty clerk. Before she could say hello, a young woman came through the door. Early twenties, well dressed, light-brown skin, and close-cropped hair. She radiated confidence.

"Amy Charles?"

"Yes. Sorry I'm late. I had a little trouble extricating myself from my other engagement." Amy held out her hand.

Jocelyn shook it. "Detective Larson. I'm glad you're here. Our artist is ready, so let's get started." She left Amy with the detective who created sketches, then went back to her desk while they worked. The process was slow and she had reports to fill out.

A half hour later, curiosity drove her down the hall to Detective Turner's workspace.

"We're just about finished," he said, looking up.

Next to him, Amy nodded. "Close enough. It was getting dark, so I'm surprised I saw him as well as I did."

The sketch artist held up his drawing. Jocelyn stared. She knew the face. Or at least she'd seen it once or twice, but couldn't place it. She turned to Amy. "Do you have time to look at mug shots? We need to see if this guy is in the criminal database."

"I have another half an hour, then I have to make a meeting. But I can come back late this afternoon."

"Great. I'll get you set up."

Detective Turner stood. "I'll photograph the drawing and send you a digital file to distribute."

"Thanks." Jocelyn led Amy to a computer station and opened their mug shot database, which contained images for witnesses to peruse. "If you find him, let me know right away. I'll be down the hall in the open workspace."

Back at her desk, Jocelyn checked her email. She had a message from the manager at Metro Mobile:

> The calls from 202-729-4593 were made
> from one of two locations: near the corner of
> 7th and D. NW Streets or Forest Hills Park. I
> hope that helps.

The first location was downtown, and the park was in a nice neighborhood farther north. Jocelyn visualized the downtown area and tried to determine what businesses were nearby. A coffee shop and BBQ-style diner came to mind. But the man who'd killed Zach Dimizaro had wanted a microchip. He had to be someone with money, power, or knowledge. The area wasn't far, and she had to go see it for herself. Her witness would be busy for a while and could call her if she found the guy.

The drive took ten minutes, and while she sat in traffic, she racked her brain for where she might have seen the perp's face. After circling the block a few times, she squeezed into a parking space not far from the corner where the calls had been made. As soon as she stepped out of her car, the connections hit her, one after another, leaving her breathless.

FBI headquarters was two blocks away, and the perp in the sketch was a dead match for Brent Haywood, the bureau's assistant director. Well, that didn't help much. But the resemblance was so uncanny, she knew she'd need to look into it further or it would drive her crazy.

Jocelyn fumbled to get her phone out of her pocket, then called her husband. She bounced on her feet while she waited for him to answer.

"Hey, Jocelyn. I hope we're still on for dinner."

"Ross, I need you to check something for me, and it's a little weird."

"What is it?"

"The home address of Brent Haywood, your AD."

A pause. "That is more than weird. I'm not sure I have access to the information. What is this about?" He was clearly worried.

"I don't even want to say it on the phone. But I'll meet you outside your office. This is really important."

"Okay. I'll see what I can find and call you back."

The AD a killer? It seemed ridiculous, and she had to be wrong. But then again, encryption was extremely critical to everyone right now— the NSA, the FBI, terrorists, and foreign governments too—which meant the price tag for the right software could be in the millions. And money had a way of revealing who people really were.

CHAPTER 44

Tuesday, March 24, 5:25 p.m., Wanapum, Washington

Bailey paced her hotel room, trying to plot her next move. She needed to get everyone away from the mine so she could search it again. But how? Call in a fire? A more immediate concern was that Crusher or one of his thugs might have followed her back to the motel and might try to kill her again. Could she make them think she'd left town with Agent Thorpe?

She stopped in the middle of the room. Before she could move forward, she had to know who she could trust. Everything about Thorpe's actions and attitude seemed genuine. And the fact that his ex-wife and son were in jeopardy made him the least likely person to pass information to Crusher. Yes, families betrayed each other. But she couldn't find a motive. And Thorpe was a long-term agent who'd been promoted to head of a field office. But if not him, then who?

She ruled out Havi, then realized she had no reason to beyond her affection for him. She reconsidered, mentally worked through her reports to him, then realized she hadn't discussed Rockwell's identity with him until very recently. That left Lennard or Haywood, both also

long-term, highly placed agents. Unease made her start pacing again.
Which one was the most logical culprit? And how could she find out
for sure?

She recalled the meeting in Lennard's office when she'd been
assigned the case. Haywood had pushed her to investigate the Australian
scientist as a serial killer. A bizarre direction to send her. Why had he
even been part of the meeting? His presence had seemed wrong at the
time, and now she wondered if he'd participated for the purpose of
steering her away from Shawn Crusher and his rare earth mine. She'd
also been pulled off the case, and Lennard had seemed uncomfortable
with the decision. So it was probably Haywood. But why? It had to be
about money or control. Or both.

The assistant director? *Oh hell.* There was only one way to find out.
And it was a risk on many levels.

She called Agent Lennard, and her boss sounded surprised to hear
from her. "Bailey. I thought you were taking some time off."

"I was. But there's more to this investigation than you realize, and
I couldn't walk away from it."

"Where are you?"

"I'm in Wanapum, Washington, at the Sagebrush Inn." If her
boss was the leak, a bullet might come through her door in ten
minutes or less.

"What's going on?" The noise in the background stopped, and
Lennard's tone shifted.

"Shawn Crusher owns a rare earth mine here, and Jerry Rockwell
works for him. Or at least he used to. Rockwell supposedly died just this
week, and Crusher lied to his wife about how. I have to assume someone
in the FBI told Crusher his thug had been identified."

A long pause. "You're working off book and leaping to conclu-
sions." Her voice held no conviction.

"I figure the traitor has to be either you or Haywood. If I get fired
after this conversation, I'll know it's you." Bailey stopped in front of

the window and peeked through the curtains. No one was out there. Lennard hadn't cut in, so she kept going. "Analysis tells me it's Haywood. He inserted himself into the investigation and tried to steer me away from the earth-metal connection. He's also the one who pulled me off the case. Correct?"

Another long silence. "I'll see what I can find out." Lennard abruptly hung up.

She'd put her boss in a delicate position. But if Haywood was working both sides of the law, agents' lives were at risk, and he had to be exposed. If Lennard handled it well, she was probably in line for the AD's position.

Bailey grabbed her travel bag and hurried out. If she was wrong about Lennard, she was a bull's-eye now and had to move. Crusher might come after her even without updated information. She headed west on I-90, back the way she'd come into town. Her plan was to loop around on a back road, come into town from the other end, and find a different motel, if there was one. None of it was probably necessary. Crusher had to be busy trying to wrap things up or move his forced-labor research effort. He probably didn't have time to send his other thug after her. Now that she knew for sure Crusher was the mastermind, she hoped to identify his hired help.

Bailey passed the city-limit sign and glanced in her rearview mirror. Another car was back there, but in the fading light, she couldn't tell the model. The vehicle hung back, but she kept an occasional eye on it, then turned right at the first road after the golf course. Was this the right way? GPS wasn't helpful in this situation, because her destination was the same as the place she'd just left. Also, the road she needed to circle around on crossed the highway and ran in both directions. Signs of civilization disappeared quickly, and rocky outcroppings lined the landscape. This couldn't be right. She was supposed to circle around the golf course and drive past the airport.

Bailey slowed, looking for a decent place to pull a U-turn. The sun had dropped behind the mountain, and visibility was suddenly minimal. The grassy roadsides looked slick and soft, and she didn't want to get stuck. She glanced in her mirror again, but didn't see any lights behind her. Not finding an ideal place, she simply eased off the road and started her turn. She stopped and backed up a few times to keep the radius tight. In the final phase of the turn, she heard another engine and jerked her head back to the road. A truck with no lights screeched to a stop thirty feet away, blocking both lanes.

Trouble! She wanted to press the gas and blow past him, but she'd have to drive off the road. The dirt and rock and whatever else was out there in the dark could disable the car. And if the driver had a gun, she'd be an open target as she approached. Bailey threw herself sideways and grabbed her weapon from the passenger seat. A shot slammed into the windshield, cracking the glass. *The bastard!* Crawling on her side, she opened the passenger door, then shoved her feet out and down, keeping crouched behind the metal door. This left her ankles unprotected, but screw it—she'd rather die standing and firing than cowering in a car. Another shot shattered the passenger window just above her head. A third shot blew out a tire.

She had to take action. Bailey straightened her legs and popped up, bringing her arms into an elevated firing position at the same time. The driver was out of the truck and coming at her. Before she could pull the trigger, a blast nailed him in the back and he stumbled, then fell, facedown. *What the hell?* She scanned the darkness behind the fallen man, her finger itching to use the gun. Friend or foe? Just because whoever it was had dropped her assailant didn't mean he wouldn't come for her. She had to wait and see. A lean figure ran alongside the truck, coming into view in her headlights.

Dukko!

"Are you hit?" he called out.

"No." Bailey's arms relaxed, but she kept her weapon ready and stepped out from behind the car door. "What are you doing here?"

"Saving your life." He knelt down and checked the man for a pulse. "But only so you can help me find Lee Nam."

Bailey walked toward him. "You followed me all the way from DC?"

"I guessed that you were flying to Seattle, then followed you from the missing scientist's home" He stood again. "Let's go up to the mine. Now! Kim Jong-un's deadline is midnight, East Coast time."

They had less than three hours to save Jake Austin's life and prevent whatever else KJU had in mind. Bailey glanced at the dead man. He was bigger and heavier than Crusher. She squatted down and rolled his shoulder so she could see his face. Was this the same bastard who'd tried to kill her in Seattle? He definitely was the kidnapper in the DC hotel video.

"That's him." Dukko spat on the dead man. "He drugged me and took Lee Nam."

Bailey pulled a wallet from the corpse's pants pocket and checked the license. *Harlan Romero.* She hadn't seen his name in ZoGo's employee files. But she was confident he worked for Crusher. She took the gun, a compact Luger, out of his still-warm hand and searched him for more ammo. There wasn't any.

She stood and sized up the North Korean bodyguard. He wasn't her first choice for backup—considering what he'd done to her in DC—but he was willing and had already proven useful. He was also correct. They were nearly out of time.

Dukko walked back the way he'd come. "We'll take my car. Yours has a flat tire."

Bailey stared after him. They needed to clear out before they got stuck answering a lot of questions. But would anyone out here even report the gunshots?

* * *

While Dukko drove, she called Thorpe, who was still on his way toward Seattle. He answered, but the connection was scratchy. "It's Thorpe. Anything changed?"

"One of Crusher's thugs just tried to kill me again. We're going back up to the mine."

"Who's *we*?"

"I'm with a foreign diplomat who's looking for Lee Nam. We only have a few hours before the execution deadline."

"What makes you think the missing North Korean is with Dana and Garrett?" A car rushed by in the background, making Thorpe hard to hear.

Bailey gave him the basics. "The thug who kidnapped Lee Nam is the same guy who just shot at me. So yes, the kidnappings are connected, and we have probable cause."

"I'm turning around to head your way. I'll call in a team too."

Bailey hung up, her throat dry and thirsty. She asked Dukko if he had any water.

"In the back."

She reached over the seat, found a bag with beef jerky and water, then gulped down half a bottle.

"Who's Crusher?" Dukko made the first turn off the main road.

"Shawn Crusher, CEO of ZoGo, a phone manufacturer. I think he's trying to produce more of the metals he needs and to develop a new one."

"Why did he take Lee Nam?"

Bailey had given that some thought. "Encryption is a critical issue. Consumers want it, but law enforcement hates it. Since Crusher has your guy, he obviously wants to embed his product with the best security available."

"So he kidnapped him?"

She couldn't resist. "Isn't that how your government operates?"

Dukko didn't rise to the bait.

"We need to form a plan," she said.

Dukko glanced at her. "We take Crusher hostage and torture him until he tells us where the victims are."

She liked his determination, but it wouldn't be that simple. "I think they're underground. And if Crusher is with them, your plan won't work. We have to find the access, and I've already looked once. Briefly."

"I will find it."

"Are you an expert at hiding prisoners?"

"We don't hide prisoners. We make examples of them." His voice was cold.

Bailey turned back to the issue. "I'm sure the access is in the bunkhouse. That's why the old guy is there, to keep an eye on them."

Dukko looked over again. "I lied. We do hide people sometimes. So I'll check closets and utility rooms first."

CHAPTER 45

An hour earlier

When Shawn reached town, he pulled into the parking lot behind the feed store and called Harlan. While the phone rang, he played out scenarios of how they would trick, shoot, and bury Agent Bailey. Well, not bury. That took too much time, and there were plenty of remote places to dump her body. He really hoped Harlan had already done the shooting. The call went to voice mail. Shawn cursed and put down the phone. He would give Harlan twenty minutes. If he didn't hear from him by then, Shawn would head straight back to the mine.

The wait seemed to go on forever. Shawn checked his phone and realized he hadn't noted the time earlier. *Fuck!* Had Harlan been killed by the agent? He couldn't think about that right now. But if it was true, he had to get back up to the mine immediately.

Shawn got on the road, and as soon as he cleared city limits he pushed the accelerator as hard as he could. This phase of the project was making him a nervous wreck, and he was desperate for it to be over. The new material, which would be used mostly in the speakers and microphones, would go into production within a few weeks, the mine was producing most of the other elements he needed, and the new-generation phones would start rolling out soon after. The encryption wasn't that critical—at least not to him. As long as he had some password-protection software installed, most customers would be happy. ZoGo would soon be the only US company making phones people could afford. The only sticking point—besides the people in the basement—was his backer. Max wanted the unbreakable encryption ASAP. Shawn was starting to think the software was just a commodity to him. Something to sell to the highest bidder.

At Palisades, the sun was dropping, the parking lot was empty, and the processing plant was still. The quiet bothered him. They'd been operating eighteen hours a day for months, and this would be a setback. Shawn pulled the gun from the glove box, tucked it into the back of his pants, and hurried down the dark dirt-and-gravel path to the bunkhouse. Halfway there, he stopped. He needed supplies. First, the phosphine gas. A few canisters were left over from when they'd used it to kill the rodents that had made nests in the buildings when the mine was shut down.

He crossed the open space, entered the shack behind the processing plant, and picked up a large red canister. All he had to do was open a valve, run for the door, and let the lethal stuff flow into the bomb shelter. He backtracked to the office and found a box of dynamite in the storage room. Wishing he'd brought a backpack or bag, he picked up four sticks and shoved two into each jacket pocket. Would that be enough? Gas, gun, dynamite. Feeling ready, Shawn hurried out the back door.

Moonlight reflected off the plastic greenhouse as he crossed the yard between the buildings. The openness made him feel vulnerable. Shawn looked around. No one was watching. He turned his gaze to the bunkhouse. A large shape on the right caught his eye. A car! Who the hell was here? He ran over and ducked behind the chicken coop. Was it Bailey? Why hadn't Harlan called and warned him? Shawn poked his head out and tried to determine the type and color of the vehicle. *Oh shit!* It was Jia's Escalade. What the hell was his wife doing here?

Maybe she'd come to say good-bye to Uncle Tai before driving back down south. That was the only possibility that made sense. Unless she doubted him and . . . Shawn wouldn't let himself think it. He sprinted to the bunkhouse and bolted inside. No one was in the living room, and the building was quiet. Uncle Tai's things were gone, and Jia was nowhere in sight. Panic flooded his chest, making it hard to breathe. *No! No! No!* he screamed silently as he ran down the hall to the laundry room.

The trapdoor was partially open. A string of curses flew from his mouth in a repetitive pattern as he pounded down the stairs, still carrying the gas canister and dynamite. He stopped in the tunnel just outside the bomb shelter door. What now? If Jia was in there, could he convince her everything would work out? Shawn put down the canister and felt in his pocket for the ski mask. He didn't have it! *Damn!* He looked behind him in the tunnel and on the stairs and didn't see it. *Just stop!* It didn't matter now. Letting the captives go wasn't an option anymore. Federal agents had been to the mine. The released mother and son would tell their story, and the feds would come back. If they found a single fiber of DNA belonging to either of the kidnapping victims, it was over for him. Life in prison. That was also not an option. He couldn't live in a cell with a bunch of common criminals. Until this moment, he hadn't let himself consider the possibility.

But what about Jia? He had to convince her to be loyal and see things his way.

Pounding from the hallway on the other side of the door grabbed his attention. What was going on? Shawn pushed through and found Jia smashing at the first doorknob with a hammer. She spun toward him, eyes wide with horror. "What have you done? Who is the man in there?" She held the hammer over her head like a weapon, her face a mask of outrage that he'd never seen before.

"Jia, it's not what you think." Shawn put down the canister and eased toward her, his voice gentle and his hands out with palms up.

"Not what I think? You kidnapped these people just like the agents said! But why? I thought the mine would produce the metals you need. I thought you had a *business* plan." Pain, betrayal, disgust. It all came out in the way she said *business*.

"Put down the hammer and walk away from this. You were never supposed to know. Just put it out of your mind the way you did with your painful childhood. I'll do the same when it's over. We can get beyond this."

She lowered the hammer to her side. "But what happens to them? Three people are down here!"

Shawn took another step toward her. "I'll let them go, I promise. They don't know where they are, and they've never seen my face. It will be all right."

For a moment, her expression softened as she considered it. Then Garrett yelled through the door. "Go get help! He's going to kill us!"

Jia hesitated for a second, then charged at him, as though she were going to knock him out of her way. Shawn jerked sideways, grabbed the wrist holding the hammer, and twisted it behind her back. Jia cried out in pain.

"I'm sorry, love, but I can't let you ruin my plans."

She kicked and fought, but he dragged her down the dark hall to the next room. The door was open because Dana Thorpe was locked in the lab at the end. With adrenaline pumping, he shoved Jia into the room, slammed the door, and locked it. She screamed profanities from the other side. Shawn ignored her and ran down to the lab. He wouldn't leave Jia. He just needed a minute to get the data and the material sample from Dana Thorpe, then extricate Lee Nam. If Jia changed her mind, he would take her with him before he used the gas and dynamite.

Shawn unlocked the lab, bracing for what might come at him. If Dana had heard the commotion, she might try to take advantage of the situation. He threw open the door, pulled his gun, and stepped in. The scientist wasn't at her bench. Shawn spun around, expecting to be assaulted. Dana wasn't behind him either. He jogged to the long table she worked at and peered over it. She was on the floor, unconscious. Another seizure? Had she completed the sample? He searched the table and didn't see any pieces of the shimmery metal. What about the data?

He ran to her laptop and looked for the files. They weren't there! Fuck! Had she deleted them? But why? Because she'd heard Jia outside the lab and thought she would be rescued?

No, she was a scientist, and she would never destroy her own work. Shawn ran around the workbench and knelt by her body. Dana was still breathing. It almost didn't matter. He just needed the finished product. Where would she put it? Maybe she hadn't put it anywhere. He pried open her right hand, and in her palm lay a silver flash drive. Thank god. The files were probably intact. Shawn tucked the drive into his front pants pocket. Where was the synthetic sample? Dana's other hand was open, so it obviously wasn't there. He had to have it! The data alone couldn't be trusted. Dana might have sabotaged the formula so his engineer couldn't replicate it.

Shawn stood and scanned the room, his eyes darting from the workbench to the desk to the shelves in back. He didn't see anything resembling the tiny sample she'd shown him the day before. Maybe the compound was in the desk. Shawn charged toward it, and his foot thunked into something on the floor. There it was. A square steel container about the size of his palm. He scooped it up and lifted the lid. Yes! A thin ribbon of silvery-green flexible metal. He wanted to shove the precious material into a pocket to keep it safe, but he had sticks of dynamite taking up those spaces. With the container in one hand and his gun in the other, he ran out of the lab and turned left, passing through an open area that had once held moldy couches. He stopped at a door near the stairs that led to an opening at the edge of the woods.

"Nam? We need to talk. I'm opening the door."

The tech guy didn't respond. But so far, he'd been a man of few words.

Shawn unlocked the door. Nam stood in the center of the room, and behind him was a desk with an active computer monitor.

"How is the software coming along?"

"It's nearly complete, but I need to test parts of it. I can't do that here, alone, with no internet."

"Are you ready to come work for me? With complete secrecy?" They'd already discussed the basics.

"Will I have access to the internet?"

"Of course." Shawn had also promised him a new ID and housing.

"Then I'm ready."

Shawn gestured for Nam to follow. He didn't fully trust the North Korean, but he needed him and would see what happened. Shawn hurried back toward the lab, then turned into the main hallway. Footsteps! Coming down the stairs under the laundry room. He froze. Who the hell could it be? He snatched the gun from his waistband and flipped off the safety. Behind him, Nam's breath quickened, but he stayed silent.

Shawn had left the door to the bomb shelter open when he'd come through, so now he could see out into the tunnel. Gun drawn, he waited, hoping it would be Harlan. But it was two people, moving stealthily. It had to be the agents, who'd come back, found the secret entrance, and were about to arrest him. Could he still get out of this? Shawn moved down the hall toward the main opening, preparing to fire.

But it wasn't Agent Thorpe. An Asian man he didn't recognize came through the door, holding a gun. Shawn had only a moment's advantage. He aimed at the man's head and squeezed the trigger. The noise deafened him, and the kick nearly made him drop his gun. The intruder collapsed to his knees, grabbing his chest. Behind the Asian man stood Bailey—with a gun aimed right at Shawn. He spun and ran, knocking Lee Nam out of his way. If he could make it to the back exit and get to his vehicle—

No. Bailey would call for help, and they would look for his truck on the highway. To survive this, he had to find another way out.

CHAPTER 46

Bailey fired two rounds before spotting the second man at the end of the hall. The missing cryptographer! She lowered her gun. *Damn!* Crusher was fleeing. He'd rounded a corner and disappeared. *Go!* Her primal instinct was to charge after him. She'd been chasing this bastard for weeks, and her victory was slipping away. She glanced around. Where was Garrett?

"Lee Nam," Dukko cried out from the floor, his voice weak. "We found him."

Bailey forced herself to forget about Garrett's safety—for the moment. The North Korea crisis had to be resolved first. She knelt next to Dukko, who was leaning against the wall. In the dim light, against his black shirt, it was hard to tell how much blood he was losing. But the look on his face told her it was bad. He was dying. "Get out your phone!" she yelled. "You have to make the call."

Dukko struggled to get his hand into his pocket, but he managed to pull the phone out and hand it to her. "Get a picture of Nam, so Dear Leader knows he's alive."

Bailey popped up, ready to run down the hall. But the timid IT guy was coming toward them. "Ki-ha!" Lee Nam cried out and dropped next to his bodyguard. "You've been shot." The cryptographer looked up at her. "We have to save him." Nam started to pull off his shirt.

"Wait! I have to get a picture." She didn't want the dying police officer in the photo. KJU was crazy, and might use it as an excuse to kill Jake Austin anyway.

The tech guy ignored her.

She shouted to get his attention. "Kim Jong-un has threatened to execute an American and possibly launch a missile if we don't show him you're safe. Keep your shirt on and stand up!"

Nam did as instructed, eyes blinking in fear and confusion.

Bailey snapped two photos, then filmed a short video to be sure she'd covered it. She squatted next to Dukko again. "Help me send this to the right person."

"Just text it to the last number I texted. Then call that number."

She went through the motions, but the message didn't send.

"Shit! We don't have a signal down here." She stood, ready to bolt upstairs to the bunkhouse.

"Bailey?" Garrett's voice came from behind the wall.

She spun toward the sound. "Are you all right?"

"Yes."

Thank god. "We'll get you out in a minute." She hated leaving Garrett. Jake Austin wasn't even that important. But placating Kim Jong-un was critical.

She charged through the tunnel, Dukko's phone in her hand. Crusher probably had the keys to the locked doors, but there had to be a sledgehammer or something she could use to free everyone. But the phone call came first. She pounded up the stairs, heart racing. In the laundry room, she paused, gulping air, and pressed Send again. An unexpected joy filled her heart. Garrett was alive and well, and she was about to prevent a war. Another reason to love this job.

The dialogue box changed color. The text had gone out. Still, North Korea was on the other side of the world. She called the same number. It rang four times, then a tight voice said something in Korean.

"English, please!"

After a rapid background exchange in Korean, someone else came on the line. "Commander Ryuk."

"This is Agent Bailey, United States Federal Bureau of Investigation. I'm calling to report that Lee Nam has been located."

"Why do you have Lieutenant Dukko's phone?" Suspicion gave his voice an edge.

"He was injured by the kidnapper, a crazy individual who has nothing to do with our government. But Lee Nam is safe. Did you get the photo and video I sent?"

"Just a moment."

"Call off the execution and release Jake Austin." She raised her voice, but he'd already put her on hold.

Out of the corner of her eye, she saw Lee Nam step out of the basement opening.

The line went dead. *Shit!* Bailey pressed the logged call and tried again, but it didn't connect. She hurried outside into the dark and tried the call again. The same commander came back on. "Kim Jong-un will honor his agreement, but he wants an apology."

She almost laughed. "I'm sorry for what happened."

"He'd like one from President Harris."

"Then he should give him a call." She heard an engine start in the distance. "I have to go."

"Your country is irresponsible, and North Korea won't send professionals to your symposiums again."

"No problem." She hung up and turned to Nam, who'd followed her outside. She pressed Dukko's phone into his hand. "Call 911 and get an ambulance. Cops too. Tell them Palisades Mine."

275

The engine revved and she spun toward the sound. It wasn't a car. Something smaller, like the quads she'd seen earlier. An ATV roared away from the processing plant, its headlight cutting through the night to shine on the trees. Crusher!

Bailey sprinted toward the facility. There had been two quads, and she could see the other one now. *Please let the key be in it.* She leapt on the little four-wheeled vehicle and reached for the starter. A push button. Yes! She flipped it on, gave it gas, and took off after Crusher's retreating headlight.

In the distance, at the edge of the trees, he turned left and rode parallel to the woods.

Where was he going? He was heading away from the parking lot where he'd left his truck. Bailey visualized the maps she'd studied of the area. South and west of the mine was a river and another small town. He had to be heading toward it. What was his plan? Steal a car? The town was at least twenty miles away, and getting across the rugged terrain would be difficult enough in daylight. At night, it seemed impossible. Did he have another vehicle stashed somewhere?

She kept the throttle wide-open, pushing the little sports vehicle to its limit. The headlight barely illuminated the dirt path, and she bounced along, hitting the ruts and bumps hard. She toggled her focus between Crusher's ATV ahead and the ground below, trying to keep him in sight and not crash her own quad. It was crazy, dangerous, and exhilarating. Bailey also expected it to be a short ride. Nothing in Crusher's background indicated he was an outdoorsman or athletic in any way. With his life and freedom on the line, he was obviously willing to challenge himself. But she would prevail. Her lack of fear was working in her favor now, and her tenacity never failed her.

The roar of their engines cut through the quiet night, startling a big bird that flew out of the trees ahead. The path began to descend, and they zigzagged through the trees and past basalt ridges. Bright moonlight glinted off the bare rocks, giving her fair warning of their presence.

After a while, her hands tingled with numbness, and she loosened her grip on the rubber handles. This could be a long ride after all. But she was slowly gaining on him.

A few minutes later, the temperature dropped and the air felt heavier, wetter. The river! They were nearly there. Would he turn and ride south toward the little town? Was there any kind of path along the bank? Maybe the area was used for horseback riding, and he was following a familiar trail.

The trees thinned out and glimpses of the river came into view. Wet rocks shimmered along the edge. Before Crusher reached the riverbank, he veered left. Bailey steered off the path and cut across the grassy area, hoping not to hit any rocks or unexpected obstacles. A thick clump of grass popped her ATV into the air, slamming her down hard into the seat. She managed to keep control. She'd also closed the gap by another twenty feet.

Bailey tried to visualize the map again but couldn't get oriented. Where was the town from here? Was it really in this direction? Her damn dysfunction made her unsure. Crusher's engine slowed, then his vehicle turned toward the river. What the hell was he doing?

She kept the throttle open and a moment later made the same turn. But she took the corner too fast. Her ATV tipped, and she rode it on two wheels, fighting to bring it back to the ground. The rough downhill path worked against her, and the quad went over. Bailey jumped free at the last moment, landing hard on one knee. Her body registered pain, but she blocked it and jumped to her feet. Her ATV had slammed into a bush, and the engine sputtered to a stop. Bailey sprinted down the path. The river was right there. Crusher had no choice but to abandon his quad too. Was he going to swim? Did he think she wouldn't get into the river?

A dock at the bottom of the slope came into view, and she spotted Crusher standing in a boat, bent over. *Oh hell!* It looked more like a fishing dingy than a speedboat, but still, it would carry him down the damn river and out of reach. He yanked a cord, and a propeller engine kicked over. Could she reach the dock and leap into the boat before he pulled away? No, he'd already freed the tie lines, and the craft sped away.

A smaller boat was moored on the other side of the dock with its outboard tipped up out of the water. Bailey ran to it, noting the tie-downs. She had a knife in the satchel that was still strapped across her chest, but getting it out might take longer than loosening the rope. Drift boats were often moored with simple loops, and this one was. She quickly freed the lines and jumped into the boat. The dock floated in a shallow bay, out of the main river current, and probably belonged to a homeowner nearby. She didn't waste time looking back for the building. The headlamp from Crusher's quad was still on, giving her just enough light to see what she was doing. She'd hunted and fished with her father during her childhood in Colorado, so this was second nature. She dropped the motor into the water, opened the gas flow, and jerked on the starter cord. It took three pulls, but the engine purred to life and she guided the boat into the river.

Where was Crusher? She'd taken her eyes off him while she'd prepped the boat, and now he was running without lights. She caught a glint of something on the water downstream and steered in that direction, cranking the little motor as high as its RPMs would allow. The sound of water breaking against the hull brought back more memories of her father, most of them good. The night was cold, and her hands were stiff, but the discomfort barely registered. Letting Crusher get away at this point was unthinkable. It wasn't even about justice for the victims. He'd tried to kill her twice, and for that, he would pay.

His outline emerged out of the darkness a few minutes later. She was rapidly gaining on him. He'd taken a boat with a weaker engine or simply wasn't running at full speed. When she was twenty yards away, she pulled her weapon, one hand still on the throttle. He became aware of her a moment later, jerking his head back to look, then facing the river again. His hand fumbled behind him, reaching into his waistband.

He was pulling his gun! She'd watched him shoot Dukko earlier with a surprising cold accuracy. But she wouldn't fire until he pointed his weapon at her. It wasn't a moral concern, simply a practical one. This capture needed to go down clean. Cops might shoot suspects in the back, but the bureau did not. She needed her peers and supervisors to respect her.

When she was fifteen feet away, Crusher finally turned and aimed his gun at her. Bailey was ready. She fired off the rest of her rounds. Two made contact and he collapsed. His boat slowed as soon as he let go of the throttle, and the weight of his body plunging sideways shot the drifter toward her in a spin. She bumped his drifter with the nose of hers to stabilize it, then let go of the throttle and leapt into the other boat. Crusher was a bounty, and she intended to bring him in. She squatted, searched for his gun, and shoved it into her satchel. She heard him breathing, but it was a ragged, dying sound.

"Crusher."

His eyes opened, and she pushed against his chest wound. He moaned in pain.

"Who is your contact at the FBI?"

He didn't answer. She pressed harder. "Tell me! You're dying and you have nothing to lose." She might find the information in his phone, and she might not. He could have used a burner that he'd already destroyed.

"Don't know." The words were barely audible.

"Who are you working with?" Someone with deep pockets had funded that underground lab.

"Max." Crusher's eyes closed and his head lolled to the side.

At least she had a name. Bailey looked downriver and spotted the lights of the little town. Thank goodness. Now that her adrenaline had stopped pumping, her thoughts turned to the victims. She had to get back up to the mine. Garrett might be injured and still locked in the basement. The thought made her heart hurt. She'd never felt another person's pain before, and it was unpleasant. Why had she thought she *wanted* this?

Suddenly, Crusher's hand came up, reaching for the side of the boat. Bailey grabbed his wrist. But it wasn't a gun. He was trying to throw his phone into the river. She pried it from his weak fingers, then secured his hands. He died while she was locking the plastic cuffs. Bailey scrolled through his phone for the last few numbers in the call log. One had a DC area code. Had he been talking to Haywood, the assistant director? Or was Max from the capital too? He'd tried to hide his associates, but she was about to uncover them.

CHAPTER 47

Jocelyn parked down the block from Brent Haywood's house and waited in the car for Ross to arrive. She put in her earbuds and listened to her favorite Stevie Wonder songs to distract her. Was she really going to confront the assistant director of the FBI about his possible involvement in a murder? What if she was wrong? Haywood would be a powerful enemy. Still, she had to ask the questions.

Ross had found the AD's address and confirmed that it was within three blocks of the park the murdered tech guy had received calls from. The same burner phone had also made calls to Zach Dimizaro from a corner near FBI headquarters. Haywood might have a good explanation, but it was certainly no coincidence. The assistant director—or someone who worked and lived in the same places he did—had made four calls to Dimizaro in the two weeks before he was murdered. Haywood might have been investigating Dimizaro, but if so, Ross hadn't found a record of it within the bureau. Her husband had even more to lose from this confrontation.

She caught the glare of headlights pulling up behind her, waited until she was sure it was Ross, then unlocked her doors. He climbed in and apologized for keeping her waiting. "Something big is going down out in Washington State, and the Critical Incident team is gathering to monitor it. The only information I could get was that the North Korean IT guy might have been found and the Seattle field office had sent out a team."

Very good news. "Does that mean Kim Jong-un is backing down from his threat?"

"I don't know. I'm not on the CI response team, so I heard everything secondhand." A note of regret in his voice.

Jocelyn made an unsettling connection. "Do you suppose the North Korean kidnapping is somehow related to my murder victim? They're both involved with encryption software."

"That would be bizarre." Ross stared at her open mouthed. "Especially if the AD orchestrated the Lee Nam abduction." He shook his head. "That would make Kim Jong-un right about the US government being involved."

"That is disturbing." Jocelyn braced herself. "Shall we go find out?" She glanced down the street at Haywood's house. The garage door was open, and a sedan was backing out. Her pulse quickened. "He's on the move."

From a distance in the dark, she couldn't be sure who the driver was, but whoever it was had broad shoulders and a large head. "Is that Haywood? Can you tell?" Jocelyn itched to start the engine but made herself wait.

"Sure looks like him. I wonder where he's going."

Both their jobs were on the line, and they needed to stay objective. "It could be an ice-cream run."

"It's almost midnight, so I don't think so. Pull out as soon as he passes the first intersection." Ross slid down in his seat. "Unless he comes this way."

She knew how to tail a suspect. But she scrunched down as well and didn't respond. This was too important. They had to function like a well-oiled law enforcement team, not an estranged married couple.

Jocelyn counted, giving the sedan time to back into the street, then heard it drive away in the opposite direction. She eased into an upright position, waited for another count of ten, then turned the key. "Maybe he's going to the park to make another clandestine call."

Two blocks later, when the sedan eased off the street, she did the same and killed the engine. She'd been right about the park, and it was the shortest tail job she'd ever done. Excited and nervous, she turned to Ross. "Did you bring a listening device?"

He grinned. "Of course. And we it call it *ears*."

"Whatever. Just get it ready. We need to get out and get closer."

"It's in my pocket and simply needs to be activated. Let's go." Ross quietly opened his door. "If he spots us, we put our heads together and start talking like drunks on their way home."

They moved quietly past big dark houses with nothing but porch lights on, walking on front lawns rather than the sidewalk. As they rounded the corner, the park came into view across the street. They spotted Haywood walking up a path toward a cluster of trees in the middle of the park.

They ducked behind a minivan parked on the street.

"Are we close enough?" Jocelyn's knees hurt from squatting.

"No. Let's cross over and sit on that first bench." Ross pulled her up, put an arm around her, and leaned in close. "Let's do this quickly."

Jocelyn wrapped her arm around him too, and they hurried across the street. They were out of Haywood's line of sight, even if he turned around. When they reached the outer bench and sat, Ross pulled her in for a long kiss.

"You're not fooling anybody," she whispered.

They were facing the same street they'd just crossed and could no longer see Haywood, who was in the park somewhere behind them. She could only hope he hadn't spotted them. If he had, he might just keep moving. She glanced over her shoulder. Through the trees, she saw a man sit on a bench near the playground. "He's in place to make a call now."

Ross pulled out the tiny device and turned it on. They heard static for a minute, then muffled footsteps. Someone was approaching Haywood! She glanced over her shoulder again. Another man, also wearing a dark coat, sat on the bench a foot from Haywood.

Through the ears, they heard Haywood say, "It's over. Crusher has been compromised, and Seattle agents are moving in. I can't stop them."

"He was reckless," the other man said. "Kidnapping the North Korean was insane. I had no idea he would do that."

"Will the NSA lose its investment?"

The other man laughed softly. "The bureau will get all his businesses through forfeiture. And whatever the North Korean and the other scientists developed for Crusher will end up with the State Department. The government will control the cell phone market and block encryption one way or another."

He was with the National Security Agency? *Holy shit!* Jocelyn's chest felt tight. She didn't know who Crusher was, but members of two government agencies had been collaborating with a kidnapper. Rage and fear gripped her. What was this really about? She met Ross' eyes. He looked overwhelmed too.

But they remained silent, listening to the clandestine conversation.

* * *

Charles Max Damper shifted on the hard wooden bench. The mission hadn't gone as planned, but it wasn't a total loss. The government's access to the synthetic would be delayed by bureaucratic processes, but they would get control of it. They'd lost the opportunity to control the cell phone market through ZoGo, but the war was just getting started. The scientist who'd been killed was unfortunate collateral damage, but they had to keep the big issues at the forefront. Accessing phone conversations remained their best tool in preventing terrorist attacks. As long as they stayed on top of encryption and kept collecting data in motion—regardless of what those idiots in Congress did—the NSA would continue to save thousands and potentially even millions of lives.

So far, he and his supervisor were in the clear. Crusher had never seen his face, and their only contact had been through the burner phone in his pocket. Once he destroyed it, the connection would be gone. The money the NSA had shifted to ZoGo was untraceable, and his FBI contact could shut down the investigation if needed. Crusher could and likely would die in custody, if he hadn't already been killed in the raid.

But unhackable encryption software, like the code he was about to acquire from his associate at the FBI, trumped everything else. The NSA had never intended to let ZoGo embed security in cell phones. That was the primary reason for trying to gain control of the market—to keep it encryption free so they could continue to access every phone conversation and text. But they still needed a copy of this particular airtight encryption's source code so they could reverse engineer it and devise a way to defeat it. This wasn't the only security code they were scrambling to defuse—as was so often the way with tech innovation. They were forced to play whack-a-mole with several separate projects popping up nearly simultaneously in the development community. The threat posed by the North Korean's algorithm was in a class by itself. Without the original code, it might really have been unhackable.

The version Max had tried to buy hadn't worked out. The tech guy hadn't shown up at their scheduled meeting, and Max had learned recently from Haywood that Dimizaro had been killed by a mugger. A thief, who'd taken the damn prototype. Fortunately, Haywood had somehow got his hands on a version. Maybe from the company Dimizaro worked for. The greedy bastard wanted a lot of cash for it, but Haywood knew its value. "Let's see the flash drive," Max said.

"I have a prototype phone, but the code is in there." Haywood spoke softly, not looking at him. The AD had been on board the mission from the beginning. The FBI, or at least a few individuals within the bureau, wanted to see only encryption-free devices on the market as much as the NSA did. But he and Haywood had been the only ones willing to take the bold steps necessary to ensure that it happened. Haywood reached into his pocket and held out a cell phone. "Do you have the cash?"

"Yes." Max pulled a package from under his coat. The five hundred thousand he was paying Haywood was a bargain. He handed the money to the FBI agent and stood to leave. The burner phone rang in his pocket. Was Crusher calling him? Had he escaped the FBI raid? A wave of anxiety rolled over Max, and he didn't dare answer.

* * *

Ross gestured excitedly. "Go around to the other side," he whispered. "We'll box them in, and I'll call for backup."

Jocelyn jumped up, pulled out her weapon, and hurried down the sidewalk. Her soft-soled shoes made little noise on the cement, but still, she was glad to leave it behind, cutting through another group of trees and crossing the grass toward the playground. The men were standing near the bench, but then the shorter guy, the NSA agent, started to walk away.

Time to go!

With her weapon raised, she rushed toward them. From the path behind the bench, she saw Ross running at them from the other direction.

Haywood spun toward her, startled.

"Hands in the air!" she yelled.

The NSA agent reached for his weapon.

"Don't do it! I'll shoot you!" Ten feet away now, Jocelyn slowed. "Put your weapons on the ground."

Ross was next to the bench now with a gun pointed at Haywood.

"You're making a huge mistake," the NSA agent said. "Walk away and forget you know anything about this."

"Put your weapon on the ground!" Jocelyn's heart pounded and adrenaline coursed through her body. *Please don't have a stroke.*

"We're high-level government agents," the NSA man said, "and we have an undercover operation going. Get out of here so you don't fuck it up." He still had his gun in his hand, but it was at his side. Haywood had stayed silent, unmoving.

Ross spoke up. "I know Haywood. You can both explain yourselves at the bureau."

A phone rang in the NSA agent's pocket. For a moment, they all froze, as the low-pitched sound cut through the night.

"I'll take that call," Jocelyn said.

The NSA man started to bring up his gun. Jocelyn fired two shots. One hit him in the shoulder. He made a startled grunt and dropped his weapon. She rushed in and cuffed him before he could make another move. Ross had done the same with Haywood, who was talking rapidly, spinning a cover-up. Jocelyn's nerves fired so wildly it was hard to process what he was saying. Two cars pulled up next to the park, and men in suits climbed out. Backup had arrived.

Jocelyn shoved the NSA agent to the ground and pulled the still-ringing cell phone from his pocket. This could turn out to be important evidence. "Hello?"

"Who is this?" The woman on the other end was assertive.

"Detective Larson, Metro Police Department. Who is this?"

"Agent Bailey, FBI. How do you know Shawn Crusher?" The woman shouted over a loud engine noise.

FBI? That surprised Jocelyn. The NSA man's phone was a cheap burner, like the one she expected Ross to find in Haywood's pocket. "This isn't my phone," Jocelyn said. "But I arrested the man it belonged to. He's an NSA agent. Why are you contacting him?"

A pause. "This isn't my phone either. I took it from Shawn Crusher, a kidnapper and killer, and I wanted to see who was calling him from DC."

Now it made sense. Bailey was one of the field agents who'd raided Crusher's Washington operation. Jocelyn briefly explained her end as she pulled the NSA man's wallet from his pocket and looked for ID. He didn't have any on him, but Ross and his fellow agents would eventually identify him.

"You said he was NSA? Not FBI?" Agent Bailey sounded disappointed. "Someone in the bureau leaked information about my investigation."

Jocelyn glanced over at the assistant director, now cuffed on the ground like a common criminal. "That would be Brent Haywood, the NSA man's contact. We just arrested him too."

"I knew it. The son of a bitch." Agent Bailey said it calmly. "Do you know Haywood's motive?"

Ross was peeling open a brown package filled with cash. How much had Haywood traded Zach Dimizaro's life for? Jocelyn shook her head. "Money, what else? I have to go. I'm sure we'll both catch up on the details later." Jocelyn hung up, wondering if she would ever hear the whole story. Or would the FBI and NSA find a way to spin this? Good thing she was dating Ross. He might get access to at least some of the truth.

CHAPTER 48

Wednesday, March 25, 3:55 p.m., Seattle, Washington

At the front desk of the Seattle field office, Bailey gave her name and asked for Agent Thorpe, who'd requested to meet her out front. She assumed he had something private to tell her.

"I'll let him know you're here." The clerk made a call and turned back. "Well done up there at the mine, by the way. You've made quite an impression with our agents."

Bailey couldn't muster a smile. She was still bone tired from an all-night search of Crusher's properties. She and the Seattle team had confiscated computers, lab equipment, and everything that could be evidence. By the time she'd made it back there in a sheriff's car after chasing down Crusher, Dana and Garrett had already been transported out on a medevac helicopter. Dukko's body had gone with them, leaving only Lee Nam to tell his part of the story. A Seattle agent had flown out with Nam this morning, headed to Washington, DC, to meet with the president for media photos. Bailey had been summoned to the White House as well, but she wouldn't leave until tomorrow. She had to see Garrett first.

Thorpe walked up and shook her hand, not letting go. "I know I said it last night, but I'll say it again. Thank you for finding my son. When I think about the gas and dynamite that bastard was going to use down there, I know how close I came to losing Garrett." He squeezed her hand again. "You saved them all."

She hadn't been alone. "Dukko Ki-ha played his part." The North Korean police officer had found the secret door to the underground prison and had given his life for his countryman. Dukko would go home in a body bag soon. It seemed unfair.

They took the elevator to a conference room on the second floor and joined a small group of agents, including the two women she'd met at the Thorpes' house. This was the room where she'd first kissed Garrett. The thought made her happy. Garrett was picking her up after the meeting, and she couldn't wait to see him.

After everyone was seated, Agent Thorpe said, "FBI director Robert Palmer will join us in about ten minutes via video, so let's get everyone up to speed. I'll go first." Thorpe summarized both of his trips to the Palisades Mine, concluding with finding his ex-wife unconscious on the lab floor and calling for medical help. Then he added, "We're still pulling together a timeline for Shawn Crusher's illegal activities, but his wife is fully cooperating."

With Crusher and both of his thugs dead, there was no one to question, no one to confess everything in exchange for a light sentence. Bailey hadn't heard anything more about the NSA man Crusher had been working with. She looked at Thorpe. "Does Jia know anything about Crusher's connection to the NSA?"

"In theory, no." Thorpe struggled to keep his face impassive. "She says her husband referred to his financial backer as Max, so we believe Charles Max Damper, possibly with the help of the NSA, funded the whole market-takeover scheme."

One of the women cut in. "Damper may have been in it for the money, but if the NSA was backing him, what was it about for the agency?"

Bailey had given it some thought. "Based on what the detective who arrested Damper told me, I have to conclude that Damper and Haywood wanted every phone manufactured to be accessible to law enforcement. By controlling the market and producing only encryption-free phones, they planned to make tracking and convicting terrorists easier."

"What about Brent Haywood's contact with Zach Dimizaro, who ended up murdered?" Thorpe had all the reports, but he was still looking for answers. "Weren't Haywood and Damper both trying to acquire encryption software?"

"Yes, but for the purpose of getting it off the market and reverse engineering it. Supposedly, a few coders have created unhackable encryption, but with the original code, it can be cracked."

"But why kill him?"

They might never know, but she'd analyzed Haywood's actions and thought she knew. "For the same reason he was feeding intel to Damper at the NSA. He wanted to quash the new encryption. Some people in law enforcement put cryptographers in the same criminal category as hackers."

"There was a witness who got a good look at him, so maybe the tech guy did too," Thorpe said. "Maybe Haywood killed him just to cover his involvement."

A beeping sound on the wall monitor indicated a call was coming in. Thorpe pressed the remote, and the big screen came to life, showing the FBI director at his desk. Bailey had met Robert Palmer once and thought he was handsome and sincere. People said that about her too, so it didn't mean much.

"Thank you all for your great work on this case," Palmer said, getting right to the point. "By locating Lee Nam before the deadline, you saved an innocent man's life and possibly averted a missile crisis." The director chuckled softly. "No one here in the capital thought to look for Mr. Lee in the other Washington."

"You have Agent Bailey to thank for that," Thorpe said. "She connected all the kidnappings and used some creative thinking to find the mine where they were being held."

The director nodded. "I was just going to say that." On the screen, his eyes shifted to her. "Special Agent Lennard resigned yesterday, so the CIRG needs a new special agent in charge, and we'll talk about the position when you return."

What? Lennard had quit? Or had she confronted Haywood, who'd forced her out? *It didn't matter.* The director was offering her the job she'd always wanted. The question burst out of her mouth before she could stop it. "Why did Agent Lennard resign?"

The director stiffened. "She said it was personal."

A vague sense of discomfort overwhelmed Bailey. It wasn't guilt, but what? Disappointment in herself? She had to speak up. "I told Lennard I suspected Haywood had leaked critical intel to Crusher. I think she might have confronted the AD and suffered the consequences."

"You suspected Haywood?" His expression was hard to read. Admiration? Disbelief?

"Yes."

"I'd like to discuss that more when you get back." Before she could respond, Palmer added, "But now that the AD is no longer with us, we'll review Lennard's resignation."

Oh hell. There went her promotion. "I look forward to our conversation."

The director's expression shifted into funeral mode. "The news of Brent Haywood's betrayal and arrest is shocking and demoralizing for all of us. But for me especially. I promoted him. I believed in him." Palmer's eyes shifted around the table. "I wanted all of you to know that Haywood made a complete confession this morning. He was driven by financial pressure and the misguided idea that his actions were for the greater good. We had hoped that with Haywood's testimony, we would be able to convict Charles Damper too." A long pause while the FBI director stared down at his desk. "But Damper was found dead in his cell this morning. He'd hanged himself."

A few hushed murmurs from the room. Bailey was skeptical. She assumed the NSA had shut him up. She asked the director, "What happens to Crusher's cell phone business? His rare earth mine?"

Palmer smiled with his eyes. "We'll sell both businesses and use the money to fight cyber crime."

Whatever brand the phones ended up with, she was sure they would be made without the unhackable encryption.

The director excused himself, and their meeting wrapped up shortly after. Bailey called Garrett to let him know she was ready.

On the drive to his house, she made polite conversation. "How's your mother?"

"She's stopped having seizures now that she's back on her medication, but she's still dehydrated and in shock. She'll be in the hospital for a few more days."

"I'm glad she's got you to take care of her."

He didn't respond for a moment. "When are you going back to DC?"

"Tomorrow. I have a funeral service for a friend, then the director wants to meet with me." She reached over and touched his shoulder. "This is our last night together."

"It doesn't have to be."

She loved hearing it, but being with Garrett was wishful thinking. "Long-distance relationships don't work. We both know that."

"What if I move to the capital? I can get a physical therapy certification anywhere."

That surprised her. "You would do that? What about your mother?"

"I found out she's dating someone. So I'll stay with her just long enough to get her through the transition and back to work." Garrett pulled off the street and shut down the engine. He turned in his seat and grabbed Bailey's hands. "I love you. I want to be with you. And I can't think of any reason we shouldn't be together."

She couldn't either. He made her happy, and there were no downsides. Not for her, anyway. In her simple cost-benefit view of the world, that was all that mattered. "I love you too. In my own way. If you're willing to make the move out east, I'm into having a relationship."

Garrett leaned in and kissed her. "Thanks for finding me. Both times."

ABOUT THE AUTHOR

L.J. Sellers writes the bestselling Detective Jackson mystery-thriller series—a four-time Readers' Favorite Award winner—as well as the Agent Dallas series and provocative stand-alone thrillers. Her seventeen novels have been highly praised by reviewers, and she's one of the highest-rated crime fiction authors on Amazon.com.

Sellers resides in Eugene, Oregon, where many of her novels are set, and is a Grand Neal Award–winning journalist. When not plotting murders, Sellers enjoys stand-up comedy, cycling, and social networking. She's also been known to jump out of airplanes.